Amber Stone Agent Zero
For The Love of Blood

Amina Warsuma

This book is dedicated to Jayson Warsuma

The Book's of Amina Warsuma

My Stars Are Still Shining
-
My Track & Field Practice And Races
-
What Am I Grateful For Today
-
The Circle of TIE
-
Amber Stone Agent Zero
For The Love of Blood
-

The night was hot and misty in the Mississippi Delta shanty town in the 1960s, with a full, red moon casting an eerie glow over the scene. The air was thick and swampy, creating an oppressive atmosphere.

At the far end of the shanty town, Irma's small, dilapidated shack had been engulfed in flames, the fire raging from the inside. Twenty-five hooded figures in white Ku Klux Klan robes had surrounded the burning home, a large burning cross illuminating their sinister presence. Suddenly, Irma had burst out the door, her body engulfed in flames. She had let out a piercing scream as she fell to the ground, the flames consuming her. The Klansmen had watched impassively as Irma was reduced to ashes, the fire casting an eerie glow on their robes.

The scene had dissolved, and Blood had found himself back in the Bronx in 1970, sitting rigidly in the passenger seat of a getaway van.

It was a cool, breezy spring night around 10 p.m. The street was dark and deserted, with only a lone, dimly lit lamp post. An oppressive air of suspense and foreboding hung heavy, punctuated by the ominous hum of electricity through the neon, sky blue sign displaying 'Benny's Supermarket'. Usually, the store would be abuzz with a mob of customers crowding the aisles until closing, but this evening the market stood eerily silent and empty, the customers having cleared out well before 8 o'clock.

Parked in the shadows of a gray, windowless van, four African American men sat in tense, anticipatory silence. Cisco, a nervous 20-year-old, peered intently out the side rear mirror, his eyes fixed on the supermarket, occasionally turning to glance at the rigid 28-year-old Blood in the passenger seat. In the back, 50-year-old Soupy and 40-year-old Jonesy sat motionless, their faces etched with a mix of anxiety and determination. The seconds ticked by with agonizing slowness as the men waited for Blood's signal.

"Blood, are you alright?" Cisco asked.

Finally, after what felt like an eternity, Blood glanced down at his watch and spoke in a low, gravelly voice, "Cisco, you've got ten seconds before he locks up. Now go."

Cisco nodded tensely, his knuckles ashy and dry as he gripped the door handle. The others braced themselves, their faces set in grim resolve as they prepared to spring into action.

The air was thick with unspoken dread; they knew all too well how this night could end, but the lure of the score was too great to resist. With Blood's signal, the dye had been cast, and there was no turning back now.

He dashed out of the van and proceeded to the supermarket's entrance. The middle-aged Latino manager approached the exit to lock it as Cisco kicked it open. Blood, Soupy, and Jonesy were dressed in black with stocking caps on their faces. They jumped out of the wagon and rushed inside with guns. Cisco looked over his shoulder as he ran, got back into the van, and turned on the motor.

Inside the market were aisles of pale pink painted walls with metal shelves of cans and bottled food products. A whiff of packaged bread rolls, cakes, and doughnuts mixed with the tang of ozone from the dry ice in the frozen department. The manager and the five diverse female cashiers in their 20s stood behind their check-out area. They stood frozen in shock as the stick-up men leveled their weapons at them, hands instinctively raised in surrender.

"Don't hurt us," pleaded the manager, his voice trembling.

"Just give us the money, and nobody will get hurt," Blood replied coolly, an edge of menace in his tone.

"What are you waiting for? Open up the registers!" Soupy yelled, his impatience palpable.

Fear coursed through the cashiers as the clinking of metal filled the room. Obediently, they pried open the registers, hearts racing.

"I want paper and double plastic," commanded Jonesy, his eyes scanning the counter with urgency. The frantic cashiers fumbled to prepare the bags, their hands shaking as they tossed in the items. Meanwhile, Jonesy hurriedly began emptying the cash from the registers into the bags, determination etched on his face.

Blood glanced at his watch, anxiety creeping into his expression.

"We have to move," he urged, his voice clipped.

"I'm going as fast as I can!" Jonesy shot back, the weight of their predicament pressing down on him. He reached the fifth register, his adrenaline spiking as he stuffed more cash into the bag. Time was slipping away, and they all knew it. Every second felt like an eternity as they raced against the clock, fear and desperation intertwining in the tense air. In the dimly lit back of the market, a middle-aged African American security guard stepped into view, his gun aimed directly at Blood.

"Hold it! Put your guns down and your hands up where I can see them!" he commanded, his voice steady yet urgent.

Blood froze, a wave of shock washing over him. He had been convinced that he was alone in the store. In a split second, he reacted, firing his pistol at the guard.

Screams erupted from the manager and the five cashiers as they dove to the floor, bodies tumbling over one another in panic. The security guard returned fire with precision, his bullets ricocheting off the checkout counters, zinging dangerously over the employees' heads.

Soupy and Jonesy, caught in the chaos, pulled out their revolvers and aimed at the guard. But he was quick, dashing behind an aisle for cover. A barrage of bullets filled the air, blasting through rows of cans and jars, sending food splattering across the area. The once serene market had transformed into a battleground, chaos reigning as adrenaline surged through every heartbeat.

The security guard emerged from behind the aisle, firing his gun at the robbers. But Blood was quicker, his pistol cracking as he shot the guard square in the chest. The man crashed to the tile floor, his hand stretching out towards his fallen weapon. Blood rushed over and kicked it away, then stood over the wounded guard, pointing his .38 revolver at the man's head.

"You lose," Blood growled, and pulled the trigger. A bullet drilled the guard between the eyes as the supermarket alarm blared to life. The sound of approaching police sirens only fueled Blood's rage. In a final act of vengeance, he grunted and kicked the dead guard's body twice.

"Come on, forget the rest of the money. Let's get out of here," Blood snapped at the others.

Soupy grabbed the bags of cash from Jonesy. "I have one more register," Jonesy protested.

"Forget it; the cops are on their way," Blood yelled.

The four men ran out of the supermarket, snatching off their stocking cap masks as they went. Soupy hurled the money bags into the waiting van, and they all piled inside as Cisco fired up the engine and peeled out, the wail of the sirens fading in the distance.

The van sped through the dark, deserted streets of the Bronx, crossing over the bridge into upper Manhattan. The coast was clear as they pulled up to a rundown building on 142nd Street in old Harlem.

Blood and the others jumped out, and Cisco walked around to the back, ripping off the temporary license plate to reveal the original.

Soupy and Jonesy grabbed the money bags and hustled inside, climbing the creaky staircase to their shabby, dust-coated hideout. Blood unlocked the door and flicked on the light, illuminating the ramshackle, brown-furnished flat. The sound of the sagging floorboards accompanied them as they approached an old card table and chairs. The men dumped the stolen cash onto the surface, the screech of a window being opened by Cisco piercing the air.

"It stinks in here; it smells like pee from the stairwell," Cisco complained.

"Hey, what do you want us to do? The bums don't have a bathroom," Soupy replied with a laugh.

"Put some lye behind the steps to burn their raggedy shoes off," Cisco shot back.

Soupy chuckled. "You're going to hear more than piss sizzling on the walls."

Cisco turned to Soupy, his voice gruff and commanding.

"That is too much work for you."

Soupy nodded, a nostalgic look crossing his features. "Yeah, I remember when I was pimping. I was known for my flashy clothes and fast money."

Blood shook his head. "You are the one who wanted to do stickups."

Soupy let out a heavy sigh. "If I would have known it was this much work, I would have stuck to pimping."

Jonesy chimed in his voice laced with weariness. "This is easier than me running numbers for the mob. I would run up and down the streets of Harlem like crazy."

Cisco snorted derisively. "Jonesy, you're getting old and lazy."

"Sit your asses down and count this money, we don't have all night," Jonesy chimed in.

The sound of police sirens blared in the distance, but the crew seemed unfazed by the crime they had just committed. They all sat down and began tallying the cash, stacking it neatly into rows.

Blood stacked the money up into neat rows. "Twelve thousand dollars, that's all we got," he announced.

"There was probably more in the back safe," Soupy said.

"Yeah, under the circumstances, you guys did your best," Cisco replied.

Blood handed each of them their share. "Here's your three thousand," he said.

The men eagerly grabbed their cash. "That security guard spooked us," Soupy remarked.

"You think he survived?" Cisco asked.

Soupy, counting his money, answered, "He's dead; he put his life on the line for chump change."

Jonesy grinned as he eyed his haul. "It's going to be hot on the streets."

Cisco slid his share into his jacket pocket. "I say we lie low for a while."

"With what? Be real, we have no money," Blood scoffed.

"We can't publicize this stickup," Soupy pointed out.

"Blood, you're full of bravado," Jonesy said.

"You guys think I'm that hungry for recognition?" Blood replied defensively.

Soupy fixed him with a hard stare. "Hell yeah, it's like you got something to prove."

Blood yelled, "I am not happy with this small money. You have a problem with that?"

Jonesy replied, "Lower your voice Blood, you don't want to wake up the neighborhood."

Blood chuckled. "No rest for the wicked," he said, flicking his money with his thumb.

"I suggest we all go out and stay on the scene in plain sight," Soupy proposed.

"Yeah, when the cops ask around, someone will say they haven't seen us," Jonesy chimed in.

"That's true. If we disappear, it will cause suspicion," Blood agreed.

"The cashiers will say it was four black men who did the stickup," Soupy said.

Blood said, "The cops always say it was black men who did the crime even if they didn't."

Soupy responded, "Thanks to you they will keep on saying it."

Blood continued, "Forget you man. You act like I am in this by myself."

Cisco chimed in, "Blood, you need a girl. It's ladies' night at The Den; all the babes show up after midnight."

"Let's go," Blood said. "It beats sitting around here arguing about my ambition. You guys don't understand me. I am way ahead of you."

Soupy responded, "Yeah, we're the only ones that do understand you."

The men rose from the table, pocketing their share of the stolen cash. Each one headed to their shabby bedrooms to shower and change. They emerged looking sharp, dressed in flashy suits - Blood in red, Soupy in blue, Cisco in green, and Jonesy in a light tan with a matching hat. Smelling sweet and looking attractive, the four robbers exited the rundown flat.

They left the building, hailing a taxi that drove them to the Den Club. A glamorous, upscale crowd in their 20s and 30s lined up behind the velvet rope, trying to get inside. The gang strutted past them and up to the entrance, where a massive African American bouncer let them in without hesitation.

Inside the upscale Den club, the line of elegantly dressed patrons leaned against the beige, art-adorned walls. The murmur of their chatter echoed through the spacious interior, mingling with the soulful sounds of music playing in the background.

At the tables and bar, servers moved deftly between the seated customers, delivering plates of french fries, hamburgers, fried chicken, and an assortment of drinks. Amid the lively atmosphere, Blood, Cisco, Soupy, and Jonesy stood alongside the walls, observing the scene and conversing amongst themselves.

Across the room, Amber Stone and her friend Dee, both dressed in sharp black suits, were seated at a nearby table, ordering their drinks from a young server.

"I'll have a Manhattan cocktail," Amber said, her sultry red lips curving into a smile.

"And I'll have a Margarita," Dee chimed in.

The server jotted down their orders and hurried away. Amber glanced over, her eyes meeting those of Blood, who stood watching her intently.

"Dee, who is that guy?" Amber asked, nodding towards the imposing figure. "He keeps staring at me."

Dee followed Amber's gaze, a knowing look crossing her face. "Oh, him? That's Blood. I used to date him," she revealed.

Amber's brow arched. "What happened?" she inquired.

The server arrived with their drinks, interrupting the charged exchange and sat their drinks on the table and rushed away.

"He's a crazy guy, but nice," Dee replied, her tone cryptic.

"Is that all?" Amber pressed.

Dee shrugged. "That's all I want to tell you," she said, taking a sip of her drink.

Sensing an opportunity, Blood suddenly strode over to their table, a confident grin on his face. "Hi, I'm Blood," he said, his gaze locked on Amber. "What's your name?"

Amber eyed him cautiously. There was an undeniable magnetism to this man, but his imposing nickname gave her pause.

"Amber Stone," she replied, taking a sip of her Manhattan cocktail.

"Hi, Dee," Blood said, nodding towards Amber's friend.

"Hey, Blood," Dee responded, a hint of familiarity in her tone.

"Amber Stone, is that your first and middle name?" Blood asked, his gaze fixed on the raven-haired beauty.

"People just don't call me Amber without the Stone," she answered, her crimson lips caressing the rim of her glass.

Amber and Dee took sips, savoring the potent cocktails. Blood watched, mesmerized as Amber's lips glistened.

"Are you a model?" he asked, his eyes roaming appreciatively over her elegant features.

Amber smiled coyly. "I'm trying desperately to be one," she replied.

Blood leaned in closer. "Amber Stone, would you like to hang out with me tonight?" he asked, his voice low and alluring.

Amber felt a flutter of excitement, but also a twinge of unease. "Well, I don't know - would I be safe?" she asked cautiously.

Sensing her hesitation, Blood reassured her. "Don't listen to Dee. You'd be very secure with me," he said, casting a sly glance at his ex-girlfriend.

Dee rolled her eyes good-naturedly.

"With a nickname like Blood, it resonates with a vampire," Amber teased, the girls giggled.

Blood chuckled, a hint of embarrassment colored his cheeks. "My name is Ray Perkman. Blood is just my street name. I know it sounds intimidating," he explained.

"No, it sounds macho," Amber purred, her eyes shining with curiosity.

Sensing an opening, Blood pulled a crisp twenty-dollar bill from his pocket and placed it on the table.

Amber looked surprised. "What's that for?"

"For you and Dee's drinks," he replied, his gaze focused solely on her.

Slowly, Amber rose from her chair, her hand slipping into Blood's outstretched palm. "The night is still new," he murmured. "I guarantee we won't be strangers for long."

Amber glanced back at Dee, a coy smile playing on her lips.

"See you later," she said, allowing Blood to lead her out of the club.

"Have fun," Dee called after them, a knowing gleam in her eye.

It was 2 a.m., when the taxi pulled up to the desolate, black-boarded storefront on Lenox Avenue. Blood and Amber Stone stepped out, making their way towards the entrance. Amber surveyed their surroundings cautiously as Blood knocked on the gate, pressing his face to the peephole. The gate swung open, and the couple stepped inside.

In the hallway of the Spot, a muscular bouncer in his 40s stood guard, casual attire concealing a waist holster with a gun and nightstick.

"Hey Blood, welcome to the Spot," the bouncer said.

"Hey, brother, what's up?" Blood replied.

"Nothing much. I haven't seen you in a while." The bouncer patted Blood down, searching for any weapons, then turned his gaze to Amber. "Miss, do you have any weapons on you?"

Amber raised her palms. "No, I don't."

"Where have you been, fellow?" the bouncer asked.

"I've been around," Blood responded.

The bouncer produced a small bag of white powder.

"Here's some coke. I cut it one time."

Blood pulled out a hundred-dollar bill, exchanging it for the aluminum foil containing the drugs. "If you say this is good, I believe you."

"You and the lady enjoy the rest of the evening," the bouncer said, allowing them to pass.

The VIP room of the Spot was a stark contrast to the gritty streets outside. Awash in the pulsing blue and red lights, the space exuded an air of exclusivity and decadence. Glamorously dressed men and women in their 30s and 40s lounged in the plush booths, casually snorting lines of cocaine between sips of expensive champagne. A hazy cloud of cigarette smoke hung in the air, adding to the clandestine atmosphere.

Blood and Amber navigated through the opulent scene, their eyes scanning the room as they sought out a secluded booth. The patrons lining the bar were equally indulgent, nursing glasses of premium liquor and puffing on lit cigarettes, their laughter and chatter mingling with the pounding bass from the speakers.

Finding an isolated corner, Blood and Amber slid into the booth, settling in as a server in her 40s, her makeup impeccably applied, approached them. With a practiced smile, she asked, "What can I get for you two tonight?"

Blood's gaze flicked over the woman, cataloguing her movements and demeanor. This was a different world from the streets he was accustomed to - one of wealth, excess, and carefully curated personas. He glanced at Amber, waiting for her lead on how to navigate these unfamiliar waters. As Amber placed their order, Blood took in the sights and sounds around them, his senses heightened.

The VIP room may seem like a sanctuary from the chaos outside, but he knew better than to let his guard down. This was still the Spot, a hub for the city's criminal elite, and he had to be vigilant. One wrong move could have serious consequences.

"I'll have a Bloody Mary," Blood ordered, his gaze steady as he met the server's eyes.

"And a Manhattan cocktail," Amber requested, flashing the server a coy smile.

As the server stepped away, Blood turned his full attention to Amber. "Did you have fun at the Den?"

"I enjoyed myself; I rarely get out," Amber replied, a touch of wistfulness in her voice.

"Where do you live?" Blood asked, his curiosity piqued.

"I live in Harlem, on 121st Street," Amber revealed.

Blood's brow furrowed slightly. "That's hard to understand. A beauty like you would have caught my eye a long time ago."

"Thanks for the compliment; I'm not uptown a lot," Amber said coyly.

"Where do you hang out?" Blood inquired, leaning in slightly.

"I go to photoshoots, and to maintain my shape, I do Judo. I am trying to stay thin to be a model," Amber explained.

"Judo!" Blood exclaimed, some surprise evident in his tone.

"It's a sport," Amber clarified, a small smile playing on her lips.

"I like a woman with a little meat on her. If I wanted bones, I would go to a butcher," Blood declared, his gaze roaming appreciatively over Amber's curves.

"I have curves," she said coyly, a hint of a challenge in her voice.

"Yes, I can see but don't get too thin on me," he cautioned, a slightly possessive edge to his words.

Suddenly, Blood produced a small bag of white powder, sniffing it deeply. He then offered it to Amber, who took it and swiftly snorted the contents into both nostrils.

"Wow! This is good," Amber said, pinching her nose.

"So you know coke as a connoisseur knows wine?" Blood prompted, a touch of approval in his tone.

"How could I not, hanging out with Dee? It kind of rubbed off," Amber admitted.

"Dee learned from me to inhale only the best. I don't put crap up my snout," Blood boasted, handing the remaining powder to Amber.

Amber carefully snorted the last of the cocaine, wincing slightly as it burned in her nasal cavity.

"Wow! This quality of snow keeps a girl thin," she remarked, sliding the empty bag back towards Blood.

Leaning in closer, Blood's gaze intensified. "You must have an abundance of pressure on you?"

"Yeah, that's why I'm sitting here with you - I can be myself," Amber confided.

"You certainly are pretty," Blood observed, a hint of admiration in his voice.

"Thanks, even beauty has its standards," Amber replied, a touch of wistfulness in her tone.

"I don't give a damn. I do what I want to do in this world," Blood declared boldly.

"That's complicated to do, but I'm trying," Amber admitted.

As the server brought their drinks, the conversation continued to flow, delving into deeper personal territory.

"You haven't told me what you do for an income?" Amber inquired, her curiosity piqued.

Blood dabbed a bit of the white powder onto his tongue. "I prefer to gamble and shoot craps," he revealed.

"You make a livelihood out of that?" Amber asked, her brow furrowed with concern.

Blood raised his glass and swallowed the liquor. "Hell yeah," he replied confidently.

Amber thoughtfully circled the rim of her glass with her finger. "You think society owes you something?"

"No, I'm making it," Blood stated matter-of-factly.

"Shooting dice is not a normal career - it's not a steady job," Amber pointed out, a touch of worry in her voice.

"Who needs security if you have the money?" Blood argued, his tone unwavering.

Amber shrugged. "Who am I to judge? I am struggling myself."

A shadow passed over Blood's features. "No one knows strife more than me; they killed my Mama," he said solemnly.

Amber's eyes widened with empathy. "I'm sorry, my mother died too; she had cancer. It was difficult for my dad and me. But for you, I can't imagine the pain you feel. You want to tell me about it?"

Blood paused, his gaze distant. "We lived in the Mississippi Delta, and it was after midnight. I was escaping and trying to make it back to my house to warn my Mama to escape. I knew they would come after my Mama looking for me."

With those words, Blood's recollection began, transporting the pair back in time to a dark and treacherous night in the Mississippi swamp of 1960.

The night was thick with the damp air, the black trunks of the trees dripping with rotting vegetation. Frogs croaked, leeches clung to slugs, and snakes curled up on the branches as a spider spun its web. An alligator slid silently through the water.

Blood ran, his clothes sticky with sweat, the moisture clinging to his skin. He slapped at a stinging insect on his neck as he splashed through the swampy ground, his wet shoes squelching with each step.

Something brushed against his leg in the water, and he lashed out with a torn branch, discovering it was just a floating fish. Climbing through the deadfall, Blood's skin was cut by the slimy rocks and trees. Leeches fell upon him, and he pulled them off one by one. The hanging moss brushed against his head as his heartbeat fluttered at every sound and splash. The mud sucked at his shoes as he stumbled and tripped, quickly bouncing back to his feet.

Beneath the shadows of the moonlight, Blood emerged from the swamp, racing across the landscape until he reached his mother's humble shack.

There, a half-circle of twenty Klansmen in white hoods held torches and a large cross, clamoring outside Irma's home. Blood peered through the thick leaves, daring not to show himself. His eyes filled with terror as he watched a Klansman light a Molotov cocktail and hurl it through the window. Irma insisted that Blood was not there, but the flaming bottle was soon followed by several more, the furniture and trash catching fire.

The flames spread swiftly, blocking the entrance and windows. Irma frantically tried to escape, but the fire consumed her. Her liquor bottle exploded, and she was enveloped in flames, twirling and screaming as she crashed out the door and fell to the ground, burning to ashes. The Klansmen stood and watched as Irma and her shack were reduced to embers and smoke.

Blood, hidden in the foliage, wept helplessly, his hands covering his face as he relived the horrific memory. Amber, shocked by the brutality of the story, gently grasped Blood's palms. "That is horrible for any child to see happen to their mother. You tell the story like Blood is not you."

"It's how I see and talk about my past like it was an out-of-body experience, yet I feel the pain, remember every smell," Blood explained.

"The coke helps?" Amber asked gently.

He squeezed her hand. "Right now, I am here with you, and I know it's marvelous."

Blood offered the remaining cocaine to Amber, and she quickly drained her cocktail, the two of them riding high on the soft jazz music playing through the Spot's speakers.

The inky darkness of the pre-dawn sky gave way to the first faint glimmers of light on the horizon. A chill hung in the air, the city streets eerily quiet in the stillness before the bustle of the day began.

Blood and Amber stumbled out of the Spot, their laughter echoing through the deserted alleyway. The VIP room had been a cocoon of excess and indulgence, but now they were confronted with the stark reality of the early morning.

Amber's makeup was smudged, her pant suit slightly disheveled from hours of sitting and drinking. Blood's suit was rumpled, his shirt loosened, a faint sheen of sweat on his brow. They had lost all track of time, entranced by the intoxicating atmosphere inside the club. The Spot had been a temporary escape, but now they faced the harsh realities that awaited them beyond its doors.

Yet, in that moment, there was a sense of camaraderie and shared experience that bound them together, even if just for a fleeting instant. Blinking in the pale light, they made their way towards the street, searching for an available taxi. The sounds of their laughter and the scuff of their shoes were the only disturbances to the tranquil silence that blanketed the city.

As Blood raised his arm to hail a cab, Amber leaned into him, her body swaying slightly. The night had clearly taken its toll, but there was an aura of exhilaration about them - a sense of having indulged in the forbidden pleasures of the Spot's VIP room. The taxi pulled up to the curb. Suddenly, Blood pulled Amber into a passionate kiss, his arms wrapping around her waist and drawing her close. Their laughter faded into the stillness of the morning as they lost themselves in the heated embrace. After a long moment, they broke apart, both slightly breathless.

"I'll call you," Blood promised, his eyes gleaming with a mix of sincerity and mischief.

Amber, with a hint of doubt in her voice, replied, "Alright."

"I promise I'll call you," he reiterated, reaching out to tuck a stray strand of her hair behind her ear.

With a shallow smile, she said, "Sure."

Blood then opened the taxi door for Amber, gesturing for her to climb inside. Amber climbed inside, sinking into the worn leather seats.

"Until next time," he murmured, his gaze locked with hers.

Amber waved goodbye as the cab pulled away, leaving Blood watching her disappear into the soft glow of the rising sun. He stood there for a moment, a small smile playing on his lips, before turning and vanishing back into the shadows of the alleyway.

Entering her studio apartment, Amber stepped behind the shutters, changing into a blue satin robe. The soft fabric clung to her curves as she moved, a stark contrast to the darkness of the room. She sat at her table, producing a dollar bill filled with cocaine from the hidden pocket of her robe.

Resisting the urge to immediately indulge, Amber glanced around her carefully curated, black-and-white decor. The fashionable clothes hanging in the closet, the lilac ostrich feathers decorating the dresser mirror, the vogue photos adorning the walls - all of it a testament to her aspirations and the image she sought to project. But the lure of the drug was too strong.

With a heavy sigh, Amber gave in, leaning forward to snort the cocaine. The sharp sting in her nose was immediately followed by a rush of euphoria, momentarily washing away her troubles. Frustrated by her weakness, she pounded her fist on the tabletop, scrunching her face as she checked for wrinkles in the vanity mirror. Facing the reality of her addiction, Amber knew she had to quit - but not today. She would delay the inevitable, telling herself she'd kick the habit tomorrow. For now, she sat in the bright sunlight filtering in through the shutters, waiting for the high to come down, determined to get through the next 24 hours without sleep aids. The promise of temporary escape was a siren's call she could never fully resist, even as it continued to chip away at her sense of control. Amber gazed into a flashback of her graduation.

The auditorium was alive with energy as Harlem Community College's graduates filed in, their navy blue robes lending a sense of formality to the celebratory atmosphere. Amber searched the crowd, her eyes finally landing on her father, Professor Stone, as he made his way to a seat in the middle section.

Amber's heart swelled with pride as she watched him settle into his chair, his gaze fixed intently on the stage. She knew how much this moment meant to him, even if he had hoped for her to pursue a more prestigious degree.

As the ceremony began, Professor Stone sat up straighter, his fingers drumming nervously against the armrest. Amber could see the mix of emotions playing across his features - the pride at her accomplishment, tempered by a hint of disappointment that she hadn't chosen the path he had envisioned for her.

When Amber's name was called, Professor Stone's eyes narrowed in focus, a small smile tugging at the corners of his mouth as he watched her confidently stride across the stage to accept her diploma in Business Management. Amber locked eyes with him for a brief moment, silently seeking his approval.

As the ceremony came to a close and the graduates began filing out, Professor Stone remained in his seat, lost in thought. Amber approached him cautiously, unsure of how he would react.

"Daddy?" she said softly, placing a hand on his shoulder.

Professor Stone looked up, his expression unreadable. "I'm proud of you, Amber," he said, his voice carrying a weight of mixed emotions. "But I must admit, I had hoped for more."

Amber nodded, bracing herself for the inevitable conversation they would have as they made their way back to the Harlem brownstone.

She knew her father's standards were high, and that her choice of a business degree over the sciences he had pushed her towards would be a point of contention.

Yet, as she looked into Professor Stone's eyes, Amber saw a glimmer of understanding. He may not have agreed with her decision, but she could see the fierce love and pride he felt for her. And in that moment, Amber knew she would need to find the strength to prove to him – and to herself – that she could still forge a successful path, even if it didn't align perfectly with his vision.

After Professor Stone and Amber returned to the Harlem brownstone, he wasted no time in voicing his disappointment.

"Amber, I'm happy you graduated, but I was hoping for a university degree in biology or science."

Amber fidgeted nervously. "I know, Daddy. But the sciences just aren't my strong suit. Business is what I'm good at."

Professor Stone nodded slowly. "I see. And that's exactly the problem. Science means you can't drink or smoke pot - you have to stay home and study, and I know you like to party. I am selling the house."

Amber's brow furrowed as she argued, "Daddy, this is the house where I grew up. Where Mom died. How can you just sell it?"

"The Brownstone has too many memories, and I'm not going to keep making the trip back and forth from Washington. I'm moving there permanently," Professor Stone stated firmly.

Amber's eyes widened. "Can I come live with you then? I could work for a corporation until I can start my own business."

Professor Stone's expression hardened. "What kind of business?

"I don't know," Amber answered.

Professor Stone responded, "That's the problem, Amber. You have no plan. You just drift along waiting for something to fall into your lap. The sciences would have given you a more strategic, focused mind."

"I can focus if I am interested," Amber answered.

He paused, his gaze unwavering. "I know you, Amber. I know you'll be out partying in Washington, and I prefer you to live on your own. I am selling the Brownstone and I will use the money to pay your rent and send you a monthly allowance until you can figure out what you want to do."

"What do you expect me to do sit home and twiddle my thumbs." Amber sassed back.

"Maybe in a couple years you'll get tired of partying or meet a well-to-do man and settle down." Professor Stone suggested.

Amber said, "In the meantime, Daddy, my friend Dee wanted to move into this studio apartment here in Harlem, but she couldn't afford the rent. It would be perfect for me."

Professor Stone's brow furrowed. "Amber, is Dee one of your college friends?"

Amber shook her head. "No, I met her at the bar."

Professor Stone let out a heavy sigh. "It figures."

Amber's eyes narrowed. "Daddy, I have to have friends. We don't all live in a perfect world like you."

Professor Stone's lips pressed into a thin line. "Yes, and that's another problem. You always seek out the down and troubled, the ones who need fixing."

"Not everyone is disciplined or goal-oriented like you." Amber said.

Professor Stone said, "No but you could be if you tried. That is the problem, you never try. Girl, I just don't know what I'm going to do with you."

Amber's shoulders slumped. "The question is, what am I going to do with myself?"

Professor Stone reached into his jacket pocket and withdrew his checkbook. "I'm going back to Washington." He jotted down a figure and handed the check to Amber.

"Here's a check for $10,000 to cover your rent until you get settled. Send your address to my PO Box and I'll send you a monthly allowance."

Amber's brow furrowed. "Daddy, can't you tell me where you're staying in Washington? The letters I sent came back."

"I'm staying at a top secret facility. EBW Tech has a government contract, so we had to relocate with no forwarding address. You have the PO Box and my number, that's all I can give you," Professor Stone replied, his tone clipped.

Amber rushed forward, wrapping her arms around her father. "I'm going to miss this house, Daddy. And I'll miss you."

Professor Stone's expression softened, and he placed a gentle kiss on her forehead. "I know, I'm sorry. But you'll have to pack your things today. The realtors are coming with buyers tomorrow."

Amber's eyes widened. "That fast?"

"Yes, no point in lingering any longer and your mother's memory will always be in my heart. I loved Vera and still love her, and I will never forget her. It is time we moved forward," Professor Stone said, his voice tinged with regret.

Amber's gaze searched his face. "Is there someone else, Daddy?"

Professor Stone's jaw tightened. "I don't want to talk about it. I must go, I don't want to miss my flight."

Professor Stone kissed Amber on the forehead. They broke their embrace.

Amber Stone said, "See you soon."

Professor Stone said, "Sure."

Amber had watched as her father departed, leaving her to face an uncertain future. She had stood there trying to digest what her father had said while she looked around the living room for the last time. Her flashback ended, and Amber was back sitting at her table in her studio apartment, sniffing cocaine and gazing into the bright, sunny room.

Later that afternoon, outside The Den Club Bar, the regulars entered for their afternoon drinks. Blood exited the building, greeted by Chang - a man in his 60s with a limp.

Their exchange was brief but hinting at a deeper connection between the two men that extended beyond the walls of the bar.

"I'm going to open a club next to The Den," Chang announced. "Why don't you come and work for me?"

"Doing what?" Blood inquired.

"Being a bouncer. I may need you for other things," Chang replied.

"I don't know," Blood hesitated.

"It'll be good for you. My brother Ejay looks out for my dealers, and my baby brother, Baby James, will be taking care of the books. Fat Bob is just my gofer. I need a bouncer," Chang explained.

"I'll think about it," Blood said.

"I'll be waiting for your answer. Take care, Blood," Chang said, limping away.

Suddenly, Dee approached Blood, throwing her arms around him.

"Hey baby, I missed you. When are we going to get together again?" Dee asked.

"You know, it's over between you and me," Blood answered.

"What do you mean it's over?" Dee protested.

"What we had was a fling," Blood clarified.

"That's not how I saw it," Dee argued.

"What did you tell Amber Stone about me?" Blood inquired.

"Nothing, just that I used to date you," Dee replied.

"Dee, the best thing you ever did was to bring Amber Stone to The Den," Blood stated.

"Don't tell me you like her?" Dee questioned, her voice tinged with jealousy.

"What if I do?" Blood responded.

"We had some good times together, Blood," Dee reminisced.

"I really do like Amber Stone," Blood admitted.

Dee grabbed his collar, pulling him close. "You can call me anytime," she purred.

"I thought Amber Stone was your friend," Blood said.

"I'm not that bitch's friend," Dee retorted.

Blood took Dee's hands off his collar and broke their embrace. "Amber Stone and I are going to be together," he declared.

Blood then strolled into The Den, heading to the payphone to call Amber. "Hey, babe, it's Blood. Why don't you meet me at The Den?" he said.

Amber's sleepy voice replied, "I'm tired. I have a shoot tomorrow, so I'll meet you in the evening."

"Get your beauty sleep, and I'll see you in the evening. Lots of kisses and hugs," Blood said with a smile.

"The same to you; see you later," Amber responded before hanging up.

Blood hung up the phone and approached the bar. He ordered a drink and couldn't help daydreaming about seeing Amber again, watching the basketball game playing on the television until he decided to head home, eager to be well-rested for his girlfriend.

The next day, at Bill's Photo Studio, Amber stood in front of the camera, modeling a high-fashion outfit. The deep crimson dress clung to her figure, accentuating her curves, while the intricate beading and lace detailing added an air of sophistication.

The 30-something Caucasian photographer, Bill, moved around her, excitedly directing her poses. He had a keen eye for composition and lighting, capturing Amber's elegance and poise through the lens. His hands gestured animatedly as he instructed her to tilt her head, to angle her body just so, to convey a sense of refined confidence.

Amber responded effortlessly, and focused on her modeling and it shined through. She moved with a natural grace, shifting her weight, striking poses that highlighted the design of the dress. There was a practiced precision to her movements, honed through countless photoshoots and runway shows.

The studio was filled with the whirring of the camera's mechanical shutter, the soft hum of the lighting equipment, and the occasional murmur of approval from Bill as he reviewed the images on his digital display. He seemed enthralled by Amber's performance, eagerly capturing every nuanced expression and subtle shift in her posture.

As the session wore on, Amber maintained her composure, her focus unwavering. But behind the polished veneer, the telltale signs of her addiction lingered - the faint tremble in her hands, the slight hollowness in her gaze. Still, she channeled that vulnerability into her work, imbuing the photographs with an intriguing depth and vulnerability.

"That's great. Try another pose," Bill instructed.

Amber moved gracefully, and Bill continued shooting.

"That's a wrap! We got it," Bill announced.

"When is this coming out?" Amber asked.

"It'll be in the Daily News next week," Bill replied.

"I can't wait to tell everybody," Amber said excitedly.

"I don't know what shot they'll use," Bill admitted.

"This is my first big job," Amber beamed.

"Congratulations, I hope you have many more," Bill said.

"I'm going to celebrate tonight. I would invite you, but it's uptown with my new boyfriend," Amber shared.

"No, thanks, I have work to do; you enjoy yourself," Bill said.

Amber accepted Bill's effusive praise with a practiced smile. She happily went into the dressing room and changed out of her fashion attire, donning casual jeans, a t-shirt, and a jacket, and left the studio, eager to celebrate her success.

CHAPTER TWO

Later that evening, at the dimly lit Den Bar, Amber sits with Soupy, Jonesy, and Cisco, the three other members of Blood's crew. They have gathered to toast Amber's first successful modeling job, excitedly sipping champagne.

Amber, dressed in her finest, can barely contain her enthusiasm. This is her big moment, and she had hoped to share it with Blood by her side. But as she scanned the crowded room, her eyes search anxiously for any sign of him.

"Where is Blood?" Amber asked, her voice laced with trepidation. The others laughed and drank their champagne. They knew better than to make excuses for their leader's tardiness.

Amber tried to push down the knot of worry in her stomach. She and Blood had played it by ear, navigating their relationship without a clear plan. But she had assumed he would be there to celebrate her success with her.

As the minutes ticked by, Amber can't help but worry that Blood may have stood her up. She had been so looking forward to this night, to sharing her triumph with the man she cared for.

"He may be at the apartment," answered Soupy.

"We'll save some champagne for him," Cisco said.

"What's it like to be a model?" Jonesy asked.

"I love it," Amber said.

"Models get paid big money," said Soupy.

"That is only If I make it," answered Amber.

"Why do you do it?" Cisco asked.

"I want to make it big," Amber replied.

"That kind of patience I don't have," said Jonesy.

"My money has to come in fast," Soupy said.

Amber poured the guys and herself a glass of champagne and toast. "Thank you guys for being here."

Amber took a sip of her champagne and glanced at her watch. Dee approached the bar.

"Hey, Amber Stone, what's up?" Dee said.

"Dee, my girl, you want a glass of champagne?" Amber asked.

"Sure, what's the occasion?" Dee inquired, sliding onto the barstool next to Amber.

"I got my first modeling job today," Amber replied.

Amber poured Dee a glass of champagne.

Dee raised her glass, "Here's to you."

The minutes ticked by agonizingly slow, and Amber couldn't help but fidget nervously, her fingers drummed against the polished wood of the bar. She took a hasty sip of her champagne, hoping to calm her nerves, but the bubbly liquid seemed to turn to ash in her mouth.

"Where is Blood? He's supposed to be here?" Amber asked.

Dee took a sip of the champagne and sat the glass down.

"Watch my drink?" Dee said.

Dee walked over to the jukebox, puts coins into it, and looked at the selection of music.

Suddenly, all eyes turned towards the entrance. There, in a swirl of leather and attitude, is Blood, his eyes scanned the room until they landed on Dee. A slow, predatory grin spreads across his face as he made his way towards her, the other patrons instinctively parted to let him pass.

Blood passed Amber, walked over to Dee, and slapped her hard across the face. She ran out of the bar crying. Amber's heart raced as he made his way towards the group, with a calm expression spreading across his face as if nothing had happened. The group continued their conversation, Amber remaining cool and composed despite the underlying tension. She knew there's more to the story between Dee and Blood, but for now, she's focused on celebrating her own success. Blood approached her and she looked into his eyes.

"What is going on?" Amber asked, her voice betraying a hint of irritability.

"Dee has been talking shit about me," Blood said.

"We are celebrating my first modeling job," Amber stated.

"Dee told you I used to date her," Blood continues, his eyes narrowing.

"It was mentioned," Amber replied, her gaze steady.

"She's been trying to get me back," Blood explained, his possessiveness on full display.

"I don't believe it. Dee's my friend," Amber said, her loyalty to her friend evident.

"She's trying to take your man from you," Blood claimed.

Amber was concerned and couldn't help but question Blood's accusation.

"Now you're my man?" she asked, her voice laced with skepticism.

"I hope so," Blood replied, his gaze fixed on Amber.

"That means you're committed?" Amber probes, her curiosity piqued.

"That's what it sounds like," Blood said as he kissed Amber.

Blood's magnetic pull he exerts over Amber is undeniable and his charisma and power threatens to consume her.

"The proof is in the pudding ," Amber said, a hint of a smile playing on her lips.

"What is that supposed to mean?" Blood asked.

"That is for me to know and for you to find out," Amber responded.

"Come on, shall you and I party," Blood suggested.

"I have an audition early in the morning," Amber said.

"Great, I hope you get it," Blood replied.

"She'll give you a judo throw," Cisco blurted.

"What about dinner tomorrow night?" Blood asked.

"I accept; what time?" Amber inquired.

"I'll meet you here at 9 o'clock," Blood said.

"Deal. Good night, Soupy, Cisco, and Jonesy. Thanks for the champagne," Amber said.

Soupy, Cisco, and Jonesy all hugged and kissed Amber Stone on the cheek and said, "Good night."

The guys watched as Blood escorted her out of the club. They turned to each other and began talking amongst themselves.

"Amber is too good for Blood," said Jonesy.

"When he slapped Dee, she didn't even flinch," said Soupy.

"Most girls would have backed out after seeing his display of violence," said Jonesy.

"She knows Judo if Blood ever hits her, she will throw him all over the place," Cisco laughed and said.

"You think she knows about what Blood did?" Soupy asked.

"She doesn't have a clue if she did; she'd drop him like a nasty habit," Cisco said.

Outside the Den Club, the neon lights cast a warm glow over Amber and Blood as they lingered, reluctant to part ways for the night. Amber looked up at Blood, her eyes shining with a mixture of excitement and trepidation. Their connection had been electric from the start, a magnetic pull that made her feel like she had known him for years, not just one date. Carefully, Blood reached out and tucked a stray hair behind Amber's ear, his touch igniting a spark between them. Amber leaned in, her hands sliding around his waist, and they shared a deep, passionate kiss—a silent promise that this was only the beginning.

When they finally parted, breathless, Amber flashed him a coy smile. Blood gazed at her, his eyes filled with an intensity that made her heart race. With great reluctance, Amber stepped away and turned to the waiting taxi, glancing back at him one more time before disappearing into the night.

Back inside the Den, Blood's crew – Soupy, Jonesy, and Cisco – continued their raucous celebration, laughter and the clinking of glasses filling the air. They were clearly unbothered by their leader's absence, secure in the knowledge that he would rejoin them soon enough.

As Blood made his way back into the bar, Soupy said, "Did I ever tell you about the time I was pimping? Me and my hoe were on the corner," and Soupy's flashback began.

The night was alive with the pulsing energy of the city streets. Soupy stood on the corner, his eyes scanning the passing cars, his hoe by his side, ready to earn their keep.

Suddenly, a red station wagon pulled up, and Soupy watched as his hoe approached the vehicle, sliding into the backseat. Something wasn't right. Soupy could sense the tension, the struggle.

Without hesitation, he darted forward, yanking the car door open and climbing in. "Hey, you better be payin' my girl, you hear?" he demanded, his voice laced with a dangerous edge.

But the man in the backseat didn't cower in fear. Instead, he flipped open a badge, the metal glinting under the streetlights.

"NYPD," he growled, his hand reaching for his holstered weapon. Soupy's heart raced, his mouth going dry as the realization sank in. This was no ordinary john – it was an undercover cop.

"Get out of the car, both of you!" the officer barked, the barrel of his gun trained on Soupy and his hoe.

Soupy and the woman complied, their hands raised in surrender as the officer ordered them to turn around and place their hands on the hood of the car. With a swift motion, he snapped the handcuffs around their wrists, the cold metal biting into their skin.

"You're under arrest," the cop stated, his voice devoid of emotion. "We're going down to the station."

Soupy's flashback ended.

Blood asked, "What happened next?"

"I thought my number was up that day," he said, shaking his head. "But I managed to sweet-talk the judge, convinced him it was all just a misunderstanding."

Blood whistled, impressed. "Damn, Soupy, you got some balls, man. What'd you do after that?"

Soupy's expression darkened. "After that, I knew I needed to start looking for bigger scores. No more pimping and hustling, I started doing stickups. I wanted big money all at once." He took a long sip of his drink, the memory still vivid in his mind.

Jonesy said, "Let me tell you about the time I thought I was going to die," and his flashback began. Jonesy stepped out of the dimly lit building, the night air chilling his bones. He quickened his pace, his eyes scanning the deserted street as he made his way up the block.

Suddenly, a car screeched to a halt beside him, the passenger door flying open. Before Jonesy could react, a figure jumped out, grabbing him by the collar and shoving him into the backseat.

"Get in the car, now!" the man growled, his voice laced with menace.

Jonesy's heart pounded in his chest as he complied, his body trembling with fear. Once inside, he was met with the cold, hard stare of another man, a handgun pressed against his temple.

"Empty your pockets," the armed man demanded, his grip on the weapon unwavering.

Jonesy's fingers fumbled as he hastily removed the contents of his pockets – his wallet, ten $100 bills, and a set of keys. The man snatched them from his hand, his eyes narrowing as he rifled through the meager items.

"A thousand dollars that's it?" he snarled, his grip on the gun tightening.

Jonesy swallowed hard, nodding his head. "Y-yes, that's all I have," he stammered, his voice barely above a whisper.

The man's lips curled into a sneer. "Not good enough," he spat, before shoving the gun against Jonesy's ribs.

The car made a sharp turn, and Jonesy was suddenly thrown against the door as it slowed to a stop. The armed man grabbed him by the collar and yanked him out of the vehicle, tossing him onto the sidewalk.

Jonesy landed with a painful thud, his hands scraping against the concrete. He looked up just in time to see the car speeding away, leaving him alone and shaken on the dark, deserted street.

Jonesy's flashback ended. Cisco nodded, understanding dawning on his face. "After that, you knew you had to get off the streets. The risk of running numbers and carrying all that money on you was too high."

Jonesy met Cisco's gaze, a silent understanding passing between them. "That's right, after that incident, I got off the streets. I knew that as long as I was running numbers, I would be a target. I met Soupy, and he asked me to join him. The risk is greater, but the money is faster, and nobody is staking me out - I'm the one doing the stake out."

Cisco chimed in, "I was the one that did the driving. One time, I barely escaped," and his flashback began.

In a flash, Cisco was transported back to another time, another life. Cisco's heart pounded as he gripped the steering wheel, the adrenaline coursing through his veins. This wasn't his first rodeo - the familiar rush of a high-speed chase felt almost nostalgic. The air thick with tension, the sound of screeching tires and blaring sirens echoing through the city streets. He remembers the weight of the stolen cash in the backseat, the panicked shouts of his accomplices, and the laser-like focus required to navigate the darkened alleys and backroads.

Cisco gritted his teeth, his knuckles were sweaty as he pushed the pedal to the floor. The sleek sedan weaved through traffic, narrowly avoiding collisions as he expertly maneuvered the tight turns. In his rearview mirror, he could see the flashing lights of the police car closing in, its siren wailing.

"Come on, come on," Cisco muttered under his breath, sweat beading on his brow. He knew he had to lose them, had to get away before it was too late. Memories of that fateful night flooded his mind - the heist going south, the panicked getaway, the crushing weight of failure.

Ahead, Cisco spotted a sharp turn leading into a dimly lit alley. Without hesitation, he jerked the wheel, the tires screeching as the car took the corner, lifting up on two wheels, almost turning over, and then slamming back down. The police car, unable to match his nimble maneuvers, lost control and slammed into a nearby parked vehicle, the impact sending it spinning out of control.

Cisco let out a breath he didn't know he was holding, his grip on the wheel finally loosening. He was in the clear, for now. Glancing in the rearview mirror, he watched as the police car came to a halt, its occupants dazed but unharmed.

With a wry smile, Cisco knew he'd lived to fight another day. The past may have come back to haunt him, but in this moment, he was the master of his own destiny, a ghost in the night, escaping the clutches of the law once again. Cisco's flashback ended.

The four men shared a weighted look, each with their own scars and experiences etched into their faces. In this world, survival was an art form, and they were the masters of their craft.

Soupy raised his glass, a knowing glint in his eye. "To us, the ones who made it out the other side. May our luck never run out."

The others joined him, the sound of glass clinking filling the air as they toasted to their shared history, a bond forged in the fires of adversity and crime. Tony — a casually dressed, brown-skinned young man — approached Jonesy, Soupy, and the others. Whatever they had to say seemed to pique his interest, drawing him into the conversation.

"What's up, Jonesy?" Tony asked.

"Hey Tony, how are you doing?" Jonesy answered.

"Fine," said Tony.

"We are going to the basement to gamble come hang out with us," Jonesy said.

"Are there any ladies on the scene?" Tony asked.

"There are some ladies waiting for us I don't know about Blood he's taken," Jonesy said.

"Amber's got him hooked," Soupy chimed in.

"It's more like, he's got her," said Cisco.

"Meaning she's not like Blood's other two women," Jonesy said.

Blood smiled and said, "You guys are full of crap."

"You are crazy Blood but you are my man," Soupy replied.

"Blood digs Deanna, she's cool a little emotional. She goes to work every day," Cisco said.

"Betty is hot she's got it together," said Soupy.

"Betty is cool. Never raises her voice. Her apartment is cool too," Cisco blurted.

"Betty doesn't give a fuck; she is dating other motherfuckers anyway," said Soupy.

"I got a fashion model," Blood bragged.

"Amber Stone has a lust for life," said Cisco.

"Unlike you Blood all you can think about is money killing and dying," Jonesy said.

Blood raised his glass of liquor and said, "I'll drink to that."

All the guys raised their glasses in a toast and gulped their liquid in merriment.

"Does Amber Stone know all about you, Blood, and she is still with you?' Jonesy asked.

"No, she doesn't know. She thinks I am some two-bit hustler," answered Blood.

"Well, Blood you are not far from it," Soupy said and laughed.

"Get the hell out of here I am the man just asked my ladies," said Blood.

"When Amber finds out boy, Blood is going to be in trouble," Jonesy said.

"Put your money where your mouth is how much do you want to bet Amber Stone knocks Betty and Deanna out of the box," Cisco said.

"What do you think this is a competition? This is love they love the ground Blood walks on," Jonesy said.

"Betty doesn't give a fuck about no other woman. She'll date anyone that will make her life easy," said Soupy.

"Come on let's go to the basement and bet on it I am the Cisco kid the ladies are waiting," Cisco said.

Soupy slapped a $100 bill on the bar to pay for their drinks before they exited.

As the night wore on, Blood and his crew – Soupy, Jonesy, Tony, and Cisco – spilled out onto the brightly lit boulevard, their boisterous laughter and chatter carrying through the air. The neon signs and streetlights cast an almost electric glow over the scene, and the men were flush with the thrill of the evening's celebration.

However, as they turned the corner, the atmosphere shifted dramatically. The boulevard gave way to a dark, shadowy block, with the street lamps casting long, ominous shadows. Undeterred, the men pressed on, their footsteps echoing along the deserted street. They passed a looming schoolyard, its gates and fences casting forbidding silhouettes against the night sky.

Ahead stood a weathered brownstone, its facade inscrutable in the gloom. Soupy, Jonesy, and Cisco led the way, with Tony and Blood following closely behind. Approaching the building, Cisco strode up to a black door set into the basement, rapping out a rhythmic pattern.

The door swung open, and the men stepped inside, the heavy portal closing behind them with a dull thud. The basement was a study in contrasts – the walls bathed in rich, royal blue and crimson, the plush red velvet sofa an inviting oasis. In the center of the room, a regal red and gold chair sat at the head of a dining table, with five other seats surrounding it. Glasses of liquor and a bowl of cocaine sat upon the table's polished surface.

Four women, dressed in clingy red and pink jersey dresses, immediately converged on the men, their arms snaking around Soupy, Cisco, Jonesy, and Tony. Blood, ever the leader, settled into the ornate chair, his crew and the women gathering around him as they indulged in the illicit pleasures displayed before them.

Blood, as he stuffs the drug up, his nose said, "This is good coke."

"That is not why I brought you guys here we got a bet," Cisco said.

"You can't bet on a woman you talking like they are horses at the races," Jonesy said.

"They are in a race to get Blood who will be the winner or loser?" Soupy asked.

"Yeah but the race isn't over yet," Blood said.

"I say Amber Stone wins and that is 7 or 11 haven't you guys ever heard of intuition?" Cisco asked.

"I bet you don't get 7 or 11," Soupy said.

Flashing his money, Cisco said, "I got $500; how much you guys got?"

Blood, Jonesy, and Soupy wave their $500 in Cisco's face.

"Let us go over to the wall and start this game," Cisco said.

"Tony would you like to join us?" Jonesy asked.

"I am staying right over here with my lady she's a doll," said Tony.

The three women, their dresses shimmering in the low light, guided Soupy and Jonesy over to the far wall of the basement lounge. Cisco stepped forward, a wad of cash clutched in his hand, and tossed it down onto the floor with a decisive thud.

Without a word, Blood, Jonesy, and Soupy followed suit, their own stacks of bills joining Cisco's growing pile. The room took on an almost electric tension as the men readied themselves for the coming game.

One of the women, her eyes sparkling with mischief, sidled up to Cisco. Gently, she took the dice from his outstretched palm, cupping them in her hands before blowing softly across them.

The gesture was both sensual and superstitious, a silent plea for good fortune. Cisco watched, transfixed, as the woman tossed the dice onto the floor. The cubes tumbled and bounced, sharp clicks echoing off the rich, velvety walls.

All eyes were trained on the dice as they came to rest, the number 11 glaring up at the assembled players.

A collective murmur of approval rippled through the group, and the woman who blew on the dice flashed Cisco a triumphant smile. The other women moved in closer, their hands caressing the men's arms and shoulders as the game began in earnest.

Blood settled back into his ornate chair, his gaze sweeping over the proceedings with a cool, calculated expression. This was his domain, his kingdom, and he would ensure that the night's events unfolded exactly as he desired.

Cisco said, "11 give me my money, man."

Soupy and Jonesy rushed to pick up the money from the floor.

"Hey man that is my money what are you all doing man," Cisco pleaded.

Soupy, and Jonesy stood before Cisco, throwing the money at him. "Here is your money," Soupy said, his voice laced with a hint of triumph.

"Take it, take it," Jonesy urged, his excitement palpable.

Cisco caught what he could, greedily grabbing the bills from the floor. He counted it quickly, his eyes darting back and forth. Soupy leaned over his shoulder, curiosity etched on his face.

"Any extra dollars is ours - how much did you win?" Soupy asked, a greedy gleam in his eye.

"Fifteen hundred, plus the five hundred I already had," Cisco answered, a satisfied smile spreading across his face.

"Come, ladies, let us have some cocaine and drinks," Soupy suggested, gesturing towards the dining table.

The group moved to the table, settling into their seats. Soupy poured generous servings of vodka, his favorite white liquor.

"Soupy loves that white liquor," Cisco blurted, a chuckle escaping his lips.

"That's right, I get fucked up off of this shit. I got to have a sniff of coke to balance my high. We old folks say let's go get stoned," Soupy retorted, a mischievous grin on his face.

They all drank and made merry. Tony sat on the sofa, getting a lap dance from his lady. Jonesy grabbed a saucer of cocaine, approached them, and offered Tony a line.

"Tony, would you like a sniff of coke?" Jonesy asked.

Tony's lady paused the dance, took the saucer, sat next to Tony, and indulged in the white powder.

"Thanks, Jonesy. I'm sorry I don't have Blood's money," Tony said, his voice laced with worry.

The mood shifts from a carefree revelry giving way to a more serious, pensive atmosphere.

Blood, overhearing the exchange, snapped. "You talk to me about money? I saw you yesterday, and you said the same thing. Let's go over in the corner and talk about what you owe me."

Tony, visibly terrified, followed Blood to a secluded corner of the basement. The confrontation was ferocious.

"Jonesy is not in charge of collecting money, I am," Blood growled.

"I know, I had the money, and I was stopped by the police, and they confiscated it," Tony pleaded, his voice trembling.

"You're a lying piece of shit. You stole and spent my money," Blood accused, his eyes narrowed.

"No, no, Blood, I swear the cops got the money," Tony begged, desperate for his life.

"I've heard this bullshit before from you," Blood spat.

Tony, terrified and bending his knees, pleaded for his life.

"Give me a chance, I can get the money," he begged.

"I want my money now," Blood demanded, his hand closing around Tony's neck.

"Please, I'll do anything you ask," Tony cried, tears streaming down his face.

"You mean it?" Blood asked, his grip tightening.

The tension in the dimly lit basement is palpable as Tony's desperate words fill the room.

"Tomorrow, tomorrow, I swear you'll have the money, tomorrow night at midnight," he promises, his voice choked with fear as Blood's unrelenting grip remains around his neck.

"I have your word?" Blood asked, his tone low and laced with menace.

"Yes, yes, I won't let you down, just don't kill me, I'm begging you," Tony sobbed, his body trembling under the gangster's unyielding gaze. With calculated slowness, Blood removed his hand from Tony's neck, reaching behind to pull a gun from under his shirt. He aimed and fired, the sound echoing through the basement, causing the women to erupt into terrified screams. Blood glared at the ladies, his eyes filled with a chilling menace.

"You ladies better shut up, or I'll kill all four of you," he growled, the threat in his words undeniable.

Jonesy stepped forward, his voice trembling. "You can't do that, Blood," he protested, brow furrowed with defiance and trepidation.

Blood's lip curled in a sneer as he levels his gaze at Jonesy.

"Watch me," he retorted, the underlying promise of violence palpable in his tone.

The women fell silent, their hands covering their mouths in a futile attempt to stifle their terrified sobs. The air thickened with dread as they realized the true extent of Blood's ruthless power and the danger they faced. Jonesy approached Tony's lifeless body and checked for a pulse.

"He's dead," he announced, his face etched with disbelief.

"Ladies, promise you won't say a word to anybody. This is a private party," Soupy said, his tone grave.

The four women, their faces streaked with tears of panic, nodded in agreement.

"Leave, go straight home, don't stop. I'll lock up. Remember, this is a private party, and if you wish to continue to live, you'll keep your mouth shut," Cisco said, handing each of them a stack of money.

The ladies grabbed their bags and rushed out, their fear palpable. Cisco paced the basement, the weight of the situation weighing heavily on him. "How are we going to get out of this?" he asked, his voice laced with desperation.

"Tony has family, they'll be looking for him. What are we going to do with his body?" Jonesy questioned, his brow furrowed.

"His family is going to want retribution. Blood, you just started an all-out war," Soupy warned, his expression grave.

"How could you be so stupid, Blood?" Jonesy asked, his voice tinged with anger.

"Fuck it, stay calm and carry on," Blood said, his tone nonchalant.

"I've got to get out of this. The cops on one side, Tony's family on the other. I can't take this heat. You didn't have to kill him, Blood," Cisco said, his panic evident.

"I didn't see you trying to stop me. Too late now, you're in this just like me. The only way out is in a coffin," Blood retorted, his words laced with venom.

"I'm not going down for this. The security guard was self-defense, but this was murder. Why did you have to kill him?" Cisco pressed, his desperation palpable.

"Be cool, Cisco, stay calm. People disappear in Gangster land every day," Jonesy said, trying to reassure his friend.

"Lay low, get rid of this body, throw him in the Hudson River before the sun comes up. Cisco, go and get the van. Don't think, just do it. I'm going home and getting some sleep," Blood ordered, already heading for the exit.

"What are we going to do about the bowl of cocaine?" Soupy asked, eyeing the remnants of the white powder.

"Take it with you and sniff it. Also, dust everything to wipe away the fingerprints," Blood said over his shoulder as he left the basement.

"Blood is crazy, and he still wants his money," Cisco said, his voice tinged with resignation.

"I agree, but he's our man, and we have to cover for him," Jonesy replied, his loyalty unwavering.

"For how long? I feel like I made a deal with the devil," Cisco asked, his brow furrowed.

"For as long as we're all together," Soupy answered, his expression grim.

"We must bury this incident, and our lips must be sealed shut. Come on, we have to clean this place," Jonesy said, already wiping down the surfaces.

"I'll be back with the van," Cisco said, hurrying out of the basement.

Soupy and Jonesy worked quickly, their movements efficient and practiced as they used their handkerchiefs to wipe away any lingering fingerprints from the chairs and glasses. Fifteen minutes later, Cisco returned with a tarp and a thick, heavy blanket.

The men carefully, yet with a grim purpose, wrapped Tony's lifeless body, ensuring every inch was covered. They then carried the bundled form out to the waiting van, Cisco slamming the basement door shut behind them with a resounding thud.

The van sped through the night, its tires eating up the asphalt as it headed towards the Hudson River at the end of Riverside Park. The area was dark and deserted, the perfect location to dispose of the body. Cisco drove the van up to the guard rail, the engine idling as Soupy and Jonesy opened the rear doors.

Together, they lifted Tony's remains, swinging the wrapped body back and forth a few times before heaving it over the edge and into the murky waters below. The men hurried back into the van, the doors slamming shut behind them. The vehicle sped off, leaving no trace of the deadly deed they had just committed, vanishing into the night as if it had never been there at all.

The only evidence that remained was the faint ripple on the surface of the river, the body's descent marked by a small, ever-widening circle that soon disappeared in the inky blackness of the water.

The following morning Amber Stone awoke, her body weary from the exertions of the previous night. She was grateful that she had left Blood to make his own way home, allowing herself the luxury of a full night's rest. Unaware of the dark events that had transpired in Blood's absence, Amber eased herself out of bed, her movements languid and unhurried as she made her way to the bath-room.

After a refreshing shower, Amber slipped into her judogi, the crisp white fabric a stark contrast to her sun-kissed skin. Grabbing her training bag, she headed out the door, her mind focused on the day's workout at the Dojo.

It was well past 1 p.m., by the time the model stepped onto the mat, her brown belt a testament to her years of dedication and discipline. Her instructor, Master Dan, a seasoned practitioner in his fifties, greeted her with a nod, his own judogi rustling as he moved to stand across from her.

The two warriors began to spar, their movements fluid and graceful. Master Dan, ever the taskmaster, threw Amber around the mat with a relentless intensity, pushing her to the limits of her abilities. Yet, Amber held her own, her years of training shining through as she managed to throw the older man not once, but twice.

As they broke apart, both participants bowed in a gesture of mutual respect, acknowledging the skill and dedication that had been displayed on the mat.

"You're doing great," Master Dan said, a hint of approval in his voice.

"I could do better, Master Dan," Amber replied, her competitive spirit shining through.

"Stop drinking. It's slowing you down," he admonished.

"It's not like I'm an alcoholic," Amber protested.

"You're a social drinker and drug user," Master Dan said, his eyes narrowing.

"I don't use drugs," Amber lied, her heart racing.

"Don't lie to me. I can tell you think I was born yesterday," Master Dan scoffed.

"This sport is tough, but it keeps me in shape," Amber said, changing the subject.

"If you don't build up your speed, you won't get your black belt," he warned.

"I can fight on a black belt level," Amber insisted.

"For the Judo tournament, you need speed to win, and using drugs slows you down," Master Dan said, his concern evident.

"Guys take steroids all the time, and no one saids anything. And I won't be in the tournament," Amber said, her tone dismissive.

"If you're content to be at the level you are, that's fine with me," Master Dan replied, his disappointment palpable.

"I'll get there at my pace. I have a fashion show to do. I'll see you next week," Amber said, already heading for the locker room.

"You're going to have to kick your habit, eventually," Master Dan called after her.

"A junky I am not; I'm functioning. I have to stay thin," Amber retorted.

"Excuses. When your life spirals out of control, I'm here if you need me," Master Dan said, his words laced with worry.

"Life is great. I'm in perfect control," Amber lied, flashing him a forced smile.

"Until you OD or have a heart attack," Master Dan said, shaking his head.

"Don't wish that on me; I'll be all right. I can kick any habit," Amber insisted, her bravado faltering.

"That's what they all say, and I'm worried you're on a fast track. Don't become a train wreck, and don't forget practice," Master Dan said, his gaze piercing.

"I get it; you're not going to go easy on me, are you?" Amber asked, a hint of resignation in her voice.

"No. The first time you miss class for any reason, I'm dropping you until you kick and get clean," Master Dan said, his tone unwavering.

Amber smiled, her competitive spirit ignited. "I love a challenge, and I'll see you next week."

Amber exited the Dojo, her mind racing with a newfound awareness. Master Dan's keen observations had clearly unsettled her, the realization that he had discerned the truth about her drug use troubled her deeply. "He knows, and he's not sure what kind? I didn't realize he was such an excellent judge of character," she mused, the weight of her secret addiction weighing heavily on her.

Amber knew all too well that she could fool the vast majority of those around her, even herself at times, but it was evident that Master Dan's perceptive eye had cut through her carefully crafted facade. "I have to watch my step and not slip up, which is hard to do when I'm high," she thought, her brow furrowed with a mix of determination and trepidation.

Stepping into the locker room, Amber quickly showered, the hot water offering a momentary respite from her turbulent thoughts. Drying her hair and dressing, she rushed out, her mind already focused on her next appointment.

Thirty minutes later, Amber arrived at the Fashion Studio Runway dressing room, where she was immediately ushered into a makeup chair. A male makeup artist and hairdresser attended to her, their skilled hands transforming her features with practiced ease. Meanwhile, two female dressers helped Amber into a stunning, high-fashion royal blue evening gown, the regal hue accentuating her natural beauty.

As she surveyed her reflection in the mirror, Amber couldn't help but wonder how much longer she could maintain this delicate balance, her addiction threatening to unravel the carefully constructed facade she had built around herself. Willie, an older woman, a real fashionista in a multi-colored pantsuit with big lacquered colored bangles and chunky rings on all her fingers, everything was overdone, even her hair, teased into an enormous rainbow-colored spike shag with pink and blue ends. She stood out as the owner of Fab Fashion Agency and surprised Amber with her presence.

"Amber Stone, you look great," Willie said.

"Thank you, Willie. I didn't expect to see you here. Are you checking up on me?" Amber asked, a sly smile on her face.

"I am," Willie replied, her expression serious.

"Oh!" Amber exclaimed, her heart rate quickening.

"Congratulations, you've had two bookings in one week," Willie said, her tone shifting to one of pride.

"I'm keeping my fingers crossed. They'll book me five days a week," Amber said, her hopes soaring.

"We'll see. I believe in you," Willie said, moving on to check on the other models.

Amber's racing heart slowly began to settle as she realized the presence of her agent was not a sign of suspicion, but rather one of unwavering support.

She couldn't afford to be consumed by paranoia, for that would only serve to hinder the success she had worked so tirelessly to achieve.

The dresser moved with practiced precision, carefully zipping up the back of Amber's regal evening gown, while the makeup artist lightly dusted her face with a delicate powder. The hairdresser then put the finishing touches on her look, primping and styling her hair to perfection.

With a deep breath, Amber glided out onto the runway, her confidence radiating as she led the pack of models. Turning elegantly at the end of the stage, she basked in the flashing of the reporters' cameras, her hard-earned success evident in every graceful movement. Yet, as Amber's confidence soared, the thought of it all crashing down should her secret addiction ever be revealed weighed heavily on her mind. She knew the consequences could be devastating, and the prospect filled her with a nagging sense of dread.

Later that night, Amber sat at the Den Bar, eagerly awaiting Blood's arrival so that she could share the news of her triumphant day. As she waited, lost in her own thoughts, a new presence caught her attention – Clair, a 30-something African American barfly with a mane of long, cascading black hair, entered the establishment and took a seat beside her.

"I'm Clair; you must be here to meet Blood?" Clair asked.

"Yes, I am. How did you know?" Amber replied, her curiosity piqued.

"I saw you with him the other night," Clair explained.

Amber peered at her, saying, "That's funny, I didn't see you."

"I used to go out with him," Clair revealed.

"You too? What happened?" Amber asked, her interest growing.

"Blood is a dynamite lover. Didn't Dee tell you?" Clair said, a hint of bitterness in her voice.

"She kept that secret," Amber replied, surprised by this new information.

"He had money problems. I started seeing another Hustler," Clair said, her tone matter-of-fact.

"Good for you," Amber said, not entirely sure how to respond.

"It was pouring rain that evening. I was sitting here; the bar was empty. I didn't expect to see anyone. Without an umbrella, I walked outside and stood in the doorway to see if I could catch a cab to go home. It startled me out of know where there was Blood; standing so close, I thought he was going to kiss me to my shock, he grabs me by the back of my neck. Then I knew he found out, and nothing good was going to come from his revelation." Clair has Amber's undivided attention as she describes her flashback to the schoolyard incident.

Blood had dragged Clair around the corner into the school-yard by her hair and neck. She had kicked and screamed. He had beaten and thrown her to the ground, continuing to pound her with his fists until she had become bloody and broken. Then he had walked away, leaving her bloody and helpless, lying on the concrete in the downpour of rain. Clair's flashback had ended. Amber had felt a sense of denial; she couldn't believe what Clair had revealed to her. In the back of her mind, she recalled how he had slapped Dee, but he had justified his violent act by claiming he was defending his reputation.

"So, what did you do?" Amber asked, her voice small.

"No one came. I lay there until I could get up, and then I went home and licked my wounds," Clair replied, her eyes downcast.

"Why didn't you go to a hospital?" Amber pressed, her concern evident.

"I would have to report the incident. I didn't want Blood looking for me," Clair explained, her fear palpable.

"That was the end of your love affair?" Amber asked, trying to make sense of it all.

"He's going with this girl Deanna now. That's his chief woman; she lives in the Bronx," Clair said, meeting Amber's gaze.

"He never told me about her," Amber said, her brow furrowed.

"Don't tell him I told you. He'll kill me," Clair pleaded, her eyes wide with terror.

"All right, I'll have to ask him about it," Amber said, her mind racing.

"I don't want to be in here when you ask him," Clair said.

"Why are you telling me this?" Amber asked.

"To warn you. You seem like a nice girl," Clair's voice trembled.

Amber sat at the bar, sipping her drink as she contemplated Clair's revelations.

"Really nice girls are competition. You still love him, don't you?" Amber asked.

"What difference does it make? I'm warning you," Clair replied, her eyes pleading.

Amber's brow arched. "Are you telling me this for my benefit or yours? I'll see what Blood has to say."

Clair, her fear palpable, quickly got up from the bar and rushed out of the club. Amber sipped her drink, lost in thought. A few minutes later, Blood strode in and approached her, a smile spreading across his face.

"Hey, what's up, baby?" he asked, leaning in to kiss Amber.

"You're late, as usual," Amber replied, her tone laced with irritation.

"I had some business to take care of," Blood said, settling onto the barstool next to her.

"Like Deanna, and who is she anyway?" Amber asked, her eyes narrowing.

"Deanna is the woman that I live with," Blood admitted, his gaze unwavering.

Amber looked him in the eye, unable to believe what she was hearing. This man had no shame in his infidelity.

"How many women do you have?" Amber asked, her voice rising.

"Well, I also live with Betty sometimes," Blood replied, his tone nonchalant.

"Oh, you do. So, where do I stand?" Amber asked, her heart sinking.

"You know I care for you," Blood said, his words doing little to soothe her.

"So does my ex-boyfriend, Gregory. He just came back to me," Amber said, her eyes gleaming with defiance.

"You know I'm a hustler, and I can't just keep one pad," Blood said, trying to justify his actions.

"Don't make it sound like it's a business arrangement," Amber snapped.

"It is, but there are strings attached," Blood said, a hint of possessiveness in his voice.

"Like what, making love? That shouldn't be too hard for you to do," Amber retorted, her sarcasm biting.

"This Gregory dude, how come I didn't hear about him in the beginning?" Blood asked, his brow furrowed.

"I've just gone back with him. Now that I see you're occupied," Amber said, rising from her seat.

Blood reached out and grabbed her arm, pulling her back to him. He kissed her passionately, the karmic bond between them undeniable. Amber broke the embrace, her emotions in turmoil.

"Can Gregory or whatever his name kiss you like that?" Blood asked, his eyes searching hers.

"This is wrong, wrong, wrong," Amber cried, her voice laced with despair.

"We got chemistry," Blood said, his grip tightening.

"I want to love and have a commitment," Amber pleaded, her eyes filled with longing.

"I've made time for you. I've treated you well," Blood argued, his tone defensive.

"It's not enough. You could do better," Amber said, her resolve weakening.

"What do you want me to do?" Blood asked, his frustration evident.

"I didn't see this coming," Amber admitted, her head spinning.

"The question is, what are you going to do about it?" Blood challenged, his eyes narrowing.

"No way, I'm not dealing with those other women. They have to go," Amber declared, her voice firm.

"All right, I'll end it," Blood conceded, surprising Amber with his capitulation.

Amber rolled her eyes, her disbelief palpable. "Just like that?"

"Yeah," Blood said, his tone nonchalant.

"How could you be so clear-cut?" Amber asked, her brow furrowed.

"You know what I've been through; I have to survive. Come on," Blood said, gesturing towards the exit.

"One thing about you, you're definitely not boring," Amber sighed, following him out the door.

They hailed a cab and drove off, the tension between them palpable.

An hour later, Blood and Amber stumbled through the door of the studio apartment, their steps slightly unsteady from the effects of their indulgence. As Amber's gaze swept across the space, her eyes widened with a newfound appreciation for the contemporary, upscale design that defined the interior.

The walls, painted a rich, earthy brown, provided a warm backdrop to the sleek, white lacquer furniture that dominated the room. A plush, shag rug covered the floor, its soft fibers inviting them to sink into its comfort.

Strategically placed beaded orange curtains sectioned off the bedroom area, lending an air of privacy and mystery to the space. A small white kitchenette with a white dining table and two contemporary matching chairs.

Futuristic floor lamps, their sleek lines and muted illumination, cast a dim glow throughout the apartment, creating an atmospheric ambiance that seemed to transport them to a different era. Amber found herself captivated by the harmonious blend of mid-century modern and avant-garde elements that permeated the studio, her senses heightened by the intoxicating effects of the evening's indulgences.

As Blood moved to explore the various nooks and crannies of their temporary abode, Amber couldn't help but feel a sense of wonder and anticipation, eager to see what other surprises this intriguing space might have in store for them.

"Wow, this pad is gorgeous. Is it yours?" Amber asked, her voice laced with awe.

"It's all mine, as long as I pay the rent," Blood replied.

As Blood led Amber towards the bedroom, she couldn't help but feel a growing sense of excitement and curiosity. The futuristic design that permeated the main living area had already piqued her interest, and she wondered what other wonders this studio apartment had in store.

Upon entering the bedroom, Amber's eyes widened with a mixture of surprise and delight. The centerpiece of the space was a massive, round bed that seemed to defy the constraints of traditional furniture. Its' sleek, curved lines and pristine white upholstery gave it an almost otherworldly appearance, as if it had been plucked from the pages of a science fiction novel.

Surrounding the bed were a series of futuristic floor lamps, their geometric shapes and muted illumination casting a warm, ethereal glow throughout the room.

The walls were adorned with a mesmerizing array of abstract art, their vibrant colors and geometric patterns adding to the sense of being transported to a different time and place.

Amber ran her fingers along the soft, plush bedding, marveling at the attention to detail that had been put into crafting this truly unique and captivating space.

She couldn't help but imagine herself sinking into the bed, allowing its comfort to envelop her and transport her to a realm of pure relaxation and indulgence.

As Blood stood back, watching Amber's reaction with a satisfied grin, she knew that this bedroom was the perfect complement to the overall design of the studio apartment. It was a space that seamlessly blended form and function, creating an environment that was both visually stunning and deeply inviting.

Amber jumped onto the bed, exclaiming, "This bedroom is to die for, and the bed is so comfortable."

Blood joined her, and they made passionate love, their bodies intertwined.

The following day, Blood and Amber were still in bed when he glanced at his watch. It was 11 a.m.

"Come on, wake up. We have to get breakfast," Blood said, gently shaking Amber.

Amber moaned and turned over. "Why can't we eat here? You have a lovely kitchen."

"There's no food in the fridge. You can take a shower first," Blood said, already getting up.

Amber crawled out of bed, showered, and got dressed. Blood did the same, and they exited the apartment building.

Hand in hand, Blood and Amber strolled around the corner, the cozy café coming into view. The inviting atmosphere and tantalizing aromas of freshly brewed coffee, sizzling bacon, and savory eggs drew them in, and they stepped through the entryway.

Once inside, they found a table and settled in, taking in the cozy ambiance. A few other patrons were already enjoying their meals, and the rhythmic sounds of the chef flipping hotcakes on the grill and the toast popping from the toaster created a comforting backdrop. She watched as the server darted from table to table, busily taking orders, and Amber couldn't help but feel a slight twinge of irritation.

Finally, the server approached their table, notepad in hand, ready to take their order.

"Bring us a large plate of bacon and eggs and toast with a pot of coffee," Blood ordered.

The server jots down their order, nodded and walked away.

Amber forced a smile, but she couldn't push aside her lingering, irritating curiosity to focus on the moment at hand.

"We could have stayed at the apartment and bought groceries, and I would have cooked breakfast for you," Amber said, her disappointment evident.

"There's something I have to tell you," Blood said, his tone serious.

"What?" Amber asked, her heart sinking.

"That was not my apartment," Blood admitted, his gaze averted.

"You told me it was yours," Amber said, her voice rising.

"I said as long as I pay the rent, it's mine," Blood corrected, his eyes meeting hers.

"Whose apartment is it?" Amber asked, her brow furrowed.

"It's Betty's apartment," Blood revealed, his expression unreadable.

"How could you do such a thing?" Amber cried, her anger bubbling to the surface.

"I pay to use the space," Blood explained, his tone nonchalant.

"You told me you would end it," Amber reminded him, her disappointment palpable.

"In my own way, I am," Blood said, his words doing little to reassure her.

"It's hardly what I call ending it. What if Betty would have walked in on us?" Amber asked, her voice tinged with fear.

"Betty and I would be through," Blood said, his confidence unwavering.

"You have a lot of nerve," Amber spat, pushing her chair back.

"I just can't say no," Blood admitted, his shoulders slumping.

"You better start learning how to. It's her or me?" Amber declared, rising from the table.

"Where are you going?" Blood asked, his eyes pleading.

"My appetite vanished, and don't fetch me a cab," Amber said, storming out of the restaurant.

Blood watched her go, his usual smirk firmly in place. No woman had ever dumped him before, and he refused to let his feelings show. He calmly opened the menu, the server approached with a tray of food and placed it on the table and walked away. Blood was determined to enjoy his breakfast alone.

It was 8 p.m., when Amber emerged from her building, dressed in a striking red pantsuit. She was determined to go out and socialize, to get Blood off her mind.

As she stepped onto the sidewalk, she was greeted by Dee, who was standing there, waiting for her.

"I'm going down south. I wanted to see you before I left," Dee said, her voice laced with regret.

"I have nothing to say to you," Amber replied, her tone icy.

"Oh, you don't? I came here to ask you for forgiveness," Dee said, her eyes downcast.

"You go behind my back and try to see Blood," Amber accused, her anger resurfacing.

"I was seeing him first, bitch," Dee retorted, her eyes flashing with jealousy.

"Yet, you didn't tell me you still had feelings for him. I'm his woman now," Amber said, her voice dripping with disdain.

"He slapped me because of you. I had a second chance," Dee said, her voice quivering.

"Sorry, I had nothing to do with it. I thought you were my friend," Amber said, turning to walk away. Dee reached out and gripped Amber's arm.

"Don't call me a bitch. Now let go of my arm." Amber demanded.

Dee quickly slapped Amber across the cheek. Amber jerked her arm free, then swiftly executed a judo sweep kick, flipping her rival onto the pavement. She landed with a thud, her cries of anger and humiliation echoing through the night.

"I hate you, Amber Stone," Dee cried, her eyes filled with rage.

"Your jealousy has consumed your heart. Believe it or not, I was your friend. I regret meeting you," Amber said, her voice laced with sorrow.

Leaving Dee in a heap on the ground, Amber strolled off, her mind racing with the events of the day. She had a lot to think about, and she knew her relationship with Blood was far from simple.

CHAPTER THREE

An hour later, Amber was frustrated from her encounter with Dee. She walked into the Den Club; it was no use for her to run and hide. She had to face her problems head-on. The dimly lit bar was alive with activity, a sea of casually dressed men and women sipping drinks and swaying to the soft soul music. Amber's gaze immediately zeroed in on Deanna, a gorgeous woman in her 20s, stood near the entrance, her young, lithe form clinging to Blood in a passionate embrace.

Amber ignored Blood and went straight to a back table and sat. Amber's jaw tightened, but she forced herself to ignore the spectacle. Settling into the worn leather seat, she watched intently as Deanna lavished Blood with attention, her hands roaming possessively over his body. She grabbed Blood and kissed and sucked his lips.

Out of the corner of his eye, Blood saw Amber's disapproval. He broke their embrace, rushed to the back, and sat at the table with Amber Stone.

"What in the hell is wrong with you?" asked Amber.

"You don't understand. I haven't seen Deanna in two weeks," Blood answered, his tone defensive.

Amber kept her composure. "You will not see her at all."

"I called you all day, and you didn't return my calls. What do you expect?" Blood said.

"Respect if I'm here or not," Amber stated.

"You know two women love me. I am the man," Blood claimed.

"You had two women," Amber responded.

"How would I know she would show up?" Blood asked.

"Blood, you told me you would end it," Amber said.

"She's here now. What shall I do?" Blood questioned.

"I want you to quit." Amber demanded.

Blood got up from the table and walked over to Deanna, and she pulled him close.

"Blood, I miss you; why haven't you've been to see me?" Deanna asked.

"Deanna, I've been busy taking care of my business," Blood replied.

"Are you coming to visit tonight?" Deanna inquired.

"Go on home. I'll meet you there," Blood said.

"I'll be waiting," Deanna responded as she exited the bar.

Blood meandered over to Amber Stone and sat down.

"Well?" Amber questioned.

"I ended it," Blood said.

Amber arched her eyebrow. "Good, so we'll be spending the next two weeks together?"

"That means you forgive me?" Blood asked, a hint of hope in his voice.

"If I find out you are cheating on me, Blood. I will cut you off," Amber warned.

Betty, a shapely woman in her 40s, strutted into the Den bar and sat at a table in the corner; Blood held his head down.

"Betty just walked in," Blood informed Amber.

Amber's eyes narrowed, her gaze shifting between Blood and the newly arrived Betty, who sat at a table in the corner.

Amber's frustration boiled she slammed her palm down on the table.

"What the devil is this, a three-ring circus? I want you to end it now."

Blood didn't know what to do; he wanted to keep Amber calm.

"Don't worry, you just sit here, and I'll talk to her," Blood said as he walked over to Betty's table and sat down.

"Betty, how are you doing?" Blood asked.

"Fine. Blood, I came here tonight to ask you to give me back my keys," Betty stated.

"Why didn't you just change the locks?" Blood inquired.

"I know there was a woman in my bed, and that woman wasn't me," Betty replied.

"I can explain," Blood said.

"I know when it's over, and this is over," Betty declared.

Blood reached into his pocket, pulled out a set of keys, and gave them to her. She took the keys and placed them in her purse. Betty stood, displaying a shapely figure, and exited the bar. Blood approached Amber Stone with her arms crossed, fuming. The contrast between the three women was striking – Deanna, the young, lithe temptress; Betty, the shapely, confident older woman; and Amber, the one who demanded Blood's full attention and loyalty.

"Say nothing it's done," Blood said.

Amber's patience was wearing thin, and she made it clear that she would not tolerate Blood's juggling of multiple relationships.

The air was thick with tension, and Amber knew she had to put her foot down if she had any hope of maintaining control over the volatile situation.

"Are you sure?" Amber questioned.

"Yeah, I recall when I was 17; I was dating a schoolgirl named Sadie, and I met Satara; you remind me of her. My Mama was alive," Blood reminisced.

Blood had a flashback to a shantytown crammed with old run-down wooden shacks. Only the most impoverished Black families lived here in the Mississippi delta, and Blood was one of them with his mother, Irma. To get money, he had two skills: shooting craps and fighting for wealthy white people.

Inside Irma's shack, she was in her 30's in a tattered gray dress; her hair was nappy and unkempt. Once, she was an attractive brown-skinned woman who now spent her days sitting at a table in the dining area and staring at a half bottle of whiskey and a grimy, filled glass. Irma scattered piles of junk all over the place. An open kitchen was in the background, with two concealed bedrooms and one bathroom. Irma gazed at her bottle of whiskey and had a flashback. She was on her knees, scrubbing the gleaming hardwood floors of the sprawling plantation home. The lady of the house, Mrs. Dawson, approached her - a strikingly beautiful young blonde woman with porcelain skin and bright blue eyes.

"Irma, it's time for you to take your lunch. Mr. Ray is out in the field and he said you can eat with him. Go on, he's waiting for you. You can finish when you come back."

"Thank you, Mrs. Dawson," Irma said, standing up and shaking out her dress.

She hurried out of the grand foyer, with its high ceilings and ornate chandeliers, and ran out of the house to the water pump. There, she pumped water and washed her hands and the sweat off her face. Then, she made her way across the manicured lawn towards the fields.

Out in the warm, golden sunlight, Irma spotted the tall, handsome figure of Mr. Ray, his strong, muscular frame and chiseled features a stark contrast to the lush, verdant surroundings. She ran into his waiting arms, and they kissed passionately, his embrace swinging her around.

"Mis Irma, I love you," the deep, rich baritone of Mr. Ray rumbled.

"Mr. Ray, I love you too," Irma replied, gazing up at him adoringly.

They broke apart and made their way over to the simple wooden picnic table, where Mr. Ray had his large metal lunch box waiting. He opened it, revealing sandwiches and soda pop inside.

"How is my boy, Little Ray, doing in school?" Mr. Ray asked, his tone tinged with a hint of wistfulness.

"Well, if you would come home early, you would know," Irma responded, a touch of exasperation in her voice.

"You know I have to work two jobs. I'm here in the field all day, and then at night I go to the bar to clean it."

"I'm working, Ray is 10 years old, and you said after ten years we would get married," Irma insisted.

"You have my name, Little Ray has my last name. What more do you want?" Mr. Ray asked.

"I want to be legally married. What if something should happen to you? Everything you've saved will go to your sister," Irma explained.

"Don't worry, nothing is going to happen to me, and marriage is just a piece of paper," Mr. Ray said.

"Yeah, to men it is, but to women, it's much more. It's security. We have a son to think about," Irma argued.

"The boy is 10, soon he'll be in junior high and high school, and he can get a job. I've been working since I was 13, he can do the same," Mr. Ray reasoned.

Irma persisted, "Why can't we get married? I've waited."

Mr. Ray sighed, "It would be unfair to you or the boy. I'm just not husband material. I love to come and go as I please, and I make a better boyfriend than a husband. Let's face it, money is scarce around here. I have to get all the work I can while I can."

Irma's eyes filled with tears, "I'm young, Little Ray is young. These are my best years as a woman. I'm ready for marriage."

Mr. Ray reached out and cupped her face, "I love you, Irma. I'm just not as ready to settle down as a family man. If you find someone who wants to marry you, you have my permission."

Irma shook her head, "Don't be stupid. You're the only one for me. I could never find another Mr. Ray."

"And I could never find another Ms. Irma," Mr. Ray replied, reaching into his pocket and handing Irma some money, which she promptly tucked into her bra. They then continued eating their lunch together.

Later that night, Mr. Ray was making his way home from his shift at the bar, trudging down the dark, lonely road towards Irma's small shack. The night air was still and heavy, the only sound the crunch of his boots on the packed earth.

Suddenly, the rumble of engines shattered the silence as two cars came barreling down the road, their headlights blinding. Mr. Ray squinted against the glare as the vehicles screeched to a halt, a group of white men spilling out.

"Where you think you're goin', boy?" one of them sneered, stalking towards Mr. Ray.

"Home," Mr. Ray replied evenly, refusing to be cowed.

"Don't you give us that lie, nigger!" the man snarled.

"Go to hell," Mr. Ray retorted, turning to continue on his way.

"You think you can disrespect us and get away with it?" the man retorted.

Enraged, the men charged at him, their fists flying. Mr. Ray fought back, his powerful blows landing squarely, but the sheer number of his attackers quickly overwhelmed him. Battered and bloody, he was dragged towards a towering oak tree, a noose already prepared.

The men hoisted Mr. Ray up, his body swinging lifelessly as the life drained from him. Whooping and hollering, they set a fire at the base of the tree, the flames licking hungrily at the dry grass as they celebrated their barbaric act.

Finally, the white men disappeared into the night, leaving Mr. Ray's lifeless form dangling from the tree, a knife embedded in the bark beside him. A note fluttered in the breeze - "Nigger disrespected a white man and got lynched."

The fire slowly burned out, the air thick with the stench of charred wood and smoldering embers. It was then that Sam, a Black man from the nearby shantytown, had been watching the gruesome scene from the bushes. Now, it was safe to approach the tree, his heart sinking as he read the chilling message left behind.

Without hesitation, Sam turned and raced back to the shantytown, a sense of dread and urgency gripping him. He had to tell the others, to warn them against this unspeakable act of violence.

Inside the small, dimly lit shack, Irma sat by the bed, watching the gentle rise and fall of Little Ray's sleeping form. The weight of the day's events hung heavy on her, but she cherished these quiet moments of peace.

A sudden knock at the door startled her from her reverie. Irma rose, her heart pounding, and pulled the door open to reveal Sam holding a lantern, and a group of five other African American men, their faces etched with grim determination.

"Irma, you've got to come quick," Sam urged, his voice tinged with anguish. "It's Mr. Ray - he's been lynched. I saw it all happen, the white men followed him from the bar. I couldn't do anything to help, there were ten of them and only me. I hid in the bushes and watched."

Irma's breath caught in her throat, a cold dread seizing her. Without a word, she snatched her shawl from its hook and threw it around her shoulders, rushing out the door with Sam and the other men.

They hurried through the woods, the crackling of twigs and the rustle of leaves the only sounds that pierced the eerie silence. And then, there it was - Mr. Ray's lifeless body, hanging from a twisted oak tree, a knife embedded in the bark beside him.

Sam and the five men gently lowered Mr. Ray's form, Irma collapsing beside him, her anguished sobs echoing through the night.

"We better bury him now," Sam murmured, his voice heavy with sorrow. "Those white men might come back, and cut his fingers, arms and legs off as souvenirs."

Without hesitation, the men lifted Mr. Ray's body and carried it to the shantytown graveyard, Irma trailing behind, her steps heavy with grief. They dug a shallow grave, their movements hurried and desperate, and laid Mr. Ray to rest, the earth covering his broken form.

Irma flung herself over the freshly turned soil, her whole body shaking with the force of her weeping. Sam and the others stood vigil, their faces etched with a mix of sorrow and resolve. This would go unanswered.

As the first hints of dawn began to peek over the horizon, Sam gently helped Irma to her feet, escorting her back to the shack. Her eyes were red-rimmed, her spirit shattered, but in the depths of her grief, the spark of determination had died with Mr. Ray.

Irma's flashback ended when the front door opened, and Little Ray was now a young Blood in a frayed shirt and pants who entered, carrying his schoolbooks.

"Welcome home, baby. To me you are still Little Ray. White folks and everybody else has renamed you Blood." Irma slurred.

"Mama, if you quit drinking, I will give up boxing and graduate from high school. I will earn enough money to get us to New York," Blood said.

Irma slurred, "We have to eat first; we don't have money to buy food."

Blood laid his books on the table. "I'll get some cash. I'll be back," he said as he exited and stood on the porch, looking at the row of shack houses a couple of yards away in the area. He spotted a crowd playing craps and strolled towards them, and stood in the middle of the action. A group of African American men playing dice surrounded him. Satara, young, scantly dressed in red, stood over him and offered her services. Blood's eyes lit up at the sight of a cash pyramid on the ground. During the crap game, he dug into his pocket and took two dollars out. An old man and a young man were taking turns throwing the dice. Neither one came up with a seven or eleven-on-one throw. Satara blew on Blood's dice, and he won the game, and she made him an offer.

"I'll increase your winnings tenfold if you give me a piece of your action," Satara said.

"I need all the aid I can get," said Blood.

"Why don't you come with me to my place?" Satara asked.

"Your place, where is it?" Blood inquired.

"Follow me through the woods," Satara replied as she grabbed his hand and led him away from the crap game into the woodlands to a deserted shack. He followed her inside.

Inside, lit candles were throughout the shack. An altar with a black skull, a red figurine, a couple of candles, and bottles of herbs soaking in them sat on a table. Raggedy curtains like spider webs hung from the ceiling and partitioned the living area, kitchen, chamber, and bathroom. Satara sprawled on the sofa, covered with different snake skins. He stood there amazed at the decor. There was an alligator skin rug on the floor on the dingy coffee table, incense, and candles burned with wax flowing from the holders. A spider had woven its web in the corners of the shack, and two rats circled each other—the sound of three chickens in a small cage. On the table, a yellow snake was in a medium-covered glass case. She grabbed his arm and escorted him to the bathroom threshold.

"You get into the empty tub," she said.

"With no water?" asked Blood.

"I have a special spell bath for you," Satara replied.

He entered; lit candles were on the wooden wall sconces. Blood's pants and shirt dropped to the floor.

He stepped into the waterless bathtub and waited a few seconds. Satara rolled a rusty tray cart in with a gallon of warm water of herbs and spices into the bathroom, and she poured the potion over Blood's head and body. She took a sea sponge, wiped his back and chest, and gradually slid the sponge down and caressed his genitals. Satara recited her spell.

"More Money For Blood, More Money For Blood, More Money For Blood," she shouted.

Satara slipped off her dress, stepped into the tub, and sat on Blood as she made love to him.

Later in Satara's bedroom, the faint light from a melted candle shone on Blood, and Satara as they lay asleep in bed. Blood awakened and glanced at the old fashion alarm clock on the tarnished lamp stand, and the large numbers read midnight. Blood got out of bed and slipped on his underwear, trousers, and shirt over his back. He glimpsed at Satara in a deep sleep; he grabbed his shoes and put them on, and the shoelace on his right shoe was missing. Blood searched around the room and didn't find it. Without waking Satara, he tiptoed out of the quarters, and he didn't break a stride with one shoe tied and the other slipping off his foot. He opened the door and sneaked out of the shack.

A few seconds passed, and Satara entered the living room wide awake with his shoelace. She took a live chicken out of a cage, cut its throat, let the blood drain in a bowl, and put the shoelace inside the bowl until it was soaked with blood. She plucked the shoelace out of the bowl with a tweezer and placed it on a white sheet of paper. She sprinkled white powder over it, rolled the paper up, and placed it on the coffee stand. The Hoodoo woman lay on her sofa and drifted off to sleep.

The following morning at Irma's, two full plates of scrambled eggs, one glass of water, and one of milk were on the table. Irma sat at the table wearing a clean dress and her hair combed. She had stacked the junk in the corners of the shack, showing some attempt that it was clean. Blood entered with his schoolbooks in his hand, surprised, and sat at the table. Irma was responding soberly.

"Mama, where did you get money from?" Blood asked.

"After you left, Daniel came by; he said he owed you $20. He gave it to me, and I went shopping for food," Irma answered.

"You cleaned up too?" Blood questioned.

"I did that yesterday when I came back," Irma replied.

"I got home late last night. I didn't notice," Blood said.

"You better eat your breakfast, so you don't be late for school," Irma urged.

"Mama, did you buy a bottle of whiskey?" Blood asked.

"What if I did?" Irma replied.

"You promised Mama," Blood reminded her.

"I said I would try to quit drinking. I didn't say I could," Irma responded.

Blood finished his breakfast and kissed Irma on the forehead.

"Are you going to be home for dinner tonight?" Irma asked.

"No, I got to go over to Sadie's to do my homework," Blood answered as he grabbed his books and left for school.

Later that afternoon at the all-African American high school, the stark contrast in social economic status among the students was evident. While some kids struggled with poverty, lacking basic necessities, others had parents who could provide for their needs.

Blood sat in his classroom, his eyes focused on the back of his girlfriend Sadie's head. The 17-year-old girl, with her youthful charm, occupied his attention as he leaned in, whispering something in her ear.

Around them, the classroom was filled with African American teenagers, their faces reflecting a range of emotions and experiences. At the front of the room, the teacher stood, her back turned to the class as she diligently wrote on the blackboard, the sound of chalk scratching against the dark surface echoing through the space. The contrasting realities of the students' lives created a palpable atmosphere, one that shaped their educational journey and the challenges they faced.

"What is the difference between George Washington and Abraham Lincoln?" the teacher asked. Sadie turned around and Blood payed attention.

"Washington was a general, and Lincoln freed the slaves," Blood responded.

"I assume you did your homework, and it will be on my desk at the end of class," the teacher said.

"I didn't have time. I was busy last night," Blood replied.

"It is a shame you are a smart boy, but you are falling behind; get your over-due assignment's to me. Maybe Sadie can help you," the teacher stated.

The droning sound of the bell signaled the end of the class, and Sadie stole a glance at Blood as she gathered their papers and approached the teacher's desk. She gently placed the documents atop the worn wooden surface, the well-worn edges a testament to the countless hands that had traversed this path before.

As the students filed out of the classroom, the hallway erupted with the cacophony of teenage voices - laughter, chatter, and the occasional shout echoing off the dented walls and scraped lockers. The scuffed floors creaked underfoot, the soles of their shoes leaving their mark on the well-trodden ground.

Sadie and Blood joined the throng, their books cradled in their arms, weaving through the crowd of their peers. The vibrant energy of the hallway enveloped them, a stark contrast to the academic focus that had just consumed their attention.

As they reached their lockers, Sadie turned to face Blood, her expression a blend of concern and curiosity. The world around them faded into the background as she sought to connect with him, her eyes searching his face for answers, for insight into the thoughts that were hidden in his mind.

"Where were you last night? We had a study date. I waited for you?" Sadie asked.

"I was with Satara; she put a good luck spell on me so I can get money," Blood answered.

"It took all night?" Sadie questioned.

"Nothing happened. It was late, so I went home," Blood replied.

"I know you Blood, it is Satara or me," Sadie stated.

"You can't fault me. You are saving yourself until after we're married," Blood argued.

"I wish to get out of Mississippi and become something other than barefoot, unwed, and pregnant," Sadie said.

"Like my Mama," Blood responded.

Sadie caressed his face. "I didn't mean that."

"It's okay, you are right. Maybe if Mama had parents who cared, who knows, I might not have been born. I promise I won't see Satara again," Blood assured her.

Sadie and Blood joined the throng of students spilling out into the yard, their steps quickening with the promise of freedom.

The worn concrete underfoot gave way to the soft grass, a verdant respite from the institutional confines they had just left behind. Pausing amid the bustling crowd, Blood pulled Sadie close, his gaze locked onto hers with an intensity that seemed to halt time.

Tenderly, he cupped her face, his calloused fingers tracing the delicate lines of her features, before leaning in and capturing her lips in a lingering, passionate embrace. The world around them faded into the background, the roar of their peers a distant echo as they lost themselves in the moment.

When at last they parted, breathless and flushed, Blood gently relieved Sadie of her books, stacking them atop his own. With a reverence born of affection, he cradled the weight of her academic burden, a silent gesture of his devotion.

Unbeknownst to the couple, a young boy, no more than ten years old, peered out from behind the school building, his eyes wide with fascination as he observed their tender exchange. For a moment, he was captivated, transfixed by the intimate display of affection. Then, with a sudden start, he turned and scurried away, disappearing into the labyrinth of the school's periphery.

Sadie and Blood, oblivious to their young observer, continued their journey, the road before them stretching out like a tapestry of endless possibilities.

But their solitude was soon interrupted by the hurried approach of a familiar face – Daniel, his bronzed skin glistening with the sheen of exertion, his ragged attire a testament to the challenges he faced.

"Blood, I've been looking for you to tell you, old man; Hawkins is having a party tonight," Daniel said.

"Daniel, you tell him my Mama doesn't want me to fight," Blood told him.

Sadie held Blood's hand. "Neither do I want him to fight."

"The match is between Black Butch and you; Hawkins will pay you $300," Daniel informed them.

Sadie hugged Blood. "Please don't go. You will break your agreement with your Mama too."

"I have to go that kind of money can last me a month. You do my homework, and I'll pick it up after the fight. I'll have enough money to buy you what you want," Blood said.

"Well, I'd like to save up for my wedding dress," Sadie replied.

"Whatever you want, Sadie, you're my girl, and don't you forget it," Blood assured her.

Blood kissed Sadie, and he and Daniel walked off, and she proceeded down the road on her way home.

The teens exited the woods, and Satara's shack came into view; she was standing on the porch dressed in black as they walked by and ignored her.

"Blood," she yelled.

"Don't stop. We have to get to old man Hawkins," Daniel said.

"I want to talk to her to end our association," he told Daniel.

Blood approached Satara, who was standing there defiantly.

"My little spy told me you were kissing a girl on the school's steps," Satara said.

"That was Sadie, my girlfriend," Blood replied.

"I feel you disrespected me; after all I've done for you, I want you to break up with her," Satara demanded.

"Our affair is over before it has begun. I am not one of the young lovers that you can cast aside whenever you wish. You seduced me. You don't own me," Blood argued.

"I put a spell on you so you could get lucky," Satara claimed.

"I won that money with my luck. You just were there, and I am not splitting anything with you," Blood stated.

"You owe me for my magic. It is not yours to steal," Satara insisted.

"I am not paying you anything if there is any magic," Blood refused.

The porch of Satara's shack had become the stage for a twisted, supernatural confrontation. Satara, her eyes wild with a desperate fury, had produced an envelope from the folds of her revealing dress, extracting a worn shoelace – a twisted memento of their shared past.

"I kept this," she had hissed, "just in case you reneged on our agreement."

The implications of her words hung in the air, a dark and ominous cloud that threatened to consume them. Her gaze had burned with an unnatural intensity as she leveled her accusation.

"I curse you," she had spat, "and if you can't love me, you will love no one in this life."

With a flick of her wrist, she had blown a plume of fine, white powder into Blood's face, the Hoodoo dust swirling in the air like a spectral mist.

In that moment, instinct had taken over, and Blood had lashed out, his hand striking Satara's outstretched arm with a re-sounding crack. The force of the blow had sent her reeling, her body crashing to the porch with a sickening thud.

But Satara's desperation had only fueled her determination. Recovering with a speed that defied her apparent fragility, she had reached for the shotgun that had been concealed beneath the near-by bench, the blast echoing through the air as Blood and Daniel had turned and fled.

Now, as they raced towards the safety of old man Hawkins' plantation house, the weight of that encounter hung heavy in their minds. What dark forces had they awakened? What ancient powers had they provoked? Blood's flashback ended.

Amber sat in rapt silence, her eyes locked on Blood as he recounted the harrowing events. She took a slow sip of her vodka cocktail, the burn of the alcohol a mere afterthought as she con-templated the gravity of his words. This was no mere story – it was a window into a world of darkness, a world where the lines between love and obsession, curse and blessing, blurred until they became indistinguishable.

"So I am a witch?" Amber asked.

"I didn't say you were you are possessives like her," Blood answered.

"Just because I don't wish to share my man doesn't mean I own you," Amber stated.

"Being a black man from the South, it's hard to think of myself as being free. There is always someone trying to clip my wings," Blood expressed.

Amber paused for a second, not wanting to disagree any-more. "I am sorry about your mother and father. So what's on the agenda for tonight?"

"We can go to my place," Blood suggested.

"I hope this time it's your place?" Amber questioned.

"It's my place; the guys live there with me," Blood replied.

"I bet," Amber responded skeptically.

"It's true, only us guys," Blood assured her.

"Before we go to your place, I deserve a night out of on the town," Amber declared.

Blood and Amber Stone exited the Den bar, stepping out into the vibrant Harlem nightlife.

He and Amber strolled the lively streets, taking in the sights and sounds of the bustling neighborhood. The couple went to Well's restaurant, and enjoyed a leisurely dinner together.

After their meal, they continued their exploration, visiting the opulent Gold Lounge, the elegant Shalimar, and the iconic Lennox Lounge. Finally, they ended up at Small's Paradise, where they cuddled closely in a secluded booth. The lovers sipped their drinks and swayed softly to the rhythmic jazz music filling the dimly lit venue.

A romantic evening was exactly what Amber needed. The day's turmoil had faded, and she had maintained her emotional poise - a feat that had clearly pleased her lover. Blood had spared no expense, showering Amber with his affection and stroking her ego. In this moment, she was the sole focus of his attention.

When their night in the city came to a close, Blood took Amber back to the stash - a shabby, dimly lit apartment that served as their private sanctuary. The couple stepped through the threshold, the day's stresses melting away as they retreated into their own intimate world.

"You bring me to this dump?" Amber snapped.

"Excuse my humble abode," Blood answered, embarrassed.

"We are going to fix this place up," Amber declared.

"We?" Blood questioned.

"Yes, you and the guys, this is the first and last night I am sleeping in this slum," Amber stated.

"Chill, Amber, I feel you," Blood assured her.

Blood entered the kitchen and came back out with a bottle of champagne and two glasses, and he popped the cork and poured Amber Stone and him a glass of champagne. She sat at the table, and Blood took out a dollar bill filled with cocaine.

"Look what I have," he said. Amber's eyes brightened; she hadn't had a sniff of the drug all day, no wonder she had the jitters. Blood and she took a sniff of the drug.

"I am the brains, and you are the brawn," Amber said.

"Whatever you say, lady," Blood smiled.

"I have some ideas for decorating," Amber mentioned.

"I don't think the guys would mind a woman's touch, just don't make the pad too girly," Blood replied.

"I'll have exquisite taste. What about this new job you have?" Amber inquired.

"It's Chang. He has a community club next door to the Den," Blood explained.

"I met him once. Dee introduced us," Amber stated.

"Where is Dee?" Blood asked.

"You scared her out of town," Amber replied.

"Good," Blood responded.

Amber and Blood kissed and sniffed cocaine and guzzled their champagne. Blood put on the 8-track player, and soul music was playing.

"I want to dance," Amber wiggled.

"Entertain me, sexy Mama; shake your body down," Blood flirted as he flopped on the chair in front of Amber.

She stripped her clothes off, revealing her red bodice and garter stockings. Blood's gun was in his waist holster. She straddled him, eased the loaded pistol into her hand, and danced provocatively with it, arousing his sexual desire as she entertained her man.

CHAPTER FOUR

The following week at the Stash apartment, Amber, Blood, Soupy, Jonesy, and Cisco set about making the space their own. They arranged the white and brown furniture—a plush sectional sofa, matching armchairs, and a sturdy wooden coffee table—comfortably in the living room. In the bedrooms, they placed heavy oak dressers, sleek metal bed frames, and cozy area rugs to define the sleeping spaces.

To give the entire apartment a more masculine, grounded feel, the group decided to paint the walls a rich, earthy shade of green. They worked together, carefully applying coat after coat of the deep, mossy color until the space felt transformed. The once-bare, shabby-looking rooms now had an inviting, rustic ambiance.

As they stepped back to admire their handiwork, the quintet knew this stash house was becoming a true home. The fresh paint, the well-appointed furnishings - it all spoke to the sense of camaraderie and purpose they shared. This was more than just a hideout - it was a sanctuary where they could plan their next moves and find respite from the chaos of their lives on the streets.

Later that evening, Amber and Blood were in bed.

"The apartment looks great. We really did a wonderful job getting this place fixed up," Amber said, gazing around the cozy, inviting space.

"I love you, Amber," Blood said, his voice sincere as he looked into her eyes.

Amber raised an eyebrow playfully. "You mean I've actually managed to pierce the player's icy heart?"

"It's true, I do love you," Blood replied earnestly. "Why is that so hard for you to believe?"

Amber considered his words for a moment. "I guess we'll just have to see how things play out," she responded, a hint of wry amusement in her tone.

Blood took the pillow and hit Amber with it, and she grabbed hers and hit him back until they have a pillow fight and burst out laughing at each other. Amber kissed Blood; he broke their embrace and took out a mini glass cocaine vial.

"Look at what I have," Blood said as he dangles the bottle in front of Amber's face. She grabs it and twists the top of it off, there is a tiny spoon attached to it, and she takes a scoop and sniffs it.

"Wow! That is potent stuff," Amber said as she hands the vial back to Blood.

"I can't lose with what I use," Blood said as he snorts the blow. Amber lies on the bed, and he feeds the drug to her nose.

"You never told me if you won the fight at the old man Hawkins plantation house," Amber said.

"You don't want to hear the story," answered Blood.

"Yes, I do, and what happened to Sadie?" Amber pressed.

"What do you care about her?" Blood replied.

"If you and she would have gotten married, you and I never would have met," Amber explained.

It was late afternoon, Daniel, and I made it to Hawkins, barely escaping Satara's shotgun. I wish I would have turned back. I regret I didn't listen to Mama. But, they made me an offer I couldn't refuse.

Blood's flashback resumes.

The sun had set at Hawkins' plantation. The upper-class Southern wealthy white partners danced cheerfully on the patio to an African American band as if they didn't have a care in the world.

It was the South; anyone with light or white-skinned the living was easy. You were white; you were right; if you were yellow, mellow, brown, please stick around black stay back. Blood was black, and so was Butch, and paid to fight and spill blood. The patio is upscale decorated with wire lights of different colors. There are tables of food and liquor-filled glasses, silverware, and plates. A crowd of guests sat around eating and drinking. Old man Hawkins and his wife are seniors chatting away. Watching a fight between colored young boys was their only excitement. He stepped away from her to the middle of the ring, waved his hand, and the music faded.

Blood and Black Butch, a large young man, stepped into the ring. Old Man Hawkins moved out of the way as both young men had their dukes up and got into a fighting stance. Blood weaved around Black Butch, who was taller, and his arms were longer jabs at Blood's face, and he ducks and moved close to him. Blood gave Black Butch an uppercut to the jaw. Black Butch swung and missed him. Then, he offered his opponent a wicked left hook in his mouth and a right to his jaw, knocking him to the ground with blood pouring out of his lip. Black Butch has been totally knocked out, and Blood was the winner of the fight.

Old man Hawkins approached him and held up his hand in victory as the guests all cheered. The champ trotted out of the ring and met Daniel, who paid him the $300 from Hawkins. Blood counted his money.

"It's all there," said Daniel.

"Don't blame me for making sure," Blood said.

"Here's a switchblade to protect you from any alligators you see on the road."

Daniel gives Blood the blade, and he puts it in his pocket and his cash.

"Thanks, Daniel, for looking out for me."

"I got my percentage off of the top. So be safe, Blood." Daniel cautioned.

Blood bustles off on his way to Sadie's house. He thought she should be finished with his homework. It was late, and Sadie was in bed. Her parents didn't allow boys in the house after 6 p.m., so he would have to throw stones up at her window, and she would wake up and tie his homework to a rope and lower it down to him. Blood felt prosperous and happy fast trotting on the country road with only the full moon's light to guide him. He heard crickets and mice skittering through the clump of weeds and the scruff of gravel under his shoes. Engines rumble, and the headlights of five cars speedily approached. The men stepped hard on their brakes as the cars encircled him. Blood, confused, looking all around for a way out, but he is blocked. Five men are in each vehicle, a total of twenty-five. They all jump out dressed in Klansmen's white robes and hoods; they close in on Blood. Two KKK men step forward to question him.

"An old white lady said a black man who fits your description stole $300 from her," said Klan's man 1.

"I didn't see no old white lady. I won this money in a fight," Blood answered.

"Boy, I don't believe you. Empty your pockets," asked Klan's man 2.

Blood takes the money out of his pocket.

"There is the money," Klan's man 1 said.

Klan's man 2 snatches the money out of Blood's hand.

"That is my money. I won it fair in a fight at old man Hawkins plantation," Blood retorted.

"That is too bad. What's a spook like you doing with this much money?" Klan's man 2 asked.

"I am going to take my Mama out of the South," Blood answered.

"You are one of them damn freedom riders, well, not with this money you won't," Klan's man 2 said as he waved the money in his face.

Blood snatched the cash out of his hand, and Klan's man 2 leaped at him and tried to take the money back. They struggled, and Blood punched him and knocked him out. The rest of the Klan's men charged him, and he flicked his switchblade open and slit a Klan man's throat. The blood gushed all over his white robe and startled the others. As they attacked Blood, he knocked them away and ran off into the woodlands. The Klan's men crowded around to get their orders.

"Let's get him to the emergency room. We'll get that nigger later, and I have his address," Klan's man 1 said.

The Klansmen carry the injured man to a car; they all get in their cars and speed off. They take the Klansmen to the hospital, and the rest drive to Blood's shack, thinking he is going there and they will capture him. Blood's flashback ended, and he and Amber are lying in bed.

"So what happened?" Amber asked.

"I told you I ran through the woodlands and came to my shack, and I witnessed my Mama busting out the door in flames and falling on the ground screaming until she burned to a crisp. So I ran and went to Sadie's house. Surprisingly she was awake and came downstairs. I told her what happened and that I had to leave Mississippi and never look back because the Klan was out to kill me. She cried, hugged and kissed me, and said she loved me. If staying alive meant that we would never marry, she was okay with it. Sadie wanted me to live, and nothing was worst than dying. I knew the Klan would visit her and Daniel to find out where I went. Still, I didn't tell her I knew I could never write. The Klan worked in the post office and intercepted all incoming and outgoing mail. I kissed her goodbye and told her to forget about me. I would never send a message to her because the Klan would spot anyone new in town, follow, torture, and kill them. I gave Sadie $50 out of the $300, and I ran until I came to a greyhound bus station. It was around 6 a.m. I got on and went to Kentucky," said Blood.

"You got away. What happened then?" Amber asked, her eyes filled with both curiosity and concern.

Blood let out a weary sigh. "I'll tell you about it later. Right now, I just need to get some sleep. I start my new job at Chang's tomorrow."

Amber nodded sympathetically. "Reliving the past must be so tragic for you."

"Nobody wants to hear those kinds of stories, and believe me, I can't forget any of it," Blood replied, his voice heavy with emotion.

Reaching out, Amber placed a gentle hand on his arm.

"Well, I'm here for you, Blood. I don't have to work tomorrow - if you'd like me to come with you to your new job, I'd be happy to."

Blood considered her offer for a moment, then the hint of a grateful smile tugged at the corners of his mouth. "I guess Chang won't mind if you tag along. It's just a recreational Penny Arcade Club, after all." Blood said as he pecks Amber on the lips, turns over and closes his eyes.

She looks at the bottle of cocaine and decides not to take a sniff. Trying to resist the lure of the drug, Amber puts it in the lamp stand drawer hidden from her sight. She turns off the lights and goes to sleep.

In the morning, Amber is in the kitchen preparing breakfast. Blood enters and asked, "Where are the guys?"

"Cisco went to stay with his aunt; Soupy and Jonesy are visiting their girlfriends," Amber said.

"You decided to fix us breakfast," Blood observed.

"Yes, a healthy diet is important, especially if you have vices," Amber replied.

"I remember when I didn't have any bad habits," Blood said.

Blood sat down at the table, and Amber grabbed a milk carton out of the fridge. He stared at the milk and said, "When Mama was alive, it was a Saturday morning."

Blood has a flashback to his shack house. Irma was drunk, sprawled out on the sofa with an empty bottle of whiskey on the coffee table. He plodded into the kitchen and opened the icebox, and took a swig of the milk. He vomited the sour milk into the sink. Blood grabbed his canteen, filled it with water, and exited the house. The scorching Delta sun beats down mercilessly as Blood trudged along the dusty country road. The fine particles of dirt swirled in the stagnant air, irritated his throat and causing him to break into a fit of harsh coughs.

He took a long, desperate sip from his rapidly warming canteen, the tepid water doing little to soothe his parched mouth. The pungent aroma of dried, withering grass assaults his nostrils with each step, mingled with the musty scent of his own sweat.

Gnats relentlessly buzzed around his face, drawn to the glistening droplets on his brow. He felt the oppressive heat radiating against the back of his neck, as if the very atmosphere was conspiring to smother him. He forced himself to keep walking, to not show any sign of fear or weakness. But the ominous pall of danger hung heavy in the air, and Blood couldn't shake the feeling that he's being watched, that unseen eyes are tracking his every step. The road ahead stretched on endlessly, offering no comfort or refuge from the hostility of this hostile, unforgiving land.

A sudden gust of wind whipped through the air, ruffling the tight naps of his hair. Blood squinted against the sting of dust, shielding his eyes as a beat-up old car came barreling down the road. The white occupants, faces ruddy from the heat and alcohol, leered at him menacingly as they pass, shouting slurs that sent a chill down his spine.

"NIGGER GET OFF THE ROAD."

They threw beer cans and bottles at him, and the young man ducked and dodged. A Mom and Pop's grocery store came into his view, and he dashed towards the entrance leaving the sound of the laughing men behind as they drove in the other direction.

A middle-aged Caucasian man, aka Pop, and his wife, Mom, were behind the counter near the cash register. Blood entered, and Pop clutched his shotgun and watched him like a hawk so he didn't steal any of the can or box food on display. A glass-front refrigerated meat counter was filled with poultry and beef, not from the best stock. Blood glanced at Mom and Pop. They pretended to be busy counting receipts. They thought he's going to steal food. Blood felt that the color of his skin judged him; it didn't matter if he was honorable or flawed; he was guilty.

Most of the fresh vegetables had rotten from the heat and lacked shipment. However, there were some collard greens on a stand. He seized them and laid them on the counter, among three cans of beans and a box of rice, as Pop added his total.

"That will be sixty-five dollars," Pop said.

"I only have five items. I didn't get no beef," Blood said.

"The supermarket is 16 miles away. If you have a car, you can get there before night," Mom said.

"I don't have a car," said Blood.

"Well, what are you going to do? I haven't got all day," Pop said.

"This is highway robbery," Blood retorted.

"If you don't like our prices, you don't have to buy our food," Pop said.

Blood took a deep breath. "I'll take everything."

He pulled a crumpled wad of bills from his pocket, carefully counting out $65 before laying the cash on the counter. Mom swiftly bagged the modest assortment of groceries, her deft hands making quick work of the task. With the purchases secured, Blood scooped up the bag and headed for the exit, the worn soles of his shoes scuffing against the linoleum floor.

Outside, the oppressive summer heat hit him like a physical force, causing him to squint against the bright sunlight. Wasting no time, Blood hurried towards home, his long strides eating up the road. As a young Black man, he knew the risks of lingering too long in public spaces - encourages, harassment, even disappearance were all too common fates for men who shared his complexion. For Blood, the road was a gauntlet to be navigated with haste and caution.

When he finally reached the rundown dwelling he shared with his mother, Irma, Blood let out a relieved sigh. Home, at last. Stepping through the threshold, he sat the grocery bag on the table, his eyes immediately drawn to Irma's wakeful form. Though her love for alcohol often eclipsed her maternal instincts, the sight of the food brought a glimmer of joy to her careworn features. She eagerly began planning to prepare Blood's favorite meal - chicken, beans, rice, collard greens, and pig knuckles.

Blood's stomach rumbled at the thought, but his excitement was tempered by the realization that the cash in his pocket had dwindled to a mere $30 - not nearly enough to ensure their next few meals. Irma's drinking habit was an ever-present burden, one that frequently left them scraping to get by. With a resigned sigh, Blood knew he'd have to venture out again, this time to the underground gambling circuit, in search of a bigger payday.

Blood's flashback is shattered as Amber appeared, pouring a frothy glass of milk and setting it before Blood, along with a plate piled high with scrambled egg whites and crisp toast, a small tub of yogurt completing the simple but nourishing meal. As he tucked in, the familiar flavors helped ground Blood, if only momentarily.

"This is a healthy breakfast," Amber said.

"What did you do with the egg yolks?" asked Blood.

"I've saved them for a cake I will bake," Amber replied.

"We never had any food to save, and my milk I had to drink it fast if I waited, it would be sour," Blood said.

"Life is refreshing, Blood; these flashbacks you are having. Don't you think you should see a therapist?" Amber suggested.

"What the fuck is wrong with you? What do you think I am crazy? I am not seeing no psychiatrist; it's an insult to me," Blood said angrily, slamming his fist on the table.

"I am sorry, it's nothing to be ashamed of," Amber said with a nervous expression.

"I am not hungry. I got to get ready for work," Blood said as he stood up.

"It's early; you don't have to go right away. I'll go with you. Think about what I said," Amber offered.

"With that attitude, you can stay here, and there isn't shit for me to consider," Blood responded.

"I apologize; it was only an offer, a suggestion," Amber said.

"Yeah, you take care of your brain, and I'll take care of mine," Blood said.

"I said I would listen," Amber insisted.

"Do it because I don't want to hear this bullshit again," Blood demanded as he stormed out of the kitchen.

Amber threw her hands in the air, frustrated. She's thwarted the only thing she could do is scrape his food into her plate and slowly eat his meal. Her man stayed in the bedroom, and Amber avoided him and cleaned the stash. Eventually, they got ready to leave; neither spoke to one another; they both got dressed casually and departed the apartment.

It was just after 6 p.m., inside Chang's Penny Arcade. The dimly lit space was abuzz with activity as the regulars gathered for their evening of recreation and camaraderie. Modern, slate-topped pool tables dominated the center of the room, their felt surfaces a pristine green. The soft clack of balls striking each other and muffled shouts of players filled the air, accompanied by the energetic chimes and bloops of the many pinball machines and video games lining the walls. Neon lights flickered over the arcade cabinets, casting an electric glow across the faces of the concentrated gamers. In one corner, a trio of men engaged in a heated game of pool. Fat Bob, in his 30s and tipping the scales at over 300 pounds, leaned over the table, his thick fingers gripping the cue as he eyed his next shot. Beside him, Baby James - tall and slim in his 20s, his thick bi-focal glasses perched on his nose - lined up his own strike.

And presiding over them was Ejay, a man in his 30s who looked the part of a pimp with his gold chains and oversized medallion dangling from his neck. Just then, the sound of a cane tapping against the worn hardwood floor drew their attention. Chang, the club's owner, limped out from the back room, his brow furrowed in a perpetual scowl as he surveyed his domain. The boys paused their game, giving the intimidating older man their full focus, knowing better than to disrupt the fragile peace of Chang's domain.

"I'm waiting on Blood to come. Baby James, have you seen him?" Chang asked.

"No, Chang, what's he's supposed to do?" Baby James asked.

"I hired him to be a bouncer, and he can do some other things for me too," said Chang.

"Everyone is at the Den," said Fat Bob.

"Who ask you, Fat Bob?" Chang asked.

"I'm just saying, we ain't going to make any money tonight," said Fat Bob.

"People will see you all playing pool and will come in," Chang said.

Amber and Blood entered the penny arcade and greeted Chang.

Blood extended his hand. "Hey Chang, what's up?"

"You're late; you have to be reliable," said Chang.

"I'm sorry, I had to bring my girl. Chang, this is Amber Stone."

Chang smiled and said, "She bought seven hundred dollars of cocaine from me. We sniffed and talked all night. She's cool."

Blood with a surprised look on his face. "You never told me that."

Amber, blushing, "I told you, I met him through Dee."

Chang chuckled. "Don't worry; your girl is not cheating on you."

Blood with a sly grin. "I'm just kidding. What do you want me to do tonight?"

Chang yawns and said, "I'm turning in early tonight; I'm tired, man. This is my brother Ejay?"

"Yeah, we've met." Blood confirmed.

"I need you to stay here and look out for the place." Chang said.

"When do you want me to leave?" Blood asked.

"About five o'clock in the morning after the crowd finishes at the Den." Change replied.

"Okay." Blood acknowledge.

Chang and Ejay left the penny arcade. There was a moment of silence.

"Hey Blood, aren't you going to introduce the lady to us?" asked Fat Bob.

"Fat Bob and Baby James, I want you to meet my girl Amber Stone."

"Please to meet you," Amber said.

"She's beautiful," said Fat Bob. Baby James smiles.

"She looks like a model."

Blood sticks out his chest with pride. "She is a model."

"I have a long way to go," Amber said.

"With your looks, you will get to the top?" Baby James said.

Amber smiled. "Yes, and it is much work, but I love it."

Baby James winked. "Good, keep on doing it; don't quit."

Amber blushed. "Can I join the game? I love to play pool."

"Sure, grab a pool stick," Baby James said.

"I'll watch the door," said Blood.

Baby James racks the pool balls. "You can relax until somebody comes in." Baby James said.

"Okay," Blood replied, and he began playing a video game. Amber, Baby James, Fat Bob started their game of pool.

Later that night, the energy at Chang's Penny Arcade had shifted to a more intimate, sultry tone. In a dim corner of the cavernous space, Amber Stone sat perched provocatively on Blood's lap, her arms draped around his neck as they engaged in a heated, passionate embrace.

Amber's long, raven black hair cascaded in soft waves around their faces, creating a veil that shielded them momentarily from the rest of the room. Their lips met in a passionate, lingering kiss, interrupted only by the occasional soft gasp or muffled moan escaping one of them.

Across the room, the hulking form of Fat Bob sat slumped in a worn armchair, his massive frame nearly swallowing the chair as he snored softly, oblivious to the amorous display nearby. The only sound that punctuated the hushed atmosphere was the muted chatter and tinny soundtrack emanating from the back room, where the glow of a flickering television cast an ethereal light. Just as things between Amber and Blood began to intensify, they reluctantly broke their embrace, both slightly flushed and breathless.

"What time is it?" Amber asked.

Blood looked at his watch, "It's midnight."

"I have a shoot tomorrow afternoon. So I'd better go," she said.

"Okay, I'll see you tomorrow?" Blood replied.

"These late nights are exciting," Amber commented.

"That's what I like about you. You're an outgoing girl," Blood said.

"Unlike my man, I have to get my rest," Amber responded.

Blood kissed Amber. "Get home safe, my lady."

Amber exited the penny arcade. Blood stepped over to Fat Bob and shook him.

Fat Bob jumpy with his eyes wide open. "What happened?"

Blood grinned. "Wake up. Let's play a game of pool."

The wobbly man got up from the chair and grabbed a pool stick. Blood placed the pool balls in the center of the table, and Fat Bob hit the balls with his pool stick.

"What happened to Amber Stone?" asked Fat Bob.

Blood, chalking his stick, replied, "She had to go home."

"I heard Tony left town. Did you ever get your money?" Fat Bob inquired.

Blood rolled his eyes. "He didn't leave town, and I killed him," he stated.

"No, you didn't," Fat Bob said.

"Yes, I did," Blood insisted.

"How did you kill him?" Fat Bob asked.

"I shot him," Blood answered.

"Show me the gun that you used on him?" Fat Bob demanded.

"I'm not showing you the gun," Blood refused.

Fat Bob smirked. "You Cats are always telling people you killed somebody."

"If I didn't do it, I wouldn't say I did it," Blood responded.

"I didn't hear nothing about no killing," Fat Bob said.

Blood pulled out the pistol from his jacket. "Here's the gun I shot him with," he said, pointing the .38-caliber pistol at the back wall.

"Let me see it?" Fat Bob requested.

Fat Bob lumbered over to where Blood was standing, his massive hand outstretched expectantly.

Without a word, Blood tossed the pistol towards his associate. Fat Bob's thick fingers wrapped around the grip, his brow furrowed as he examined the weapon.

For a moment, the hulking man considered the firearm, then, with a sudden flick of his wrist, sent it hurtling back towards Blood. The two men fell into a playful rhythm, chuckling as they tossed the pistol back and forth between them a couple of times. The men grinned with excitement. It was amusing until the light-hearted game took a dramatic turn, however, when the gun landed squarely in Blood's outstretched palm. In an instant, his finger brushed the trigger, and the weapon discharged with a deafening crack. The bullet tore through the wall, disappearing into the back room.

Stunned silence hung in the air for a heartbeat before the sound of shattering glass shattered the stillness. Blood and Fat Bob rushed towards the commotion, finding Baby James sprawled on the floor, one hand clutching his ringing ear. The large television screen behind him was reduced to a spiderweb of broken shards.

Panic etched across their features, the two men hurried to Baby James' side, hands hovering uncertainly. Blood gently helped the younger man to his feet, checking him over for any signs of injury. Aside from the graze on his ear and the obvious shock, Baby James appeared unharmed - but the terrifying incident had clearly left him shaken to the core.

Blood, frantic, said, "It was an accident."

Fat Bob explained, "We didn't mean for this to happen."

Blood brushed the pieces of glass off of his clothes. "We are so sorry, are you okay?"

Baby James takes a deep breath. "What the hell is wrong with you guys?"

Blood is fussing over him and straightens his shirt. "I'm sorry, Baby James."

Baby James rubs his head. "Wait outside. I got to get myself together."

Blood patting him on the shoulders. "You okay, man?"

Baby James sat in the chair. "Yeah, I'm all right. The bullet grazed my ear, and my heart is beating fast."

Blood and Fat Bob exited the back room after the incident, closing the door behind them.

Baby James glanced at the phone on the desk and quickly called Chang.

"Chang, it's Baby James. I almost got killed!" he said, with tears swelling in his eyes.

There was a pause, then Chang's smooth voice came over the phone. "By who?"

"Blood and Fat Bob," Baby James replied.

"Be cool; leave quickly. I'll talk to them tomorrow night," Chang said.

"Sure." Baby James placed the receiver back on the phone and emerged from the back room. Blood and Fat Bob were standing by the pool table, looking bewildered.

"I'm leaving. You guys lock up," Baby James said calmly, eyes fixed on the door.

Blood wiped the sweat from his temples. "Are you alright?"

Fat Bob moved in close, pleading, "I'm sorry."

"See you later," Baby James said, then exited the penny arcade.

"What now?" asked Blood.

Fat Bob swiped a hand over his forehead. "Do as he said."

"That was close," Blood remarked.

"Everything's cool," Fat Bob reassured.

The men put the pool cues away, straightened the chairs, and locked up the penny arcade at 5 a.m. They then went their separate ways. Blood took a cab to the stash apartment, showered, and went to sleep before the sun had risen.

Meanwhile, at precisely 7 a.m., Amber awoke with a start. She quickly slipped out of bed and made her way to the bathroom, bathing efficiently but thoroughly. Emerging refreshed, Amber changed into a pair of well-worn jeans and a simple, form-fitting shirt, throwing on her trusty black motorcycle jacket over it. Grabbing her handbag and portfolio, Amber gave her small apartment one final once-over before scrambling out the door.

Hailing a taxi, Amber provided the address for Bill's Studio. Her leg bounced anxiously during the short drive. Time was of the essence; she had a critical shoot that afternoon and needed to look her absolute best. As the taxi pulled up to the familiar building, Amber paid the driver and hurried inside, her heels clicking against the polished floors.

The model was greeted by the cosmetologist and hairdresser, both men in their early 30s, who immediately set to work transforming Amber's natural beauty. They applied her makeup with expert precision, carefully shaping her features, then set about styling her raven locks into an elegant, runway-ready coiffure.

Once her beauty team had worked their magic, Amber slipped into the stunning ice blue gown that had been laid out for her. The high fashion garment draped elegantly over her lithe frame, the shimmering fabric accentuating her curves.

With a final glance in the mirror, Amber stepped out onto the backdrop, an air of confident poise radiating from her. Bill, the renowned photographer, began snapping away, capturing Amber in a variety of captivating poses. She moved with a natural grace, her expressions shifting from sultry to pensive, adapting seamlessly to Bill's creative direction. The camera's shutter clicked rapidly as he worked, intent on preserving Amber's ethereal beauty for the world to see.

Bill snaps the photo. "That's great! Could you step to the side."

Amber stepped to the side and continues to pose.

He snaps another shot. "That's beautiful. I got it, Amber Stone. You are fabulous."

Amber stepped off the backdrop paper and approaches him.

"Thank you, what happened to the pictures we took?" she asked.

He pointed. "The contact sheets are on the table."

"I am amazed they look amazing. I can't believe how terrific the shots are. Bill, you are the best," Amber said.

"You have defined features, and you are photographed well; you are a photographer's dream," said Bill.

"I have to work on my concentration," Amber said.

"Your agent Willie called," said Bill.

"Did I get the job?" asked Amber.

"No one has told me anything yet," replied Bill.

Amber primped her hair. "A hundred girls are up for that job."

"It's a top gig for the model who lands it. She wants to see you," said Bill.

"I'd better not keep Her Majesty waiting," Amber replied as she hurried out of the studio.

"She's just an agent," Bill said.

"Willie is so intimidating; I'd better hurry," Amber insisted.

"I hope you get the assignment," Bill said encouragingly.

"Thanks, Bill," Amber responded.

Amber exited the studio and stepped into the dressing room. After changing into her clothes, she grabbed her things, waved goodbye to the guys, and dashed out of the studio.

An hour later, Amber Stone sashayed into the Fab Fashion Agency. The walls of the contemporary, well-appointed office were covered in rows of glamorous model headshots and portfolio images.

Amber took in the display, her eyes scanned the faces of the polished, picture-perfect women whose photos adorned the space. She moved with a confident, runway-ready stride, hoping that one day her own image will be immortalized among them as a top model. Amber's gaze swept across the sleek, sophisticated space of the Fab Fashion Agency. The minimalist décor exudes an air of exclusivity - gleaming marble, polished chrome, and potted plants that lent pops of verdant greenery.

The waiting area was furnished with chic, black leather seats, where a handful of hopefuls sat anxiously, no doubt anticipating their turn to impress the agency's owner. Amber was unwilling to betray the butterflies swirling in the pit of her stomach.

Instead, she focused on projecting an aura of quiet confidence, her gaze swept across the modern light fixtures and the minimalist reception desk. This is where the magic happens, she knew - where dreams of superstardom were made a reality, where the industry's greatest talents were cultivated.

With each step Amber took across the gleaming hardwood floors, her self-assurance grew. One day, she vowed, her face will grace these hallowed walls, a testament to her hard work and determination. For now, she savored the anticipation, the palpable energy of ambition and success that permeates every inch of this space.

At the front of the room, a pretty blonde receptionist in her 20s sat behind the sleek, minimalist reception desk, her gaze following Amber as she entered. The atmosphere exuded a sense of style, success, and opportunity—a tantalizing preview of the career Amber aspired to achieve.

"I'm Amber Stone. I'm here to see Willie," Amber said.

The receptionist smiles. "She's expecting you; she's in her office."

Amber entered the office, her gaze immediately drawn to the drawn shades that cast the space in a warm, subdued glow. The room had a distinct air of sophistication and authority, reflecting the stature of the agency's owner.

At the center of the office, Willie sat behind the massive mahogany desk, her imposing presence commanded the room. The desk's surface was covered in an array of neatly organized files, a vintage rotary telephone, and a few carefully placed decorative elements. Behind Willie, the wall was adorned with a striking, abstract painting of Willie that commanded attention, its bold strokes and vibrant hues provided a captivating focal point.

Plush, leather armchairs were positioned in front of the desk, inviting visitors to sink into their cushions as they discussed business. A matching credenza along the far wall houses an array of awards and accolades, a testament to Willie's impressive achievements within the industry. The overall aesthetic is one of refined elegance, with rich textures, muted tones, and a minimalist sensibility that exuded an air of professional gravitas. It was a space that demanded respect and conveyed the power and influence wielded by the overly dressed and done, colorful woman who presided over it.

Amber took a moment to absorb the details of the office; her eyes lingered on the drawn shades that cast an intimate, introspective atmosphere over the proceedings. She knew that this was where the decisions that would shape her profession were made, and she steeled herself for the pivotal conversation that was henceforth.

"Amber Stone, I am glad you are here; sit down," said Willie.

"It is a pleasure to see you, Willie," Amber said.

Willie immediately reached over and pulled open the shades, flooding the office with bright sunlight. Amber squinted, the light illuminating every detail of her face. Willie leaned forward, her gaze intently scrutinizing Amber's features, searching for any perceived flaws or imperfections that could jeopardize her chances of securing the coveted position. The intensity of Willie's examination made Amber's heart race, as she felt exposed and vulnerable under the harsh glare of the sun. She held her breath, waiting anxiously to see if the agent would find any fault in her appearance that could cost her the opportunity she had been so ardently pursuing.

After a long, tense moment, Willie finally leaned back in her chair, a slight smile tugged at the corners of her mouth.

"You'll be boarding a plane to Washington, D.C. tomorrow at 8 p.m.," she said calmly.

Amber's eyes widen in disbelief. "Willie, do you mean I got the job? Great!" she exclaims, unable to contain her excitement.

Willie nods, the smile on her face broadening. "Yes, Amber Stone, and you'll get five thousand dollars for the week's shoot," she said.

Amber's mouth drops open. "Oh my God! How many pages will I be in?" she asked.

"You have a twenty-page shoot," Willie replied.

With a renewed sense of determination, Amber knew that this opportunity was hers to seize, and she was ready to take on the challenges that were in her profession.

"What's my next job?" Amber asked.

"You have to take it as it comes," Willie said.

"I just have so much anxiety about my ability," Amber admitted.

"There is a market for your look," Willie reassured her.

"That gives me hope," Amber said.

"I can't make any promises. How's your personal life?" Willie asked.

"You mean, do I have a boyfriend? Yes, I do," Amber replied.

"Is he going to interfere with your career?" Willie questioned.

"No, he's supportive. He's like, 'go for it," Amber said.

"Model's boyfriends sometimes get insecure," Willie warned.

"Willie, it's hard to keep a relationship when you're traveling a lot," Amber acknowledged.

"Yes, I used to be a top model; you have to keep moving forward no matter what," Willie shared.

"Thanks for the tip," Amber said.

Willie took a folder out of the desk drawer and opened it.

"Here are your tickets and your hotel reservation. Also, a check for $2,500 - the other half you'll get when you come back."

Willie hands Amber the check, tickets, and reservation.

"Thank you, Willie," Amber said.

They hug each other.

"Amber Stone, you have a wonderful trip and an awesome shoot. You call me if there's anything you need," Willie said.

"I will," Amber replied.

The model exited Willie's office and hailed a cab; she was on her way to her Judo class. Amber didn't have to leave for D.C. until the next day, so she was eager to celebrate. She couldn't stop thinking about how much money she would make from this job.

Facing Professor Stone, her father who lived and worked in Washington, she would be delighted if he approved of her new-found success, as it was better than taking his allowance. The cab stopped, she paid the driver, hopped out, and darted into the Dojo.

Inside the Dojo locker room, she changed into her judogi. Master Dan waited silently on the mat in his judogi. Amber approached him; they bowed to one another and began. Amber threw Master Dan around on the mat. She felt energized. The excitement of her success sped her up. Amber realized this was the motivation she had been missing. The possibility of career success was what she needed. He got up and threw her around the mat. Amber broke his hold on her, threw him over her back, grabbed his arm, and threw him again. Master Dan stood up, and they both bowed to one another.

"Master Dan, I'm going to Washington tomorrow night. I got a modeling gig," Amber said.

"Amber Stone, I'm happy you're attaining your goals," Master Dan replied.

"I've earned it," Amber said confidently.

"Have you been practicing?" Master Dan asked.

"My so-called friend Dee attacked me," Amber explained.

"You don't seem too happy about it," Master Dan observed.

"I did the judo throw perfectly," Amber stated.

"With speed?" Master Dan inquired.

"Yes, Master Dan, like lightning fast," Amber replied.

"Tell me, are you going to see your father?" Master Dan asked.

"Yes, I'm going to try and see him if he's not too busy for his daughter," Amber said.

"I remember this angry, rebellious woman coming to my class," Master Dan reminisced.

"I was the angry Black woman, Master Dan; you've taught me a lot. I must admit, I still have my vices," Amber confessed.

"Your drinking and drug use?" Master Dan asked.

"Okay, I drink and use cocaine on occasion," Amber admitted.

"I can tell you're an addict trying to control her drug use," Master Dan said.

"I can stop whenever I want. I'm not addicted," Amber insisted.

"Stop lying to yourself. It's either all or nothing, and the strength is within you," Master Dan asserted.

"I understand this week in Washington. I won't be drinking or using drugs," Amber declared.

"Amber Stone, I'll see you in a week," Master Dan replied.

"Yes, I'll be back in top shape," Amber assured him.

"You were superb; consistency is vital. You must take care of your health," Master Dan emphasized.

"Thank you, Master Dan," Amber said.

Amber stepped out of the dojo and entered the locker room, where she usually showered. Her muscles ached pleasantly after a grueling training session. She walked into the cramped, dimly lit locker room, the familiar smell of sweat and leather permeating the air. Normally, she would linger here, rinsing off the grime of the day in a hot, rejuvenating shower. But today, Amber was eager to get home—she had big plans that night. With a sense of urgency, she peeled off her sweat-soaked judogi, tossing it haphazardly into her gym bag. Impatient, she wanted to pack her clothes, take a long hot bubble bath, and primp herself before seeing Blood. She quickly threw on her clothes and rushed out of the dojo.

The streets had been bustling with the afternoon commute as Amber rushed to the curb, waving down the first available taxi. As she slid into the backseat, her mind raced with excitement and anticipation. Blood and she had never been apart for a whole week; Amber felt strange, as if she had never been alone. This had been her big break, and Amber had to take it. No model could just work locally for the sake of a romantic relationship. Tomorrow it would be Washington; next, it would be Europe. After all, she had told Willie that her boyfriend was 100% supportive of her career and success. Now she had to prove it to herself and everyone else.

It was 6 p.m, and Amber was dressed to the nines, her lithe frame encased in a stunning emerald green pantsuit. The luxurious fabric clung in all the right places, accentuating her fashionable figure. She was ready to party with her man and live it up before leaving town the next day for her big opportunity.

With a confident, almost regal gait, the model breezed into Chang's Penny Arcade as if she had glided on the fashion catwalks of Paris. Her arrival commanded attention, every eye in the establishment drawn to her magnetic presence. But Amber's triumphant entrance was quickly shattered when she spotted Blood and his friend Fat Bob standing against the wall, their bodies tense and expressions etched with fear. Before she could react, the club owner, Chang, suddenly produced a pistol, leveling it at the two men.

Shock and confusion washed over Amber's features as she watched the scene unfold. Ejay and Baby James, known enforcers for Chang, stood ominously on guard, their faces betraying no emotion.

Without warning, Chang began pistol-whipping Blood and Fat Bob, the sickening sound of metal colliding with flesh echoing through the smoky air. Fat Bob, unable to withstand the assault, turned and fled the club, his desperate sobs fading as he disappeared into the night.

Blood, however, stood his ground, weathering the blows from Chang's weapon. As the club owner continued his relentless attack, Amber swiftly approached, her heart pounding with a mixture of fear and determination. She had to end this madness before it was too late.

"Chang, what happened?" Amber asked.

He gave her a hairy eyeball. "They almost shot Baby James in the head," Chang said.

"What?" asked Amber.

"Playing around in here with a pistol, I'm going to kill them both," said Chang.

Chang hits Blood in the face with the gun.

Amber cried. "Please, Chang, don't kill him," pleaded Amber.

Chang waved his weapon. "Why should I spare this dumb punk?" He hit him in the face again, and his wounds dripped with blood.

A wellspring of emotions burst forth from Amber that had been suppressed. Their spicy romance splashed across her mind. They always kissed and made up, but now he was about to die. The reality of being sober set in, and the depth of her feelings for him astonished her.

She pleaded, "Please don't kill him. I love him."

"Are you responsible for this punk? Because he almost killed my baby brother. Are you, are you?" asked Chang.

"Yes, I am. Please don't kill him. I love him," Amber said.

Chang pointed the weapon at Blood's head. "I ought to kill him, and I got the power to blow your brains out, and don't you forget it." Chang hit Blood across his head and face with the butt of the pistol.

Amber, with a crying scream, "That's enough. You're killing him."

"What the hell do you think I'm trying to do?" asked Chang.

"He won't do it again. Please let him go," Amber pleaded.

The gangster held Blood up by the collar with one hand, while the other pointed a gun at his head.

"Amber Stone, get on your hands and knees in a praying position," ordered Chang.

Sobbing, she dropped to her knees, clasped her hands together in a prayer position, and hesitated. He pointed the revolver at Blood's head.

Chang said, "Repeat after me. For the love of Blood, please, Chang, I beg you not to kill him."

Amber had hesitated, not understanding his orders.

"If you love him, keep this dumb punk out of my sight," he said, holding the gun to Blood's head.

"I will please don't shoot him," Amber said.

"Say what I told you to say, or I'll blow this bastard's brains out," threatened Chang.

Amber wept and said, "For the love of Blood, please, Chang. I beg you not to kill him."

"The only reason I'm letting him live is because of you. You got a good heart," said Chang.

Amber Stone stood up from the floor and wiped the tears from her face.

"I promise you, Chang, he won't retaliate," Amber said.

"You can control this punk?" asked Chang.

"Yes, I can," replied Amber.

"I'm going to let this punk live; get this motherfucker out of here," said Chang.

Chang pushed him toward Amber Stone. She held Blood and let him lean on her shoulder.

"Thank you, Chang," Amber said.

Ejay put a small spoon to Chang's nose, his eyes narrowed as he took a snort of the cocaine, the white powder burning his nostrils. With his gun still in his hand, he keenly watched as Amber supported the injured Blood, who was leaning heavily on her, as they exited the arcade.

Outside on the deserted street, the arcade and the Den Club were dimly lit, with a neon sign casting an eerie glow over the empty sidewalk. The air was thick with the lingering scent of cigarette smoke and the faint sound of music pulsing from within the club's walls. The muted thump of the club's bass line provided a discordant backdrop to the tense moment as Amber and the injured Blood made their way to the curb.

Amber glanced around anxiously, searching for an available cab to take them to the hospital. Blood's face was etched with pain and bloodied from the blow to his head. Amber desperately needed to find transportation to get him medical attention.

"Blood, you have to go to the hospital. You got walloped in the head," Amber said.

"Amber Stone, I don't need no doctor. I can't report this; you are going to have to clean me up," said Blood.

"Blood, I am oblivious. I've never seen a pistol-whipping before, except in the movies, I am no emergency room medic," Amber said.

"Woman, will you do what I tell you to and deal with it? Don't go all mushy on me," said Blood.

"All right, keep calm. I'll do my best," Amber said.

A taxi cab pulled up to the curb; they got inside and drove away.

The couple entered the stash, and Amber laid him down on the sofa. She then galloped into the bathroom and emerged with a first aid kit. Amber took out cotton pads and bandages. Quickly, she grabbed a bowl from the kitchen cabinet, filled it with water, and dashed back into the living room. She wiped the blood from his lips and dabbed the peroxide on his wounded face and head. He winced from the stinging of the antiseptic as she applied a bandage to his cheek and head.

"Boy, that stings," said Blood.

Amber had put her hands on her hips, her stance firm. "We can have that talk you have been avoiding."

Blood closed his eyes as if he's resting. "Not now," he mumbles, his voice laced with fatigue.

Amber was concerned. "Blood, we have been naive skating around real commitment and intimacy and playing the game, and indulging in our casual romance, we are both blinded by the chemistry between us. After what happened tonight, we have to move forward. I want a real monogamous legal relationship, and I know that is not what you are used to, just like the fashion business is not used to a black curvy 30-year-old woman who is not 21, blond, white, or thin. The image of beauty can change. There will be a market for me, and I can sell to millions of women who look like me in color and size. That is why I keep pushing myself; my break is coming. I want success in all areas of my life, and we can have that together if you try, but you have to change your life. I can't put the cart before the horse in this situation and hope that you get enough money from hustling to go legit," Amber said, her voice firm yet tinged with a hint of vulnerability.

Blood opened his eyes and met her gaze. "Look who's talking. You are a cocaine addict, just like me," he said, his words laced with a touch of defensive accusation.

Amber's patience began to wear thin, her frustration evident in her expression. She can't continue to sit on the fence; he must choose, and she is irritated by his defensive response, and how dare he judge her. She stepped closer, her eyes narrowing.

"Eventually, I will alleviate my habit. I don't wish to be looking over my shoulder for the rest of my existence and worrying if my man will come home or not? We need to solve your problems immediately. For us as a couple to evolve, do you realize you almost got killed?" She asked, her voice rising with a hint of desperation, echoing the urgency that filled the air.

"It's a dog-eat-dog world," Blood said, his tone resigned.

"You can change if you make an effort," Amber counters, her expression a mix of determination and hope.

"That's the way it is," Blood responded, his shoulders sagging slightly.

Amber simmered, taking a deep breath to calm her nerves, and refused to argue with Blood. He had been as hard-headed and stubborn as she was. "Sure, in the South, but this is New York. I'm going to Washington. I want you to look for employment," she said, her voice calmer but still firm.

"I am an ex-con; who's going to hire me?" Blood asked, his expression filled with uncertainty.

Amber's eyes widen, and her expression shifts to one of surprise. "Wait a minute; you never told me you were in jail. What else are you hiding?" she asked, her tone laced with a mix of concern and suspicion.

"I told you I escaped to Kentucky and wandered around," said Blood, his eyes distant as the vivid memories flooded his mind.

It was a bright, sunny day when Blood found himself walking down the dusty main street of the small Kentucky town. The warm rays of the afternoon sun beat down, casting long shadows across the weathered wooden storefronts and hitching posts that lined the sidewalk. The air was filled with the familiar sounds of rural America - the occasional clip-clop of horse hooves, the jingle of harnesses, and the friendly chatter of the townspeople going about their daily business.

A gentle breeze rustled the leaves of the ancient oak trees that arched over the street, providing pockets of welcome shade. Blood's boots scuffed against the packed dirt as he strolled casually, taking in the sights and smells of this unfamiliar place he now found himself in. He was still getting his bearings, trying to put as much distance as possible between himself and the horrors he had fled from back home.

As he neared the end of the block, a sudden commotion up ahead caught his attention. The wail of a siren pierced the tranquil afternoon, and Blood watched as a Sheriff's patrol car screeched to a halt, the two lawmen inside quickly jumping out and advancing towards him, hands on their holstered firearms.

Blood tensed, his instincts kicking in, as the officers approached and he realized they had him in their sights. It was in that moment that he knew his brief respite in Kentucky was about to come to a dramatic and potentially devastating end. A Sheriff and his Deputy hopped out of a patrol car pointing their guns. The Deputy quickly searches Blood's pocket and takes out the switchblade stained with blood and his money.

"We got a telegram with your description; you are wanted for the assault and the death of Homer Dills," said the Sheriff.

"Who is he? I've never heard of him?" asked Blood.

"The man's throat you slit is dead from the injury. Mr. Hawkins witnessed your friend Daniel give you the knife. He was the last one that had seen you. The mob tortured him and kicked his teeth out; he's in the hospital in a coma and in no condition to vouch for your character," said the Sheriff.

"Old Homer bled to death, so turn around, boy, we got to arrest you," said the Deputy.

He handcuffed Blood and put him into the car. The Sheriff and his Deputy got in and drove off to the department. Blood didn't give them any trouble or try to escape; he was sure he would be vindicated. It had been self-defense, and he had no idea how deeply he had cut Homer because there had been a white sheet over his head. That night, the Deputy fed him dinner in jail; after sunrise, he was shackled and taken to court to appear before a judge.

At 9 a.m., inside the courtroom, there was no jury, attorney, or witness present; he was denied due process and a trial. Blood's eyes darted nervously between the officers, glancing frequently at the large clock on the wall and the doorway. He became increasingly aware of his surroundings; he had never been in a courtroom before.

Sweat poured from his face, shackled at the ankles, his legs became restless. A few seconds seemed like hours had passed.
A judge, a colossal monster of a man in a black robe, entered the courtroom and sat on his bench. Blood's thirst increased, yet there was no water to quench it; his stomach started to churn. Then, with a tightening of his chest and quivering insides, his breathing began to accelerate.

The Bailiff said, "All rise."

To show respect the Sheriff and Deputy jerked Blood up from his seat.

The judge, in a deep baritone voice, said, "You have assaulted a law-abiding citizen who has died. Since there was a fight, it is murder in the 2nd degree. I am not sending you back to Mississippi, and if I do, they will lynch you. Do you have anything to say in your defense?" asked the judge.

Blood took a short breath to gain control over his tingling limbs. "25 Klansmen attacked me. I had to defend myself. I am innocent," said Blood.

"Therefore, to put some distance between you and the Klan, I hereby sentence you to 3 years in the Louisiana Juvenile Correctional Facility and seven years in the adult state penitentiary. This court is adjourned," said the judge and banged his mallet on the desk.

The Sheriff and the Deputy accompanied Blood out of the courtroom. A prison bus had been parked in front; an officer loaded the prisoner onto the bus, and it drove away. After a twelve-hour ride through the hot, dusty South, only four prisoners accompanied Blood on the bus. They arrived in Louisiana at 9 p.m., and were taken inside the juvenile prison. Blood was shuffled into the penitentiary, given his white shirt and pants, and a guard led him to the showers. After his bath, he was taken to his cell. He worked in the laundry and attended high school with the other young prisoners. When Blood was in the yard, he participated in boxing matches, with the guards betting on him and winning money. Naturally, the champion was favored and received special attention.

**

Two years later, he graduated from the facility's high school and was transferred to the adult correctional state prison. Where his luck deserted him as soon as he was lead-in, the guard gave him a towel, a new outfit, and hygiene items. They ordered him to take a shower.

He entered the bathroom, and the guard locked the door and turned his back. Blood searched the area with his eyes and didn't see anyone, yet he didn't feel alone.

He turned on the shower and let the water run. Suddenly a large bald black man in his late 30s exited the stall thinking the young man was bathing. Blood stepped into view; there was silence. The man looked at him up and down. They gazed upon each other when he knew he was a chicken about to be defiled. He stepped aside, and the man blocked his way. The hardened prisoner grabbed him, and Blood hit him so hard in the face and broke his jaw, and he continued to beat him until the man's eyes swelled closed and he's totally knocked out. Then, Blood calmly stepped into the shower and bathed. After he slipped on his black and white striped jumpsuit and knocked on the door, the guard opened it.

"Is everything all right?" asked the guard.

"Yeah, your buddy slipped and fell. I think he needs to go to the infirmary," said Blood.

"I'll send someone to take care of it. Come on," said the guard.

The guard locked the entrance and took him to his cell. As he entered, the echo of the steel bars slamming shut rang in his ears. After twenty-four months, Blood hadn't gotten used to it; there were bunk beds. He climbed to the top and lay down with his feet toward the door, assuming he would be ready if a future cell-mate or a gang of guards attacked.

Hector cautiously entered the cell, his eyes scanning the small space and its sole occupant—a man named Blood. Blood looked up as the new prisoner was brought in, studying him curiously.

"What are you in for?" Blood asked, his tone blunt.

Hector had hesitated, the memories of that fateful night flooding back. "I, uh, I got into a fight in a bar," he begins, his voice wavering slightly. "I was just passing through Louisiana, on my way to Florida, and then on to Colombia." He paused, the images of the chaos, the violence, the fear of being caught, played out in his mind.

"It was just supposed to be a quick stop, you know?" Hector continued, his gaze distant. "I was in this bar, having a few drinks, and some guy, he starts mouthing off, getting in my face. I don't know what happened, but the next thing I know, there's chaos, and the other guy, he's on the ground, seriously hurt." Hector shook his head, still struggling to make sense of it all.

"The cops came, and they arrested me. Thirty days, that's what the judge said." Hector lets out a humorless chuckle. "Thirty days in this place, for one stupid mistake. I was just trying to make my way to Colombia, to see my cousin, and now..." His voice trailed off, the weight of his situation settling heavily on his shoulders.

Blood listened, his expression unreadable. He sensed the fear and uncertainty in Hector's voice, the way the memory of that night still haunted him. Without a word, he nodded, acknowledging the other man's story.

Later, in the prison mess hall, Hector tentatively walked to get his food tray. Suddenly, a large, burly inmate bumped into him, causing Hector to drop his tray. The inmate started yelling and shoving Hector, who cowered in fear.

But before the situation could escalate further, Blood stepped in. Without hesitation, he grabbed the burly inmate and slammed him against the wall. The other prisoners fell silent, watching as Blood landed a series of brutal punches, quickly subduing the would-be attacker.

Hector looked on, amazed at Blood's raw power and willingness to protect him. He realized that this man, this stranger, was someone he could trust. From that moment on, Hector was in Blood's debt, grateful for his intervention and eager to repay him however he could.

The days in the cramped prison cell had fallen into a familiar rhythm for Hector and Blood. After Blood had stepped in to protect Hector from the other inmates, a tentative trust had formed between the two men. Hector often watched in awe as Blood navigated the treacherous social dynamics of prison life, his imposing presence and reputation as a fierce fighter kept the other inmates at bay. Whenever someone had tried to test their boundaries, Blood simply leveled them with a steely glare, his muscles tensing under his skin.

In return, Hector did what he could to make their shared space more comfortable. He meticulously tidied the cell, ensuring their meager belongings were neatly organized. When Blood's demons surfaced, manifesting in restless nights and haunted silences, Hector offered a listening ear, his empathy and understanding slowly chipping away at the other man's walls.

As the days turned into weeks, Hector found himself confiding in Blood about his dreams of a better life in Colombia. He spoke of his cousin Banderos and the opportunities that awaited him, his eyes shining with a blend of hope and trepidation.

Blood, in turn, simply nodded, his expression unreadable. However, Hector sensed a glimmer of interest in his gaze, as if the prospect of starting anew somewhere far from the prison walls held a certain appeal.

It had been 30 days since Hector was brought into the cell, sharing the cramped space with the enigmatic man known as Blood.

The two had formed an unlikely bond; Blood protected Hector from the other inmates, and Hector felt grateful for Blood's strength and willingness to fight.

On the day of Hector's release, he gathered his meager belongings, preparing to leave the prison behind.

Blood watched him, curiosity glimmering in his eyes. "So, you're finally getting out of this place," Blood said, his voice low.

Hector nodded, pausing in his packing. "Yeah, man, my time's up. Back to the real world, I guess."

He glanced over at Blood, a contemplative expression on his face.

Just then, a guard approached the cell and unlocked the door. "Alright, Ramirez, time's up. Let's go."

Hector turned to Blood one last time. "Listen, Blood, I wanted to make you an offer before I go. My cousin, Banderos, he's got all kinds of work down in Colombia. I will tell him about you, how you had my back in here, and he could use a man like you."

Blood's brow furrowed, a mix of interest and uncertainty on his face. "Colombia, huh? What kind of work are we talking about?"

Hector shrugged, a wry smile on his lips. "Ah, you know, this and that. Banderos has his fingers in all kinds of pies. But he's a powerful guy, and he could give you a fresh start, you know?" He paused, studying Blood's expression. "You've never been out of America, right?"

Blood nodded, silent for a moment. "No, never." He looks away, his mind clearly churning.

"Well, if you ever need to get out of here, to start over somewhere new, the offer's there," Hector said, placing a hand on Blood's shoulder. "Banderos, he'd be happy to have you. There's no coming back, though, so you gotta be sure."

Blood met Hector's gaze, a spark of interest flickering in his eyes. "I'll... I'll think about it," he said, his voice low.

Hector nodded, satisfied. "Fair enough. The invitation's there, my friend. Just remember, if you need a way out, Banderos is waiting." With that, he turned and followed the guard out of the cell, leaving Blood alone with his thoughts.

***

Seven years later, the sun-drenched streets of the small Louisiana town seemed almost mocking in their serenity as Cisco hurried along, his heart pounding with a mixture of fear and adrenaline. Just a few hours earlier, he had enjoyed a casual game of poker with the local sheriff, a stroke of luck leading him to call out the lawman's dubious tactics. It had been a moment of brash youthful defiance—one that Cisco already deeply regretted.

As the sheriff's deputies had descended upon him, their faces twisted with fury, Cisco realized the gravity of his mistake. He had pleaded and protested, but his cries fell on deaf ears as he was roughly hauled away, the distant wail of a siren cutting through the quiet afternoon.

The jail cell had been cramped and oppressive, the stale air heavy with the scent of despair. Cisco had huddled in the corner, his New York bravado withering in the face of this harsh new reality. He had been far from home, trapped in a system he barely understood, and the fear of what might come next had gnawed at his every waking moment.

Then, a new presence had emerged from the shadows—a weathered, imposing figure that Cisco had instinctively shrunk away from. But as the man had approached, there had been a surprising gentleness in his movements, a calming presence that had slowly eased Cisco's panic.

"You're new here, aren't you, kid?" the man said, his voice gruff but not unkind. "Name's Blood. I can see you're in over your head, and I reckon I can help you out. But you're gonna have to trust me."

Cisco had hesitated, his gaze flickering between the man and the barred window beyond, weighing his options. In the end, with no other choice but to brave the unknown alone, he had nodded, his eyes reflecting a fragile hope.

"Okay," he said, his voice barely above a whisper. "I'll trust you."

And so began an unlikely alliance, forged in the crucible of incarceration, that ultimately shaped the course of both their lives. Blood's flashback ended. Amber stood over him as he sat on the sofa, holding his bandaged head.

"I spent seven years in the most horrible penitentiary. Juvie was a breeze, but in prison, I was constantly fighting with an inmate who was trying to step on me. I was young; the rest of the dudes were older than I. They put me in the hole, and once I came out, I was on the chain gang hammering nuts and bolts on the freight railroad in the blistering sun. In my last incarcerated year, on some false charges, Cisco became my cellmate. He was on his vacation from New York in Louisiana, and he was put in an adult prison for a year. They would put a black male in jail for looking at a white man wrong. I had to protect the teen from the rapists and thugs, and in return, he hooked me up in Harlem. After that, I promised myself I was never going back to jail," said Blood.

"Something's got to give. You can't go back to the streets. This cycle has to end. I want you to find a vocation,"Amber said, her tone firm yet tinged with concern.

"With what? I lost all my money in a crap game," Blood replied, his voice heavy with resignation.

Amber Stone opened her purse, took out her checkbook, quickly wrote a check, and handed it to him. "Here is a check for fifteen hundred dollars."

"For what?" Blood asked, his brow furrowed in confusion.

"I want you to buy a business suit. Like a Wall Street banker," Amber stated, her eyes meeting his steadily.

"You're serious?" Blood exclaimed, surprise evident in his voice.

Amber pointed her finger at him, her expression serious. "You listen to me."

"I can't believe it," Blood said, shaking his head slightly in disbelief.

"Chang will kill you if you go back to the streets," Amber warned, a hint of worry creeping into her voice.

"I'm not afraid of Chang," Blood replied, determination setting his jaw in a firm line.

"Go ahead, be the macho man," Amber challenged, frustration lacing her tone. "It's not just about courage; it's about living— and living well."

Blood's eyes sparked with a glimmer of hope as he asked, "Are you going to come with me to buy the suits?"

"No, I'll be back in a week," Amber said, her voice steady and reassuring.

"You think I can change my life in a week?" Blood's skepticism rang clear, echoing his doubts.

"All you have to do is get the suits and try," Amber encouraged, her expression radiant with optimism.

Blood searched Amber's eyes, uncertainty flickering in his gaze. "What else do you want me to do?"

"Circle the job ads," Amber replied, her tone matter-of-fact. "Then, go on the interviews."

He furrowed his brow, disbelief clouding his features. "It's really that easy?"

Amber settled beside him on the sofa, her arm wrapping around his shoulders in a comforting gesture.

"All you have to do is show up," she reassured him, her voice soft yet filled with determination.

His doubt hung heavy in the air. "I'm a convicted felon. Who's going to give me a job?"

"The state will give your employer extra money to hire you," Amber said, holding his gaze steadily.

Just then, Blood winced as a sharp pain pierced through his head like a sudden storm.

"You thought of all the angles?" he asked, his voice laced with a mix of surprise and reluctant appreciation.

"I'll even pay your rent. Until you get back on your feet," Amber offered, her hand gently squeezing his shoulder.

"What other choice do I have?" Blood replied, his shoulders sagging slightly under the weight of his circumstances.

"It's the right thing to do," Amber asserted, her voice firm yet understanding.

"I've got to have money; I can't stand it," Blood stated, his frustration palpable.

"You were in jail; you can stand anything," Amber countered, her eyes filled with quiet determination.

"I'm not afraid of dying," said Blood, his gaze unwavering.

"You're afraid of living," Amber responded, her words cutting to the heart of the matter.

"You got money, a promising career. What do I have?" asked Blood, his voice tinged with a hint of bitterness.

"You have me. Aren't I worth a hundred Changs' or some macho dice game?" asked Amber, her expression earnest.

"What do you think?" asked Blood, his eyes searching hers.

"I think you and I are worth more than just a buck," Amber said, her hand reaching out to gently cup his face.

Blood glanced at his watch. "It's 1 a.m.; you can stay here," he said, his voice low.

"I can't. I'll see you when I get back," Amber said, giving him a small, reassuring smile. Amber had kissed him gently on the lips before exiting the apartment. Blood had taken off his shirt, trying to sleep, but swelling with perturbation, he poured himself a drink. He took a dollar bill out of his pocket, snorted some cocaine, and contemplated Amber Stone's advice, his expression a mix of uncertainty and desperation.

CHAPTER FIVE

Amber entered her studio apartment, exhausted. She opened the dresser drawer and removed a dollar bill filled with cocaine, sniffing it to give her the energy to pack her suitcase. Quickly, she grabbed her toiletries, underwear, a pair of jeans, and an elegant black dress for dinner with her father. Amber needed to appear conservative and respectable; otherwise, she would be scolded by her picky, critical, controlling dad. Because of his work, he could never enforce his standards upon her. He was the hammer, and she was the nail. This was her vacation from New York—a week completely free from blood, cocaine, and liquor. She placed the drug back into the drawer to help overcome her anxieties.

Amber had been in denial, indulging in the drug out of a need to escape or numb her emotions. Being with Blood had been more compelling than the narcotic, as her heart and karmic bond with him had ruled her head. After taking a short period away from her love to regain her mental equilibrium, Amber had taken a hot shower to sweat the drug out of her system. Then, she had slid into bed and put on her eye pads to block out the rising sunlight. Tossing and finally falling asleep to suppress her jitters, she had known she needed to be alert and energetic in Washington.

It was 10 a.m., and while Amber slept peacefully, unaware of his actions, Blood stood in the busy bank lobby, trying to project an air of calm despite the adrenaline coursing through his veins. The sterile, clinical atmosphere of the bank grated against his senses - the harsh fluorescent lights, the cold marble floors, the imposing mahogany teller counters. Around him, the other patrons moved with a sense of practiced routine, their faces impassive as they conducted their transactions.

Blood felt the weight of their gazes upon him as he waited in line, conscious of how out of place he had looked amongst the sea of well-dressed, middle-class white customers. The security guard at the entrance eyed him suspiciously, no doubt noting the bandage on his cheek and the tension in his movements.

When Blood finally reached the teller, a young woman in her 20s, he forced himself to maintain a neutral expression as he handed over the check and his driver's license. He watched her brow furrowed slightly as she examined the documents, and he held his breath, praying she wouldn't detect any signs of his true intentions.

The teller disappeared into the back, leaving Blood alone with his thoughts. His eyes darted around the bank, taking in every detail - the cameras mounted in the corners, the armed guard by the exit, the quiet murmurs of the other customers.

When the teller returned, Blood accepted the cash with a calm, measured movements, tucking it safely into his wallet. As he turned to leave, he felt the guard's eyes on him, watching his every step. Blood couldn't wait to be out of this place, to put this nerve-wracking encounter behind him, and disappear back into the world.

Later that evening, at 8 p.m., Amber was on her flight to D.C. while Blood entered Chang's Penny Arcade Club. He scurried to the back room, where baby James, Ejay, and Chang sat at a dimly lit table. The air was thick with cigar smoke and the clink of coins as they counted their earnings from the day.

"Chang, please give me another chance," Blood pleaded.

"Why so you can screw up again?" asked Chang.

"I need these streets," Blood said.

"If you hurt any of my brothers, I'm coming after you," Chang warned.

"I wouldn't do anything to you or your family," Blood assured.

"Good, I need you to prove yourself. I'm going to give you $3,000 to hit Underwood," Chang said.

"Who is he?" Blood asked.

"One of my cocaine dealers in East Harlem; he owes me money," Chang explained.

"I'll do anything for you, Chang," Blood promised.

"I'm going to give you 2 grand when the job is done," Chang said.

"Anything you say," Blood agreed.

"I'm driving the get-away car. We want that scum dead," Ejay said.

The gangster gave Blood the payment, and he put the cash in his pocket. Ejay and he exited the back room.

"Chang, are you crazy? Why did you give him all that money?" Baby James asked.

"When pops died, I became the father of this family, and don't question my judgment. He's going to buy so much cocaine from me," Chang said.

"I am sorry for what I said. You're going to get the cash back," Baby James said.

"That's right either way, I profit," Chang said.

"You have more faith in him than I do," Baby James commented.

"Come on, Baby James, let's count our financial gains," Chang said.

Chang dumps a bag of money on the table, and he and his brother count it.

At Morningside Park, the dim glow of the streetlights cast long shadows across the isolated grounds. The park was shrouded in darkness, giving the scene an ominous, foreboding atmosphere. Blood and Ejay's car, its lights off, quietly pulled in and parked a few paces away. They spotted a parked gold Cadillac in the distance, its occupants unaware of the impending danger.

Inside the car, they observed Underwood, a man in his thirties, and Rosy, an attractive woman in her twenties, with long, thick, teased, and sprayed hair styled into a bouffant hairpiece. The two lovers were locked in a passionate embrace, kissing and caressing each other, oblivious to the watchful eyes in the shadows.

Ejay gripped the steering wheel tightly, his hands sweating.

"We can't have no witnesses," he growls.

Blood and Ejay quickly exited their car and approached Underwood's vehicle, their movements swift and predatory. The darkness of the park seemed to envelope them, amplifying the sense of danger and vulnerability. Blood positioned himself by the driver's side door, while Ejay moved to the passenger side. Without hesitation, Blood started firing his pistol into the car, the sharp cracks echoing through the quiet, isolated park.

"No, Ejay, don't shoot me," Rosy yells.

Ejay fired five shots into her head. Rosy and Underwood lie lifeless as the killers scramble away from the car.

"Ejay, I heard her call your name. Isn't that Rosy? She's the sister of the powerful drug dealer Louie. Why did you shoot her?" Blood asked.

"She just happened to be in the wrong place," Ejay replied.

"Underwood is dead," Blood said.

"You did well, Blood," Ejay commended.

The men got into the getaway car and drove off. They decided to split up, with Ejay dropping Blood off at the Den Club, and parking the vehicle out of sight.

Blood entered the Den Club and bumped into Deanna, who was standing there looking sexy in her cutout spandex mini red dress.

"Hey, Blood, you have been missing in action," Deanna said.

"Deanna, I've been busy," Blood replied.

"I heard you're with Amber Stone," Deanna mentioned.

"That's her name," Blood confirmed.

"Where is the Diva?" Deanna asked.

"She's out of town," Blood answered.

Deanna moved close to him and threw her arms around his neck.

"Does that mean, while the cat is away, the mouse is out to play?" Deanna purred.

"What do you mean by that?" Blood questioned.

"I was always there for you," Deanna said.

"Yeah, you were," Blood acknowledged.

"I still am," Deanna insisted.

"I'm dating Amber Stone?" Blood said, sounding uncertain.

"I don't care, as long as I get what I want," Deanna declared.

"What would that be?" Blood asked.

"You, I want you," Deanna answered.

Deanna kissed Blood passionately, and he kissed her back and broke their embrace.

"What are you doing for the rest of the evening?" Deanna inquired.

"Does it look like I'm doing anything?" Blood replied.

"No," Deanna said.

"Let's go to your place," Deanna suggested.

"Okay, I got some cocaine and liquor. Why not?" Blood agreed.

Blood and Deanna grabbed each other's arms and moseyed away.

Later at the stash apartment, Deanna and Blood were in bed making passionate love, and she froze.

Blood staring her in the eyes asked, "What's the matter with you?"

"Give me another blow of that cocaine you have?" asked Deanna.

"Why?" Blood asked.

"I perform better with it. Do you want to give me a blow or not?" Deanna demanded.

Blood took the dollar bill filled with cocaine from the bedside table and handed it to Deanna. She inhaled a line of cocaine through each nostril. Then, she kissed Blood passionately, and they continued to make love.

Meanwhile, at Harlem Hospital, Rosy lay in the intensive care unit, her condition critical. At her bedside, a man in his 40s with wavy black hair and gold chains draping around his neck - Louie, also known as "Pretty Louie" - sat, holding her hand gently.

He was dressed in a navy blue suit, a testament to his status. Louie's two burly bodyguards, clad in black suits, stood guard at the door, ensuring no unwanted visitors interrupted this delicate moment.

Suddenly, Rosy's eyes flickered open. She struggled to speak, her voice barely above a whisper. "Louie..." she managed, gripping his hand weakly.

Louie leaned in closer, his brow creased with concern. "Shh, Rosy, don't try to talk. I'm here." He brushed a stray lock of hair from her face, his expression softening.

"Wh-what happened?" Rosy breathed, her eyes searching his face for answers.

Louie , unwilling to upset her further in her fragile state. "That don't matter now, chica. What's important is that you're alive and safe." He squeezed her hand reassuringly. "I'm gonna take care of you, you hear?"

Rosy nodded slightly, some of the tension leaving her features as she took comfort in her brother's presence. Whatever had happened, she knew Louie would protect her - that was a promise.

"Rosy, who did this to you?" he asked in a low tone.

"Louie, it was Ejay Chang's brother. They shot Underwood too," Rosy said weakly.

"Who else was with Ejay?" Louie pressed.

"I couldn't see the other man; I only saw Ejay," she replied.

"The doctor said the bullets were caught in your hair, and it is what saved your life. You rest, Rosy. I will take care of this," Louie assured her.

He kissed the back of her hand, then rose to his full height and approached one of the bodyguards.

"You stay here with my sister just in case Ejay comes back to finish the job. I am all she's got; I am like her father, and it's my responsibility to take care of her," Louie said sternly.

The bodyguard nodded in acknowledgment. Louie and the other bodyguard then left the room, intent on exacting justice for his wounded sister.

Away from the horrors back home in Harlem, the sun had barely risen over the nation's capital in Washington D.C., but Amber was already at the iconic Cleopatra's Needle monument.

Dressed in a stunning white suit, she posed gracefully in front of the towering obelisk as her photographer, Bill, snapped away with his camera.

Soon, eleven other models joined Amber, all of them adorned in bold red and blue suits. The group came together, posing playfully and elegantly as Bill captured the scene. The vibrant colors of their outfits contrasted beautifully against the ancient stone of the Needle, creating a striking visual statement.

Amber beamed, reveling in the energy of the photoshoot. This was a welcome respite from the chaos and violence plaguing her community back in New York. Here, in the shadow of one of D.C.'s most renowned landmarks, she could momentarily forget her troubles and simply focus on her craft.

As the models struck pose after pose, Bill worked tirelessly to immortalize their beauty and fashion-forward style. The clicks of his camera echoed across the plaza, drawing curious onlookers who paused to admire the impromptu display of elegance and glamour.

For Amber, this was more than just another job - it was a chance to escape, to find solace in the art of modeling. And as she twirled and smiled for the camera, she felt a renewed sense of purpose, a determination to succeed in this industry.

"Bill, I am so glad you got the job," Amber said.

"Thank Willie; the client was going with another photographer, and she said if they didn't hire me, they couldn't use her models," said Bill.

"You told me she was just an agent," Amber said.

"Obviously, I was wrong. I see why you are so intimidated by Willie," Bill acknowledged.

"Heck yeah, she could make or break a career," Amber agreed.

"I heard the rumors, but I didn't believe it. Speaking of careers, you girls better look alive. This is America, and we're celebrating the 4th of July," Bill said.

Amber Stone and the eleven models perked up and continued to pose. Bill shot the photos from different angles.

After the photoshoot, it was early evening. Amber returned to her hotel and took a shower. She frantically got ready to meet her father for dinner. Amber had not taken a bump of coke or a shot of whiskey since the night before. The absence left her body slightly shaking, so she held her hand to try to calm down. Amber told herself to remain stoic and not give away any signals. She wanted to talk about her new boyfriend and their life together.

Slipping on her evening gown, it conservatively hugged her shapely figure, not too sexy or avant-garde. She was his daughter, not his girlfriend, whoever she might be. There was a distance between them; they didn't share each other's lives. Tonight she was going to break the ice and spill the tea about her boyfriend in hopes of her father opening up about his life. Since her mom died, he had made her feel it was inappropriate to ask or pry into his private affairs.

Admiring herself in the wardrobe mirror, the phone had rung. She had answered it and said, "I'll be right down." Amber had hung up the phone, grabbed her purse, and exited the room.

Outside the hotel, a driver and limousine waited for her. He politely opened the door; she got in, and he entered the driver's side before driving away. Washington, D.C., looked beautiful at night, with the White House in the backdrop. Her father must have been living a wealthy life far from her in Harlem; it was her choice. He had sent her a lump sum to live wherever she wanted. The allowance was enough to cover her bills, but she needed to earn the rest independently. It felt like economic slavery; she was an adult woman. He was not obligated to support her; still, she felt under his control. Modeling would grant her independence, and she had a man she loved in her life. Together, they could make it. Professor Stone didn't care where she lived as long as it wasn't with him.

The limousine glided smoothly and pulled up in front of the illustrious Delmonico's restaurant. The chauffeur dutifully opened the car door, and Amber emerged, her presence commanding attention as she strode confidently along the plush red carpet and into the establishment.

Amber was escorted by the maître d' to her father's private booth. Delmonico's catered to an affluent clientele, the patrons adorned in their finest black-tie attire. They dined in lively conversation, the air abuzz with the low hum of chatter. Seated at the table, Professor Stone, a distinguished African American man in his sixties, awaited his daughter's arrival.

"Hello, Daddy," Amber greeted, sliding gracefully into the booth across from him.

"I presumed you might be tardy, my dear, and so I took the liberty of ordering ahead. How are you faring this evening?" Professor Stone inquired.

"Quite perplexed, I'm afraid," Amber replied.

"And what seems to be troubling you?" he asked.

"I'm simply trying to find my way, to make the most of my life," she confessed.

"But I provide you with the financial means to do so," Professor Stone reminded her.

"It's not the same as having you actively present in my life. I am concerned for you, Daddy, and I wish to be a more integral part of your world," Amber expressed.

"I'm afraid my availability is limited, as I am currently engaged in a highly confidential project," Professor Stone explained.

"And what might that project entail?" Amber asked, her curiosity piqued.

"It is something I believe could greatly benefit humanity," he revealed.

Amber let out a slight chuckle. "Truly, Daddy, aside from vitamin C and a generous pour of whiskey, what else could it possibly accomplish?"

Professor Stone's brow furrowed. "Your flippant attitude troubles me, my dear. Surely, you're not still indulging in those unsavory habits?"

"I've made a promise to myself to abstain from alcohol while I'm in Washington," Amber assured him.

"And what other activities have you been occupying your time with?" he inquired.

"Nothing of particular note, Daddy," she replied evasively.

"But you just confessed to drinking," he pressed.

Amber's expression took on a sheepish quality. "The fashion industry, you know, is a rather champagne-soaked endeavor."

Professor Stone's tone grew stern. "My dear, you must be mindful. Social drinking is a slippery slope, and one drink is never enough for you."

"That was in the past," Amber attempted to interject.

"I cannot bear the thought of my daughter falling ill," Professor Stone interjected, his concern palpable.

"But you won't be there to care for me," Amber lamented.

"Amber Stone, I am right here, and you should be grateful for my presence," Professor Stone admonished.

"For heaven's sake, Daddy, I am your daughter!" Amber exclaimed, her frustration evident.

"You are a grown woman now, and I had expected you to have secured the companionship of a well-to-do suitor, someone who could properly provide for you," Professor Stone stated matter-of-factly.

Amber took a deep breath. "That, actually, is what I had wished to discuss with you. I am, in fact, seeing a gentleman."

Professor Stone's expression darkened. "I sincerely hope this man is not some never-do-well you've picked up, wasting his life away and destined for failure. Your track record with men has been nothing short of disastrous. Where on earth do you find these parasites?"

"If you'd let me finish, you'd know that he is not after my money. In fact, I've offered to assist him financially," Amber explained.

Professor Stone's brow furrowed. "My dear child, must I constantly monitor you to ensure you conduct yourself accordingly? I insist you cease this relationship at once, for he clearly does not meet my standards."

Amber's eyes narrowed. "Forget it, Daddy. You live in a world of pristine perfection that I simply cannot seem to inhabit."

"Believe me, the fate of humanity hangs in the balance," Professor Stone proclaimed solemnly.

"I hardly see how that is my concern," Amber replied dismissively.

"But it is my greatest priority!" Professor Stone asserted.

"Except, it seems, when it comes to your own daughter," Amber retorted.

Professor Stone's expression darkened. "Why can you not afford me the same respect that any stranger would?"

Amber sighed heavily. "Could we perhaps enjoy our dinner without the constant barrage of criticism? I truly did not mean to upset you, Daddy."

The waiter, a poised gentleman in his thirties, approached their table and gently placed their plates before them. Amber and her father ate their dinner without a word, the weight of unspoken emotions permeating the atmosphere. Delicate silence blanketed the air as Amber and her esteemed father, Professor Stone, concluded their meal at the refined Delmonico's.

After they consumed their dinner, Professor Stone and Amber exited the restaurant and entered a luxurious limousine, which drove them to the stately Washington Hotel. As Professor Stone escorted Amber out of the limo, he turned to his daughter, a flicker of paternal regret flickering across his features. "This is where I say goodnight. I wish the best for you," he uttered, his baritone voice tinged with a somber cadence.

Amber's eyes grew slightly moist as she mustered the courage to speak. "Daddy, is there a chance? That we'll see each other again?" she asked, her voice laced with a delicate longing.

Professor Stone's expression softened, the lines of his weathered face betraying a deeper well of emotion. "It depends on my itinerary. I'm sorry your mother died," he replied, the weight of his words hanging in the air between them.

Amber's heart ached at the mention of her mother's passing. "I miss her and not having a father," she confessed, her words carrying the heavy burden of a lifetime's worth of yearning.

Professor Stone had , a flicker of paternal regret flickering across his features. "I'm sorry, baby. But I will try and see you again," he promised, the sincerity in his tone belying the distance that had long separated them.

"What about for Christmas?" Amber inquired, a glimmer of hope igniting in her eyes.

"Call me, and I'll see what I can do," Professor Stone replied, his hand reaching out to gently cup his daughter's cheek.

Amber embraced her father, her lips pressing a tender kiss upon his weathered cheek. "Goodbye, Daddy. It was great seeing you," she murmured, her words laced with a bittersweet melody.

"Thanks for dinner. I have to get back to work," Professor Stone responded, his gaze lingering on Amber as she turned and ambled into the grand hotel. With a heavy heart, he slid into the waiting limousine and drove away, the distance between them once again a palpable weight.

Inside Amber's hotel room, she had entered and sat down, accepting that no package from Blood had arrived. Her skin crawled as she found herself in the grips of withdrawal. Amber had entered the bathroom, stripped nude, and stepped into a cold shower, allowing the icy water to wash over her.

After she slid into bed, Amber tossed and turned with unbridled anxiety. Every nerve in her body screamed for a sniff of cocaine or a shot of liquor, even though she desperately told herself, "I am not a junkie."

The clock on the nightstand ticked relentlessly, its every chime occupying her frantic thoughts. It had been 1 a.m., and Amber had known she needed to be near the source of her addiction. Steeling her resolve, she had picked up the phone.

"Hello, Operator, could you ring the Den Bar Club in New York," Amber said, her voice trembling with desperation.

"One moment, please," the Operator's dispassionate tone came over the line.

"Thank you for calling The Den," a Bartender answered.

"Can I speak to Blood?" Amber pleaded.

"Blood is not here. Can I take a message?" the Bartender replied.

"This is Amber Stone. My job ended early; tell Blood I will see him tomorrow afternoon," Amber said, her words laced with anticipation.

"I'll give him the message," the Bartender stated, before the line went dead.

Frustrated, Amber angrily hung up the receiver, her mind consumed with the need to reunite with her love. He was like a subsequent drug, and she couldn't stand being away from him and the pleasures he had to offer. The clock ticked mercilessly forward, until eventually, Amber succumbed to an uneasy sleep.

It was 11 a.m. Amber impatiently checked out of the hotel and entered a taxi that dropped her off at the airport. She caught her flight back to New York.

By 2 p.m., at the stash apartment, a knock echoed through the room. Blood opened the door, revealing Amber standing there, a wave of relief washing over her.

"Amber Stone, come on in, baby," he said.

"I didn't think you got my message," she said. Amber entered the apartment.

Blood gave her a passionate kiss. She broke their embrace and glanced at the dining table, which was set with food and a bottle of wine.

"Baby, I miss you. Welcome home," Blood said.

"I feel the same. I am glad to be back," Amber said.

She whooshed to the dining room table.

"I made an Italian lunch for you," Blood said.

"When did you learn how to cook?" Amber asked.

"I can't but, I can make spaghetti and a meat sauce," Blood replied.

Amber admired the table. "At least you can boil water. Thanks, darling. That's so nice of you," Amber said.

Blood pulled out the seat for her. "Just sit down and relax. Have a glass of wine," he said as he poured her a full glass.

She took a sip and licked her lips. Without vodka coursing through her veins, the smoothness and taste were what Amber had longed for. "Um, that's savory," Amber said.

Blood sat down, and he and Amber tasted the meal.

"This is tasty, and I like the sauce. Thank you, sweetie, for this is delicious, and I haven't eaten anything," Amber said.

"You're trying to keep your weight down," Blood said.

"It's been a struggle," Amber replied.

"I want to hear all about Washington, D.C. It must have been exciting?" Blood asked.

"We took the shots for Fashion Magazine. It was a breeze, and I came home early," Amber said.

"Yeah, I didn't expect you back so soon! I'll bet you looked gorgeous," Blood replied.

Amber Stone picked up her glass and took a sip. "This is the first drink I've had," Amber said.

"How did it feel?" Blood asked.

"Nervous," Amber replied.

"I can't do that," Blood said.

"I didn't want my father to think. I was this coke addict and alcoholic," Amber explained.

"How is the old man?" Blood asked.

"Good," Amber replied.

"I guess it's kind of nice to be a scientist in all," Blood said.

"Yeah, he's very proud of himself," Amber agrees.

"Did you mention me to your father?" Blood asked.

"No, I wanted to, and then I decided to wait until you got a job," Amber responded.

"You wanted to wait?" Blood questioned.

"Yes," Amber confirmed.

"I see," Blood said.

"By the way, how is your job search coming along? I can't wait to see your suits," Amber said.

"They're being altered to fit my size," Blood told her.

"When can they be picked up?" Amber asked.

"I'm not sure," Blood replied.

"Give me the number to the store. I'll call and check," Amber said.

Blood hesitated and poured himself a glass of wine. "I miss placed the number," he said.

"What's the name of the store? I can get the number from the Operator," Amber pressed.

"You're determined to see those suits aren't you?" Blood asked.

"Yes, I am," Amber affirmed.

"Amber Stone, I have to tell you the truth. There are no suits; there never were, and I never went to buy them," Blood confessed.

"What? Then where is my money?" Amber demanded.

"I lost it in a crap game," Blood admitted.

"What is the matter with you?" Amber exclaimed.

"Don't worry, I'll get the money back," Blood tried to reassure her.

"I gave you that money for you to jumpstart a new life," Amber stated.

"I'll give you five hundred dollars worth of cocaine," Blood offered. He reached into his pocket, removed a small bag of cocaine, and placed it on the table.

"I'll take it, but you still owe me a thousand dollars," Amber said as she took the cocaine and put it in her bosom.

"I'm sorry," Blood apologized.

"Sorry, I didn't do it. You did," Amber retorted as she got up from the dining table, entered the bathroom, and slammed the door. Blood drank his wine, opened a dollar bill, and took a sniff of cocaine.

Amber stormed into the dining area with a pair of pink panties in her hand and confronted Blood.

"Blood, what is this?" Amber demanded, holding the panties in front of him.

"I don't know," Blood responded.

"It's panties and FYI. There are not mine. You had one of your women in here? You had her in the bed we share. Are you crazy?" Amber threw the panties in Blood's face.

"Well, while you were away..." Blood begins.

Amber placed her hands on her hips. "I'm listening," she said.

"Deanna started talking to me," Blood explained.

"You brought Deanna in here?" Amber asked, upset.

"Baby, she seduced me. I was alone thinking about you," Blood tried to justify.

"A loser, that's what you are a loser. My father was right," Amber declared.

"I love you; I really do," Blood said.

"I don't even think you love yourself," Amber retorted.

Amber cried and wiped the tears from her face.

Blood got up from the table and tried to hug her; Amber pushed him away.

"Come here, let me put my arms around you," Blood said.

"Don't touch me," Amber refused.

"Listen to your heart. You love me?" Blood asked.

She looked into his eyes. "I've listened to my heart. That's why it's broken. I'm gonna listen to my head, and I'm out of here," Amber declares, turning away.

Blood grabbed her arm. "Wait," he said.

She jerked her arm away from him. "Wait for what?" Amber demanded.

"What are you going to do?" Blood asked.

"Deanna and the other women can have you. You just get my money," Amber stated firmly as she left the apartment.

Blood sat down at the table, opened the dollar bill, took a sniff of the narcotic, and experienced a flashback. He and Cisco had been released from jail and had arrived in New York. They followed Soupy upstairs to the stash apartment. Soupy opened the door, and the men entered. The lights came on. Jonesy, Dee, Betty, and Deanna yelled, "Surprise!" The ladies were dressed up in the shabby apartment, where balloons and ribbons adorned the space. The table was filled with liquor and food. Blood was drawn to narcotics, champagne, women, and vice.

The women led him into the bedroom, where they took turns kissing him and undressing him. They had put cocaine up to his nose to sniff and sprinkled it over his body, licking the drug off him as they all made love to him. Filled with euphoria, he was engulfed in a dreamscape.

The following morning, Blood woke up naked and alone, nursing a hangover. He spotted small thank-you cards in envelopes on the bedside table from Betty, Dee, and Deanna. As he opened one of the cards, he discovered a door key tucked inside. Just then, Soupy entered the bedroom with an illegal proposition for him.

"Did you enjoy yourself?" Soupy asked.

"I never had three women at once," Blood said.

"You have been in jail. I didn't think one woman was enough for you," Soupy responds.

"I guess there is an introductory to everything, thanks," Blood said.

"This is your new home, and you can make a bundle of money," Soupy told him.

"May I ask doing what?" Blood inquired.

"Supermarket stickups," Soupy revealed.

"When and where?" Blood asked.

"You had a hard night. I'll inform you as to when. Get some sleep," Soupy said as he exited the bedroom and closed the entrance. Blood's flashback ended. He realized Amber was gone, but he was convinced she would return. Blood poured himself a glass of wine and continued to sniff the cocaine.

Amber entered her studio apartment and took a seat at her table. She retrieved the cocaine from her bosom, opened the small bag, and inhaled the powdery substance. Though she had spent countless nights by Blood's side, her apartment now felt alien to her —a stark reminder that her time with him had come to an end.

Amber had long warned Blood that his infidelity would be the undoing of their relationship, and she now found herself forced to uphold that vow, despite the immense pain it caused. Her father's warnings had fallen on deaf ears, but the truth of his wisdom had become painfully apparent.

After two days of restless agitation and distraction, Amber had managed to abstain from indulging in both her addiction to Blood and her chemical vice. Yet, like a bee drawn inexorably to the sweetness of nectar, she found herself unable to resist the allure of the cocaine before her. Tears flowed freely down her cheeks, for all she had left was the narcotic's temporary solace.

Amber's objective then was to break the shackles of self-denial and cultivate the willpower necessary to resist her addiction. The question that lingered was whether she would possess the strength to do so in the coming days.

That evening at Chang's Penny Arcade Club, Baby James, Ejay, and Chang were casually dressed, shooting pool when Blood entered, wearing jeans and a shirt.

"Hey, Chang! What's going on?" Blood asked, his eyes sparkling with curiosity.

"Not much, really," Chang replied, a subtle smile playing at the corners of his mouth.

Blood leaned against the doorframe, his expression resolute.

"I came to tell you I won't be working for you anymore. I thought about it, and I can make more money shooting craps."

Chang shrugged, his indifference apparent. "That's fine; I can get somebody else. Let me give you the $2,000 I promised you."

He reached into his pocket, retrieving a roll of cash, and handed it to Blood.

Blood eyed the money, then glanced back at Chang. "You okay with that?"

"Yeah, we're cool," Chang assured him.

"I want to go back to doing stickups," Blood stated, his voice steady.

"It's all right with me," Chang replied, his tone casual.

Blood smirked, leaning closer. "Hitting drug dealers is safe."

"To the pigs, we're all scum of the earth," Chang responded with a wry smile.

"Well, I'm glad you're cool with it," Blood said, a hint of excitement flickering in his eyes. "I gave Amber Stone my last batch of cocaine. Could you sell me $1,500 worth?"

"Baby James, please give Blood what he wants," Chang instructed.

With a hesitant nod, Baby James handed Blood the drugs in exchange for the money. Blood opened the pouch, took a sniff of the contents, and grimaced as he held his nose.

"I sell nothing but the best—it's strong, and it's almost pure," Chang boasted.

"Yeah? Nobody else is selling this but you?" Blood shot back, his skepticism rising.

"Now that you've gotten rid of that punk Underwood, he was cutting up my drugs, selling them, and pocketing my cash for himself. But you took care of that, right?" Chang's eyes sparkled with a dark satisfaction.

"Yeah, he's six feet under. Where's Fat Bob?" Blood asked, scanning the room for familiar faces.

"He's out running some errands for me; he'll be back tomorrow," Chang replied, a hint of impatience in his voice.

"Tell him I said hello. I have to go. Thanks, Chang," Blood said, flashing a brief nod before striding out of the club.

Chang turned to his brother, Baby James. "Did you see that transaction?"

"He almost spent the whole $2,000 on you, Chang," Baby James observed.

"It's just a matter of time; I'm going to get every dime back in profit. I want to finish this game of pool before the crowd arrives," Chang replied.

Outside, Blood stood at the curb as a taxi pulled up. He got in and went to the stash apartment.

Soupy, Jonesy, and Cisco were casually dressed, sitting at the dining table, playing 21 blackjack. When Blood entered, he pulled up a seat and placed the pouch of cocaine on the table.

"Game over, we got business to discuss; take a blow of this coke so we can get started," Blood said.

Soupy took a sniff, passed it to Jonesy, who did the same, then gave the drug to Cisco, who snorted it; they all held their noses.

"Where did you get this from?" Soupy asked.

"Chang, listen, I cased the joint, and it's ready for the taking," Blood said.

"What are you talking about?" Jonesy asked.

"Amber Stone's bank," Blood replied.

"Are you nuts? It's too close for comfort? How do you think she will feel?" Cisco questioned.

"She'll never guess it was us; it's just another supermarket," Blood declared.

"Blood, that's where you're wrong. A bank has much more security," Soupy countered.

"Not this one. It has an armed guard on duty. We won't touch the vault; we'll grab the teller's cash. We'll be out of there in fifteen minutes before the police arrive," Blood replied confidently.

"How did you come up with that calculation?" Cisco asked, raising an eyebrow.

"We'll hit the bank during the lunch rush. The nearest precinct is ten blocks away. The police will have to fight through the traffic jam to reach us, which should take about thirty minutes," Blood explained.

"So, when do you want us to pull off this heist?" Soupy inquired.

"Tomorrow at lunchtime. We'll leave early and arrive by noon when the bank will be swarming with customers," Blood answered, a glint of excitement in his eyes.

"We get in and escape, but how do we drive away?" Cisco asked.

"Cisco, you park around the corner. After Soupy, Jonesy, and I put the money in our backpacks with our guns, we'll give it to you. You drive off, and then we take separate routes on the subway. They'll be looking for men with backpacks. Besides, it's supposed to rain heavily tomorrow. Everyone will be inside or in their cars with foggy windows," explained Blood.

The gentlemen unanimously agreed, continuing their spirited game of blackjack and sipping their frothy ales as they meticulously planned the next day's daring heist.

Before noon, the heavens had wept endlessly, and the dreary weather mirrored the downward trajectory of Amber's psyche. Ensconced within her domicile, she succumbed to the siren's call of

drink and cocaine. Tears streamed down her cheeks as she lan-
guished, awaiting a fateful phone call. Perhaps Willie or Bill would
ring with news of employment, or, dare she hope, the return of the
mercurial Blood. Even the chastising tone of her father would have
been a welcome balm, his "I warned you" pronouncements not-
withstanding. In her anguished state, Amber craved any familiar
voice—a comforting presence to soothe her shattered heart.

Suddenly, the shrill ring of the telephone pierced through
the melancholic haze. Snatching up the receiver in desperation, she
cried out, "Hello! Hello!" only to be met with the apologetic response of a woman who had dialed the wrong number. Amber
hung up, raising the bottle of vodka to her trembling lips. She took
a deep draught, weeping as she drowned in a sea of her own sorrows, mirroring the anguished Irma. She berated herself—how
could she have been so foolish, so blind to the warning signs?

What dark enchantment did this toxic man hold over her
very psyche? Resolving to break free from her addictions, Amber
nonetheless remained uncertain of when she might muster the
willpower to abstain from indulging in her pity party. The relentless
rain tapped a melancholic rhythm against the windowpane.

While Amber wallowed in her misery downtown, a nonde-
script blue van idled around the corner from her bank. Inside,
Blood, Soupy, and Jonesy readied themselves, Cisco at the wheel.
Faces obscured by stocking caps, the men cocked their weapons and
unfurled their black umbrellas.

"I'm going in. You follow. Cisco, keep the engine running,"
Blood commanded, his tone brooking no argument.

The men sprinted through the driving rain, umbrellas aloft,
bursting into the bank. A security guard, his greying temples a testament to years of faithful service, approached Blood, grappling to
disarm the intruder.

In the ensuing scuffle, Blood's mask was torn away, and
with a decisive shot, the guard fell, his life's blood seeping into the
polished floor. The terrified customers scream they scattered like
startled pigeons as Blood strode to the teller, backpack outstretched.

"All right, everybody, this is a stickup. Get on the floor and
lay down, and nobody will get hurt," Blood yelled.

The customers lay down on the floor. Soupy Jonesy gave
their backpacks to the tellers to fill up with the money.

Blood stepped up to the teller, who filled his backpack with
money and handed it to him.

"Let's go," said Blood.

He fired his gun at the walls to scare the customers; they screamed and scurried together on the floor. The gun smoke filled the room. Soupy and Jonesy dashed through the exit, with Blood right behind them. He slammed the door shut, removed a nightstick from his jacket, and locked the bank's door handles to trap everyone inside.

Under the thick veil of the storm, the men raced through the swirling mist, their umbrellas barely shielding them from the driving rain. The streetlights cast a hazy, diffused glow that barely penetrated the opaque fog, making it difficult to see more than a few feet away.

As they reached the van, the men's faces were obscured by the gray shroud, their features indistinct. They quickly opened the doors, throwing their backpacks inside before shutting them with a muffled thud. The sound seemed dampened, the usual crisp slam dulled by the damp, heavy air.

Cisco behind the steering wheel, the van's engine roaring to life, the sound muffled and distorted as if heard from a distance. Carefully navigating the street, the vehicle disappeared into the fog, its taillights reduced to faint crimson embers in the pearlescent haze.

In the diffused lighting, their faces were almost indistinguishable, the sharp features blurred by the fog. Hoping the police would be looking for men in black jackets, they merged into the hazy, indistinct atmosphere of the subway station, their identities concealed under the veil of the storm.

Descending into the subway, the men found refuge from the rain on the platform. Turning their jackets inside out, they revealed different colors - greens, blues, and browns - blending into the shadows and obscuring their previous black attire.

Blood's mind raced as he stood on the platform, the weight of the heist heavy on his conscience. The operation had gone off without a hitch, but the security guard's injury weighed heavily on him.

He knew the authorities would be searching for them with fervor. He steeled himself - he had to get to the stash to get his hands on the money. The adrenaline was still coursing through Soupy's veins. The violence of the robbery replayed in his mind. He couldn't shake the image of the guard's body on the floor. This was supposed to be a clean job, in and out. But Blood had gotten carried away.

Now they were fugitives, and Blood's face would surely be plastered across the news. Soupy just wanted to get as far away from this mess as possible. Jonesy fidgeted nervously, glancing around the platform.

The roar of the approaching train filled the air as he contemplated his next moves. The money would set him up for a while, but he knew the noose was tightening. Blood's single-minded focus troubled him. This was supposed to be a simple heist, but it had turned into a powder keg.

As the train pulled into the station, Jonesy took a deep breath, hoping he could get to the stash without being caught by the authorities.

The train doors slid open, and the men boarded separate cars, blending in with the sparse crowd of civilians and vagrants huddled in the corners and sleeping in their seats, oblivious to the fugitives in their midst. As the train lurched forward, the men sat in tense silence, the weight of their crimes heavy in the air. The express train flickered past street stops in the windows, a visual metaphor for the uncertain fate that they shared.

An hour later, Cisco drove the van to the stash. He parked, carried the backpacks upstairs, and dumped them on the table. Afterward, he dropped the van off at the paint shop to have it painted red. The mechanic informed him to pick it up in a week. Keeping it off the streets would allow it to cool down in case anyone had spotted it. Cisco paid him a thousand dollars and exited the shop, taking the subway back to the stash. He was filled with delight as he anticipated the large sum of money waiting for him; he knew the bank they had robbed was famous for cashing checks in substantial amounts.

Upon entering the stash, he found Soupy, Blood, and Jonesy counting the money.

"Cisco, come get your share of the money!" Soupy called out.

"Okay, Soupy, let me hang up my wet coat," Cisco replied.

Jonesy asked, "Cisco, did you dump the van?"

"Yes, Jonesy. It will be in the shop for a week," Cisco answered. Blood was separating the money into four stacks.

"You have to leave the van there indefinitely. They can identify Blood if the armed guard dies; they'll want him for robbery and murder. Soupy and I are leaving town for good, and you should too," Jonesy said.

Cisco asked, "Jonesy, you mean it's over?"

Jonesy responded, "Cisco, if you want to stay here and go to jail for life, that's fine with us. I'm going to Philly, and Soupy is heading to Chicago."

Cisco said, "I've always wanted to live in Vegas to gamble."

Jonesy handed Cisco his stack of money. "Here's your share: seventy-five thousand dollars. Blood, where are you going?"

Blood replied, "It will be divulged sooner or later, but you didn't hear it from me. I've got some business to take care of."

He flicked his dead presidents with his thumb.

Jonesy looked at him. "You mean Amber Stone."

"Yeah, I have to show her I'm not the loser she thinks I am. As for the guard, I had to put a bullet in his ass," Blood admitted.

The guys all laughed as they counted their money from the heist. After stowing their cash in their backpacks, they donned their raincoats, grabbed their umbrellas, and exited the apartment.

It was pouring rain as Blood, Soupy, Jonesy, and Cisco walked to the subway and took the train to 34th Street Union Station. They each bought one-way tickets to their destination, each carrying a sack full of money, ready to start anew with only the clothes on their backs.

Soupy looked at the others solemnly. "This is it. We have to disappear. The cops will have our phones tapped to anyone we call. We have the money to go our separate ways and lay low. Blood, where are you going?"

"I'm going to New Jersey, and I have a car waiting to pick me up. Like I said, you'll find out soon enough, but I will make one phone call before my departure," Blood replied.

Jonesy raised an eyebrow. "Let me guess, to Amber Stone?"

Cisco chuckled. "You can't forget about the woman."

Blood nodded thoughtfully. "I have a feeling we'll see each other again."

They embraced in a final hug goodbye and proceeded to their respective Amtrak train stations. As the trains pulled out of the station, the men boarded, each heading to a different destination—Soupy to Chicago, Jonesy to Philadelphia, Cisco to Las Vegas, and Blood to New Jersey. The city of New York faded into the distance through the rain-streaked windows, the weight of their crimes and the uncertainty of their lives hung heavy in the air.

In the aftermath of an hour's passage, FBI Agents Moore, an African American, and McCormick, a Caucasian, both in their thirties, arrived at Blood's stash apartment.

Accompanied by a contingent of six heavily armed backup officers clad in bulletproof tactical gear, the federal law enforcement personnel executed a sudden, forceful incursion into the suspect's residence, violently breaching the premises without warning.

"FBI!"Agent McCormick yelled.

"Search the premises. I want this place dusted for fingerprints. We need to know who was here and where they went," Agent Moore ordered. The agents opened drawers and pulled clothes from the closets; all of the suspect's possessions were left behind. Agent McCormick stepped in close to Agent Moore.

"What do you think, Moore?" he asked.

"It's a nice place, but you wouldn't know it from the piss-smelling hallway,"Agent Moore responded. "They left in a hurry and needed to travel light."

"I reviewed the bank's surveillance footage. Blood was there yesterday morning, cashing a check from a Ms. Amber Stone. We need to bring her in,"Agent McCormick said.

"On what charge?" Agent Moore inquired.

"Under the New World Order charge," Agent McCormick explained. "Certain figures must be removed before the NWO can seize complete power. Banderos is one of those people, and he needs to be taken out by any means necessary."

Agent Moore acknowledged, "Of course, all this will be kept under wraps. We can't let her know that the NWO is pulling the strings."

Agent McCormick continued, "Blood made a connection with Hector when he was in prison—a henchman who works for the drug lord Banderos. We know he has obtained cocaine from the cartel for his drug-dealing associates. However, we don't know how to reach Banderos, and Blood might be our entrance. I'm sure he's leaving the country, and Agent Cortez will inform us once he arrives in Colombia. Put a tap on Ms. Stone's phone ASAP."

Agent Moore asked, "What if he doesn't call her?"

Agent McCormick stated, "If he does, she's the key we need to open the door. All right, men, let us gather any evidence and get to the station; those guys are long gone." The FBI agents gathered the fingerprints and followed Agent McCormick and Agent Moore out of the building. The heavens opened up, unleashing a torrential downpour upon the deserted city streets. Sheets of rain cascaded from the blackened skies, obscuring visibility and dampening the surroundings. No crowds gathered to witness the flurry of activity, as FBI vehicles lined the curb around Blood's apartment building.

Agent McCormick, Agent Moore, and their cohort of tactical agents, clutching their evidence. Scurrying through the deluge, they quickly filed into their cars and sped away, leaving the now empty, rain-soaked premises in their wake.

The relentless downpour battered Amber's studio apartment, howling winds whipping rain against her windows. The tempestuous weather mirrored the turmoil that raged within her mind as she sat up in the middle of her bed, her eyes transfixed on the television screen.

"Good evening. I am Carla Sands, reporting a special bulletin. This afternoon, a bank robbery of $300,000 took place at the Central Bank, executed by three masked men. One of the suspects has been identified as Ray Perkman, also known as Blood. He shot and killed the bank's security guard during the robbery. This same gang is also suspected of killing a security guard in the Bronx during a supermarket heist. The FBI has issued a warrant for Perkman's arrest. He is known to be armed and dangerous."

Amber's heart sank as Blood's picture flashed across the screen. Grabbing the remote, she switched off the television, plunging the room into semi-darkness while the storm raged on outside. The shrill ring of her phone startled her, and she reluctantly answered.

"Hello…"

"Hello, Amber Stone. It's me, Blood," the voice on the other end replied.

Amber's breath caught in her throat as she listened to his voice. The pounding rain and howling wind provided an ominous backdrop to their conversation. Blood's words cut through her; his audacity in calling her despite the manhunt was both infuriating and strangely alluring.

"What are you doing calling me?" Amber asked.

"You don't want to speak to me?" Blood responded.

"You're all over the news. The police are looking for you," Amber told him.

"Good! I always knew I would be famous," Blood said.

"It didn't have to be this way," Amber lamented.

"It's my destiny, and you're a part of it," Blood declared.

"Blood, you have a lot of nerve," Amber criticized.

"It's FDIC insured; you didn't lose any money," Blood argued.

"Is everything and everybody around you consumable?" Amber questioned.

"If it takes blood to get what I want, so be it," Blood stated coldly.

"What do you want from me?" Amber asked, exasperated.

"I'll send you your money in a money order," Blood offered.

"Why?" Amber pressed.

"Because I still love you," Blood confessed.

"Where are you?" Amber asked.

"I can't say," Blood replied, then hung up the phone.

Amber lay down on her bed and wept in sorrow. He had destroyed every plan she had for them. Amber was glad she hadn't told her father his name; he would have said, "I told you so." His words echoed in her memory. Even though her heart ached, the beat between them was unstoppable.

They couldn't stay away from each other. Blood was irresistible to her; no matter how much he emotionally abused her, she just couldn't leave him, even though she desired to. Amber's face brightened as she shed tears of relief, knowing that even if they wanted to see each other, they couldn't because he was on the run. The howling wind and rain lashed against her window. She crawled under her covers, grateful for her apartment and independence. All Amber could do was close her eyes and hope for the best, for she had no idea what would happen next.

In New Jersey, on a desolate, deserted road, the rain poured down in sheets, driven by a fierce wind. Blood stood sheltered in a dimly lit phone booth, the zero visibility reminding him of the stormy nights in the Mississippi Delta. The only things missing were the sounds of crickets and the alligators slowly trotting across the wet, muddy ground. He clutched a sack full of stolen money, his mind racing with thoughts of his new life. He had never been out of the country before.

Suddenly, headlights emerged from the misty gloom, and a sleek black limousine pulled up in front of the phone booth. Blood couldn't see inside, but he opened the door and climbed in without a moment's hesitation.

As the limo sped off, loud thunderclaps boomed overhead, and jagged forks of lightning sliced through the sky. The limousine drove to an empty hangar where a small private jet waited, its engines idling. Major airlines had canceled flights due to the weather. Although he couldn't be seen at the airport—due to being on the FBI's most-wanted list—Transportation Security Agents would apprehend him. This was a discreet, illegal private transport.

Blood hurried from the limo to the plane, boarding quickly as the storm raged around him. The jet bumped and jostled as it taxied down the tarmac, fighting against the gusting winds and torrential downpour.

This was Blood's first time flying in such treacherous weather, and he could only hope the plane would reach its destination safely. With a lurch, the small jet lifted off the ground, pitching and rolling as it climbed through the roiling storm clouds. Rain lashed against the windows, and turbulence buffeted the aircraft, forcing Blood to grip the armrests tightly. Occasionally, blinding flashes of lightning illuminated the cabin, followed by the deafening boom of thunder that shook the plane. Despite the hostile conditions, the pilot pressed on, guiding the jet higher and higher into the turbulent skies. Blood had never experienced anything like this: the roar of the engines, the bone-rattling vibrations, and the constant threat of being torn apart by the raging elements. God had never shown mercy to him, but all he could do was pray that they would make it through the storm intact.

Visibility had dropped to near zero as the jet entered the heart of the storm. All traces of the ground below were obscured by impenetrable darkness, save for the occasional glimpse of churning clouds illuminated by flashes of lightning. The plane shuddered violently as it encountered a powerful updraft, forcing the pilot to wrestle with the controls in a desperate attempt to maintain stability. Blood's stomach lurched when the jet suddenly dropped several hundred feet, ensnared in a brutal downdraft. The engines strained to keep the aircraft aloft, battered by the relentless wind gusts.

Suddenly, a blinding flash of lightning streaked past the cockpit, followed immediately by an earsplitting crack of thunder that made the windows rattle. The pilot cursed under his breath and concentrated as he fought to keep the plane on course.

In the cabin, Blood stared out the window, a mix of terror and exhilaration coursing through him as he watched the jet become completely engulfed by the storm. Visibility had dwindled to a mere few feet, the world outside transforming into an inky void, pierced only by the occasional crack of lightning. The roar of the engines and the howling wind were the only sounds echoing around him as the plane plunged into the very heart of the tempest, its fate hanging in the balance.

Eleven miles away, in the heart of Upper Manhattan, the bustling city streets had been reduced to a ghost town. Sheets of rain lashed the pavement, blown sideways by howling winds, as the rare passerby dashed for shelter.

In the dim glow of the streetlights, a sleek black sedan suddenly pulled up in front of Chang's Penny Arcade, its engine idling amidst the pounding rain.

The driver's side door swung open, and a tall, imposing African American man emerged, his long black raincoat billowing in the gusting wind. Tucked under his arm was a Thompson submachine gun, its menacing profile barely visible in the shadows. The man strode purposefully toward the entrance of the dimly lit arcade, water dripping from the brim of his fedora as he stepped through the doorway.

Inside, the familiar sounds of racked balls and idle chatter filled the air. Chang, Ejay, Baby James, and Fat Bob stood around the worn pool tables, engrossed in their games. Unaware of the dangerous intruder who had just entered, the group remained oblivious to the looming threat that had come calling on this stormy night.

The newcomer's dark eyes swept the room, taking in every detail as he slowly advanced further into the arcade. His grip tightened on the Tommy gun, the metal stock cool and reassuring against his palm. Whatever business had brought him here, it was clear he was prepared to use extreme measures to see it through. Just then, Ejay glanced up and noticed the newcomer. His eyes widened in alarm as he recognized the weapon the man was carrying.

"Hey, what's going on here?" Ejay called out, his voice cracking with nervousness.

The other men turned to see what had caught Ejay's attention, and their faces drained of color as they, too, registered the deadly firearm. Panic set in as the group scrambled to find cover, knocking over the pool table in their haste.

"I have a message from Pretty Louie," the hitman growled before opening fire with his automatic weapon. The pool players had no time to escape; they were cut down, their bodies crumpling to the floor. He fired again, killing Chang, Ejay, Baby James, and Fat Bob before they could run or duck under the tables. The hitman rampaged through the arcade, destroying the pool tables, games, and walls.

He riddled the place with bullets, turning the once vibrant venue into a scene of chaos. Finally, he exited the gun-smoked, bullet-ridden club, disappearing back into the stormy night.

CHAPTER SIX

The following day dawned sunny and bright. The police and coroner loaded lifeless bodies onto a truck outside Chang's Penny Arcade Club. Amber remained blissfully unaware of the shootings; she had turned off the news and cried herself to sleep the night before. Relieved that Blood was gone, she focused on her career—the only thing she had left to fall back on. Just then, her phone rang with a rush call to work. Forced to pull herself together, she relied on sniffs of coke and eye drops to clear her puffy eyes. Numb as she was, she knew she could concentrate on the upcoming job. Amber felt a spark of happiness at the thought of hurrying downtown to the studio—anything to dissipate her funk.

She arrived, her makeup and hair perfectly done, a smile on her face, yet too ashamed to reveal her torrid love affair or even admit that she knew Blood. She slipped into her high-fashion pinstripe pantsuit and stepped onto the set, where Bill photographed her, taking ten shots from various angles.

When Agent Moore and Agent McCormick entered the studio, nothing about them stood out; they looked utterly ordinary, certainly not fitting for the fashion industry. Bill took one glance at them and assumed they were lost, mistakenly at the wrong address.

"There is a photoshoot happening here. Can I help you guys with something?" Bill asked.

Agent Moore and Agent McCormick flashed their FBI badges and identification. Amber stepped off the photo background paper.

"Amber Stone," Agent Moore said.

"Yes," Amber answered, confused.

"I am Agent Moore, and this is Agent McCormick. You are under arrest for conspiracy in a bank robbery. Please come with us."

"Wait a minute! I didn't have anything to do with it," Amber protested.

"You have the right to remain silent. You have the right to an attorney. Anything you say can be used against you in a court of law," Agent McCormick stated. He handcuffed Amber while Agent Moore spotted her handbag on a chair and searched it, discovering a bag of cocaine inside.

Flinging his switchblade out of his pocket, the agent slashed into the bag and tasted the contents.

"This is cocaine. Add possession to the charges," said Agent Moore.

McCormick escorted Amber Stone from the studio, with Moore following closely behind, clutching her handbag.

Bill, confounded, called the Fab Fashion Agency. "Hello, Willie... Amber Stone has been arrested."

"Arrested? What the hell is going on?" she shouted through the phone.

"I'm just a photographer. You'll need to go to the police station to find out. They discovered drugs and something about a robbery. It was the FBI. I'm totally upset, and Amber is shocked. Keep me posted. I have to go." Bill hung up the phone and anxiously paced on the floor.

At One Police Plaza, a throng of reporters stood poised with cameras in hand, eagerly awaiting news. McCormick and Moore's car pulled up to the curb, and they hurriedly exited the vehicle, escorting Amber toward the station. The press jostled for position, snapping pictures as the trio moved forward.

Inside, the interrogation room was a stark, utilitarian space—its bare walls painted a dull, institutional gray, a metal table bolted to the floor, and two uncomfortable-looking chairs positioned on either side. Harsh fluorescent lighting overhead cast an unflattering, almost brutal glow that made the room feel oppressive and impersonal. As Agent Moore led Amber into the room and took up his position by the door, a sense of dread and unease began to settle over her.

When Amber sat down across from the imposing figure of Agent McCormick, she couldn't help but feel small and intimidated. Her heart raced as she realized this was no longer just a fashion shoot gone wrong—her freedom, and perhaps even her life, was now at stake. In that moment, Amber's confidence and bravado melted away, replaced by a growing sense of panic and uncertainty.

The glamorous, untouchable persona she projected on set had been stripped away, leaving her feeling exposed and vulnerable. She steeled herself, determined not to show any weakness, but deep down, she was terrified. McCormick's stern expression and the thick file he slammed down on the table only heightened her anxiety. The interrogation had begun, and she knew her future hung in the balance.

"Raymond Perkman was arrested at 17 for murder and spent ten years in prison. At 27, he was released and moved up north. He looted several supermarkets, but we couldn't prove it until he turned 28. We have observed him for a lengthy period, and finally, we have photographic evidence of him robbing a bank. We suspect he killed the security guard in the Bronx; it matches his modus operandi, and he has also been involved in cocaine trafficking. He's a lifelong criminal. The guard he shot during the bank robbery is dead, and his family wants justice," McCormick stated.

"I had no idea he was that bad," Amber said.

"You should be careful with whom you associate," McCormick replied.

"It's too late for advice," Amber retorted.

"Ms. Stone, we want your absolute cooperation." McCormick pressed.

Amber glanced at Agent Moore, who leaned against the wall, and then back at McCormick, recognizing the good cop, bad cop routine she had never experienced before her arrest.

"Or what?" Amber asked, her voice laced with defiance.

"You'll be sent to prison," McCormick warned.

"You're bluffing! You've got nothing on me except possession of cocaine. I'm a user, not a seller," Amber shot back.

McCormick took a deep breath before speaking. "Blood is a small-time guy. Compared to whom he's working for, he's in South America, working for a drug lord named Banderos."

"What do you want me to do?" Amber asked warily.

Agent Moore glanced at Amber. She returned his gaze with a harsh look, sitting back in her chair.

"Fly down to South America," McCormick stated.

"You want me to put my life on the line?" Amber questioned, her voice laced with skepticism.

"We have it on tape that Blood cashed your check. What female gives a man that kind of money if she isn't involved?" McCormick pressed.

"It was a loan, not a gift. You still can't prove I had anything to do with the robbery. I don't want to see Blood ever again, and you can't make me. I want to see my lawyer. I'm allowed one phone call," Amber insisted.

"Blood is in love with you, and you can help us," McCormick argued.

"I'm just a girl to party with. He doesn't care about me," Amber said dismissively.

"If you're not part of the solution, you're part of the problem. We have a special case here that demands we operate above the law. Agent Moore, please take Ms. Stone to the holding cell and leave her there until she's ready to cooperate," McCormick ordered.

"Are you crazy? I deserve due process! Just wait until my father hears about this; you'll be sued," Amber protested.

Agent Moore escorted Amber from the interrogation room, handing her over to a female guard, who provided her with an orange jumpsuit and led her to the showers for a bath.

As the heavy metal door clanged shut behind her, Amber felt a wave of dread wash over her. The small, sparse cell was a far cry from the lavish hotel suites and luxury penthouses to which she was accustomed. The bare concrete walls felt oppressive, closing in around her, and the thin, scratchy mattress of the cot offered little comfort.

Amber sank down onto the edge of the bed, a sense of panic rising in her chest. This was real—not the controlled environments of her photo shoots or the glamorous parties where she could easily indulge her vices. Here, she was cut off from the cocaine, the alcohol, the endless flow of substances that had become a crutch, a way to cope with the pressures of her high-profile lifestyle.

Looking around the cell, Amber was suddenly hyper-aware of her addiction. The four bare walls seemed to taunt her, a constant reminder that she would have no means to soothe her cravings, to numb the anxiety and paranoia that now gripped her. The adrenaline rush of the arrest had worn off, leaving her feeling vulnerable, exposed, and desperately craving her next fix.

Amber wrapped her arms around herself, fighting back the rising tide of withdrawal symptoms. In this stark, unforgiving space, she was forced to confront the harsh realities of her addiction, with no designer handbags or designer drugs to mask the pain. For the first time, the glamorous facade she had built began to crumble, and Amber was left facing the grim truth – that her freedom, and perhaps even her life, now hung in the balance.

Later that evening, Amber was withdrawing from the cocaine and alcohol; she was restless, dashing to the toilet to vomit. Her skin was sweating profusely. The model turned on the sink faucet and splashed water on her face, desperate to alleviate the panic coursing through her mind and body. Large shadows seemed to float around the cell, and Amber began to hallucinate, screaming in fear.

The guard rushed to the cell and flung open the door, stepping inside. She lunged for Amber, mistakenly assuming the prisoner was trying to take her own life. But Amber lashed out like an enraged, caged ape, employing judo skills to toss the guard around the cell. The women wrestled fiercely, and the guard screamed for help.

Moments later, a male guard hurried in, wielding a nightstick. He swung it, striking Amber over the head and knocking her unconscious. With swift efficiency, they threw her onto the cot and exited the cell.

"What happened?" the male guard asked, glancing back over his shoulder.

"The prisoner must be withdrawing from drugs," responded the female guard, her voice steady.

"Do not open the cell. I don't care if the bitch is hanging herself," the male guard declared with cold authority.

The guards walked away, leaving Amber motionless on the cot.

As dawn broke, Amber slowly regained consciousness, her vision still blurred. She sat on the cot, clutching her head as a sharp pain pierced the back of her skull. The female guard approached the cell door, tray in hand.

"Here's your breakfast," she said.

Amber rose from the cot, her expression wild, her hair a tangled mess. She made her way to the food slot in the cell bars."Why am I here? Why can't I be released?" Amber demanded.

"You mean you don't remember? You were caught with drugs, and you're in cahoots with America's FBI's Most Wanted," the guard replied.

"Oh, so it's guilty until proven innocent? Is that why I kicked your butt?" Amber shot back.

"For that, my dear, you will pay. You'll stay here and face cold turkey. I brought you some coffee. Drink it."

"What about water? I'm thirsty," Amber asked, her voice edged with desperation.

"You see the sink over there? Put your mouth to the faucet and suck on it," the female guard instructed, her tone as cold as the concrete walls surrounding them.

Amber grabbed her breakfast tray and settled onto the cot, watching the guard walk away with a mix of relief and trepidation. She set the steaming cup of coffee aside and lifted the plastic lid off her breakfast plate. Leaning in close, her nose inches from the food, she inhaled deeply, scrutinizing the scrambled eggs, toast, and small portion of fruit. She searched for any signs of tampering, her heart racing at the thought.

Seemingly satisfied that her breakfast appeared untainted, she picked up a piece of toast, holding it in her trembling fingers. With a hesitant pause, she brought it to her mouth, her mind swirling with uncertainty. Taking a tentative bite, she chewed slowly, her eyes darting around the cell, evaluating the taste and consistency. Each chew echoed in the silence of her confinement, a stark reminder of her captivity. In that moment, breakfast was more than a meal; it was a small act of rebellion against the monotony of her situation, a flicker of determination sparking within her, even amidst the despair that threatened to consume her.

As the days melted into one another, Amber lay in her small cell, tossing and turning, trembling, and sweating less with each passing moment. The narcotic that had once clouded her mind was fading from her system, and with it, her hands grew steadier. A week of solitude had passed, and she began to focus on gentle exercises, seeking relief for the aches and knots in her muscles. Showers were her only luxury, and she yearned for a hot bath to ease both her weary body and restless mind. With no books to absorb her thoughts, pacing back and forth within the confines of her cell became her solitary refuge, a ritual to stave off the creeping edges of madness.

As the weeks dragged on, the glamorous persona that once defined her began to slip away. Without the artifice of makeup and the thrill of posing before a camera, Amber rediscovered her true self, stripped bare and vulnerable. She had lost track of time; it felt like years since she had basked in the spotlight, and the weight of her disconnection from reality pressed heavily upon her.

In this stark environment, she was forced to confront the shadows of her mind, realizing that perhaps, in this very solitude, she might find the strength to rebuild herself anew.

Finally, the guard swung open the heavy door of Amber's cell, a gleam of anticipation in his eyes as he beckoned her forward. She stepped out, her heart racing, and followed him down the dimly lit corridor toward the interrogation room.

The atmosphere felt charged as she entered and took a seat at the table opposite Agent McCormick and Moore.

"Are you ready to be a part of the solution?" McCormick asked, his voice steady and probing.

Amber raised an eyebrow. "Do I have an option?"

"Blood cares for you," Moore interjected, his tone serious.

"What's to keep him from killing me?" Amber shot back, her apprehension palpable.

"He won't suspect you," Moore replied, leaning forward, a glimmer of reassurance in his gaze.

"I suspect my arrest has been splashed all over the newspapers," she said, her voice barely a whisper.

Moore leaned closer, his eyes glinting with a mix of determination and arrogance. "We can build a case on you to bury you," he replied, his tone steely.

"We don't care about Blood. He's just a little fish in the sea. We want his boss—Banderos. And you can lead us to Blood. He'll take us to his leader. What's it going to be, Ms. Stone? Your career is over as it stands. Life as you once knew it is finished." McCormick stated.

Amber took a deep breath, her heart racing as she folded her arms across her chest, a fortress of defiance.

"If my life is over, then what are the benefits you're offering me?" she challenged, her gaze unwavering. "I don't want to be merely alive; I want a purpose. I want all the bells and whistles, the perks and accolades that come with the life I've lived. Being just another girl to party with won't do."

The silence that followed crackled with tension, each word hanging in the air, a challenge ignited between them.

"No, but you can pretend to be that - that is the only way Blood is going to get back in your arms again and spill his guts," said McCormick.

"If I get caught, a snitch gets no mercy," Amber said.

"You are not a snitch; you are a spy. We have the Agent
Zero program. It's new - we capture minor victims before they
go off the deep end; we recruit them into the program. People
like you keep criminals in business. This is your opportunity to
help us to do our duty to put your associates behind bars, or
would you instead take their place?" Moore asked.

"You leave me no choice. What are the pros and cons?"
Amber asked.

"Cortez is our man down there; he'll get you connected.
We have a top-secret program called Agent Zero. We need people like you who are at a crossroads in life," McCormick said.

"My life has altered drastically," Amber said.

"Join us and get rich. You'll have a 6-figure salary. Plus,
you can confiscate some of Banderos' funds - the government
will want ten percent of your earnings," Moore said.

"This Banderos must be very important to you?" Amber
asked.

McCormick chimed in, "We suspect he's funding terror-
ist cells. National Security Administration is our top priority. We
have started recruiting, and you're our selection. Help us elimi-
nate Banderos."

"All this is a shock to me," Amber said.

"Do we have your cooperation, or do you wish to go
back in your cell and stay indefinitely?" Moore asked.

"I have to think about it," Amber said.

As the heavy door creaked open, the female guard
strode into the office with an air of authority. Amber glanced
up, her heart pounding, as she was led away from the chaos of
the bustling facility and toward the stark silence of her cell. The
cold, sterile walls loomed closer, and a knot of doubt began to
tighten in her stomach. Had she made the right decision to
stand her ground?

Once within the dim confines of her cell, Amber's spirit
wavered. She recalled her mantra: "Never let them see you
sweat." With determination simmering in her soul, she began to
pace, her footsteps echoing against the unforgiving concrete
floor. Each step was a battle against the anxiety gnawing at her
resolve, a dance of defiance against the uncertainty that loomed
larger with each passing second.

The sound of Willie's footsteps echoed as she approached the cell, her fashionable attire contrasting sharply with
the grim surroundings.

The guard stepped aside, allowing her entry, and an expression of sheer happiness lit up the women's faces as they embraced each other tightly.

"Willie, I am so glad to see you!" Amber exclaimed, her voice a mixture of relief and sorrow.

"Amber Stone, are you okay?" Willie asked, concern etched in her eyes.

"Yes, but who called the press?" Amber questioned, her brow furrowed.

"I did. I want your arrest to be a sensation," Willie replied, a glint of determination in her gaze.

"My modeling career is over," Amber lamented, her tone heavy with despair.

"What do you mean?" Willie probed, her heart racing.

Amber sank down onto the cot, her shoulders slumping.

"I'm part of an ongoing investigation," she confessed, her voice barely above a whisper.

"Give them what they want, and they'll leave you alone," Willie urged, desperation creeping into her words.

"It's not that simple," Amber countered, shaking her head.

"It's such a shame; you were becoming a top model," Willie said, her voice laden with empathy.

"I've destroyed my career," Amber whispered, the weight of her words hanging in the air like a dark cloud. Willie reached for her hand, vowing silently to do whatever it took to help her friend reclaim her life. In that small, dimly lit cell, the echoes of hope mingled with the reality of their situation, igniting a spark of determination in Willie's heart.

"Do you want me to bail you out?" Willie asked.

"No, I'll have to leave town; that was the deal," Amber said.

Willie sat on the cot and put her arms around Amber.

"What should I do?" Willie asked.

"Go on with your agency. Kiss Bill and Master Dan goodbye for me," Amber said.

"I'm going to miss you. Can you talk about it?" Willie asked.

"No, fashion was fun while it lasted," Amber agreed.

"Amber Stone, take care of yourself," Willie said.

"You too, Willie," Amber responded.

The guard appeared at the cell door, signaling Willie to leave. She hugged Amber and exited the cell. Amber lay on her cot, and cried herself to sleep.

It's 7 a.m., and Amber was fast asleep. Suddenly, the guard swung open the cell door, and Agent Moore stepped inside.

He shouted, "Rise and shine!"

Amber stirred, sitting up on the edge of her bed.

"Good morning, Amber Stone. What's it going to be: yes or no?" he asks.

Amber rubbed the sleep from her eyes and replied, "Yes. Get me out of here."

"Follow me. We have fresh coffee and clean clothes waiting for you," said Moore.

"Don't I get a shower?" Amber questioned, her brow furrowed.

"You can do that when you go home," Moore assured her.

"I'm going home?" Amber asks, disbelief colored her voice.

"Yes, to pack your things. Your flight to Colombia, South America, leaves tonight," Moore confirmed.

"I need to say goodbye to my friends," Amber insisted.

"We'll have someone contact them and explain you'll be on an extensive modeling trip," Moore responded.

Agent Moore and Amber Stone exited the cell, his presence reassuring as he escorted her to the interrogation office.

She stepped inside, and he positioned himself resolutely at the door. "I'll wait here," he said, his voice steady.

Once inside the room, Amber's gaze fell upon a black suit, meticulously folded and waiting for her on the table, accompanied by a large manila envelope. With a sense of determination, she changed into the outfit, feeling bland—not like the fashion fabrics that would cling to her form like armor.

She shouted, "You can come in. I am fully dressed." Moore entered the room and sat down at the table; he handed her the manila envelope.

"Your passport, work visa, and $10,000 in cash should help you out. Cortez is your contact and trainer," Moore said.

Amber peeked into the envelope and asked, "What makes you so sure Blood won't suspect me?"

"I'm not; it's your job to make sure he doesn't," Moore said.

"What if he finds out that I am working as a spy?" Amber asked.

"Then you are on your own," Moore said.

"If I refuse?" Amber asked.

"Then you will be a fugitive like Blood. It's your decision," Moore said.

"It sounds like a suicide mission to me," Amber said.

"You could stay here and go to prison. We meant what we said - you do the mission or do lengthy solitary confinement," Moore said.

"What about my father?" Amber asked.

"He won't find out that you were arrested, not even with his top-secret clearance. It will only state that you work undercover for the government," Moore said.

"I'm supposed to be happy?" Amber asked.

"You better get going; you don't want to miss your plane," Moore said.

"Tell McCormick I agreed," Amber said.

"He's at lunch. I'll give him your regards - bon voyage," Moore said.

Amber, with the envelope clutched in her hand, shot him a stern look before she exited the office.

Outside the police station, a Secret Service agent waited beside a black car with the door open. Amber descended the steps of the building and climbed into the vehicle. The agent took the driver's seat and drove her to her apartment, parking in front. She quickly exited the car and hurried into her building.

Once inside her apartment, she gazed out the window, spotting the black car still waiting to take her to the airport. Even if she wanted to escape, it would be futile; the agent would follow and drag her back to jail. She hoped never to endure the horrors of kicking a drug habit again.

Amber took out her suitcase and packed her clothes. In her top drawer, she found a dollar bill filled with cocaine. She opened her window and let the wind carry the narcotic away, along with her past.

A new life awaited her, filled with danger and intrigue; she needed all her faculties to be in top form to deal with her mission. Amber bathed and put on the bland black suit that Moore had given her.

She would blend into the background and feel comfortable during her long flight. She couldn't recall ever being sober in her apartment. Taking a somber glance at the space she would never see again, she realized the door to her new life was open; all she had to do was march through it. She felt relieved to be free from addiction, yet still trapped. The question in her mind is, has she traded one prison to step into another?

Only fate can predict what lies beyond, but being kicked out of her comfort zone left her with nowhere to go but forward into the future. The Agent Zero program promised to tie up all the loose ends in her life, including the liquidation of her possessions. Amber stood in the middle of her small studio apartment, taking one last look around. So many memories had been made within these walls—memories she wasn't quite ready to let go of.

Her mind drifted back to the days when she and Dee had been inseparable. They had met at the Gold Lounge bar, quickly bonding over their shared love of partying. Amber had always had money, thanks to her father's generous allowance, and she would happily spend it on Dee—buying her cocaine, fashionable clothes, dinners, and covering the tab when they went out. Dee, on the other hand, was a street girl, always able to get money from the men she dated. Together, they had been the perfect party duo, living life to the fullest and never worrying about the consequences. Amber felt a pang of nostalgia as she remembered the laughter, the music, and the endless nights of dancing, getting lost in a haze of drugs and alcohol.

Amber and Dee stumbled into the Gold Lounge, already a few drinks in. Amber grabbed Dee's arm, leaning in close as the music pulsed around them.

"I can't believe my dad just doubled my allowance!" Amber shouted over the music, her eyes sparkling with excitement. "We're gonna party like rockstars tonight!"

Dee grinned, her own eyes alight with mischief. "That's what I like to hear, girl! Let's make this the best night ever!" Dee insisted.

The two women made their way to the bar, ordering round after round of drinks and shots, their laughter echoing through the crowded club.

The two then found themselves huddled in the corner booth of their favorite diner, plates of half-eaten food in front of them. Amber pulled a small baggie out of her purse, passing it to Dee under the table.

"Here, this should keep us going for the rest of the night," Amber said with a wink.

Dee eagerly snatched the bag, already rolling a line of cocaine on the table. "You're the best, you know that?" she said, leaning in close to Amber. "I don't know what I'd do without you."

Amber smiled, placing her hand on Dee's arm. "That's what best friends are for, right? Now let's finish this up and go paint the town red!"

The two women giggled, their heads bent close together as they indulged in their illicit pleasures, the rest of the memories fading away around them as Amber snapped back to the present day reality in her studio apartment. Those had been the best days of her life, and now it was all coming to an end. With a heavy sigh, Amber turned and walked out the door, closing that chapter of her life for good. Amber stepped into the hallway with her luggage in hand and descended the staircase. She got into the car and was driven to the airport.

Amber arrived at the JFK Airport - it was crowded with passengers. She was hoping no one noticed that a secret serviceman was tailing her. He was a tall, big white man with a mustache in a black suit, appearing more like a cop on her trail. It looked like she was a suspect, embarrassed as all eyes were on her. She checked her bags in as the secret service man followed her into the boarding area. He watched her board the plane.

Five hours and fifteen minutes later, the plane landed at the Jose Maria Cordoba Airport in Rionegro, Colombia. It was hot, bright, and sunny.

Amber exited the airport with her suitcase. A celery-green Corvette pulled up, and a casually dressed Latino man in his thirties, attractive and confident, jumped out and approached her.

"Ms. Amber Stone?" Miguel asked.

"Yes," Amber replied.

"I'm Miguel. I work for Cortez; he sent me to pick you up," Miguel explained.

"Why?" Amber inquired.

"He wants you to meet Ray; he's doing very well," Miguel said.

"Where are we going?" Amber asked.

"To Medellín, twenty-one miles away," Miguel answered.

"Do you have a last name?" Amber queried.

"No, just call me Miguel," he replied with a smile.

"Nice car," Amber remarked.

"It's yours; get in, and you can drive. I'll show you the way," Miguel said.

Miguel threw her the keys, grabbed her suitcase, and put it in the trunk.

"I am beginning to like the perks already," Amber said.

Amber and Miguel got into the car, and she sped off.

The celery green Corvette sped through the forgotten roads, standing out from the beautiful lush trees on both sides. There were no cars - a man could get lost in this rural area. She had a full view of the forest as the car did 70 mph, not a police in sight. No wonder Blood escaped to Colombia. He could roam free, which scared her because there was no one to check him. Miguel remained quiet the entire trip. He was quite the chaperone. No matter how fast she drove, Miguel stayed calm. He knew Amber was testing him. She hadn't sat behind the stirring wheel in a while. In New York, there was a cab service, but driving is like riding a bike; you never forget once you learn.

Amber and Miguel arrived at Cortez's mansion in the secluded hills. They exited the car, and he retrieved her suitcase from the trunk, handing it to her. As they marched to the entrance, he knocked. A middle-aged Latino maid opened the door. Amber stepped inside, and Miguel completed his task and left.

Inside, the upscale, spacious drawing room boasted deep pumpkin-colored walls and elegant wood furniture. A wide floor-length bronze-framed mirror reflected her as she stood in the corridor. From the sofa and dining area, one could see anyone entering the house.

Amber stood at the base of a long staircase, her eyes drawn to a chandelier above, its brilliance dimmed by the lurking presence of hidden cameras. The unsettling thought crossed her mind: this place was rigged with surveillance. Even if she wanted to escape, it seemed impossible.

"Welcome, Señorita. Will you please follow me?" the maid said, her tone polite yet firm.

"Thank you," Amber replied, her heart racing.

The maid ascended the staircase, with Amber trailing behind her. They entered a gallery adorned with paintings of Spanish settlers covering the walls; Amber suspected that cameras were hidden behind them.

The maid led her to a lavish bedroom painted in light beige, featuring a deep brown bed set and bronze sconces. In Colombia, it felt like an eternal spring or summer, filled with rainy spells. Yet, Cortez's house exuded a warm fall or winter atmosphere, set against the backdrop of lush green trees and endless mountains.

"Señor Cortez will expect you at 6 p.m., for dinner in the dining area," said the maid.

"Tell him I'll be there, thank you," Amber said.

The maid exited and closed the door, leaving Amber relieved to be alone. However, Cortez spied on her through the sconces and strategically placed pictures on the walls.
The bathroom would be camera-free, as they could see everything she took in or out with her. Throwing her suitcase onto the chest, Amber swung open the closet doors and discovered it was filled with clothes that fit her perfectly. The message was loud and clear—there was no need to unpack. Was this another form of control or an attempt to erase her independent choices? Amber thought back to the car, right down to her shoes. Everything had been selected by someone else. She took a moment to find her favorite comb and hairbrush, grabbing them from her bag before rushing into the bathroom.

Once inside, a hairbrush, comb, makeup set, toothbrush, and soap are spread out on the sprawling ecru-colored marble counter. Amber placed her personal items on the counter, slipped out of her clothes, and stepped into the shower. Though tired, she prepared her attitude for dinner.

At 6 p.m., Cortez's dining area was elaborately set. Amber entered wearing a white evening gown and pump shoes, her hair pinned up elegantly. She glided over to the table, sat down, took a sip of water, and noticed the absence of liquor or wine. The table was filled with rice and beans, ajiaco soup, sliced avocados, empanadas, plantains, meatballs, sausages, arepas, a torta de milo, and rice pudding. She recalled hearing about South America's love for pork and bacon.

On occasions, she would have some collard greens with a smoked pig knuckle, aka soul food ham hock. Cortez entered the room in a tuxedo; he was tall in his 40s, distinguished, dark-haired with a touch of gray on the sides. He looked like a Spanish version of Clark Gable with a well-groomed mustache. Amber stood up in awe to greet him.

"Ms. Amber Stone, I am Diego Cortez. You can call me Cortez," he said.

"Pleased to meet you," Amber replied, extending her hand. He gently took it and kissed the back of her hand.

"My pleasure. Have a seat; we have much to discuss," Cortez urged.

They sat across from one another.

"No liquor or wine?" Amber asked, raising an eyebrow.

"I see you noticed. And there's no meat either—it's all vegan," Cortez explained.

"I'm used to having fried chicken, bacon, and eggs for breakfast," Amber said, with a hint of nostalgia.

"Well, we're going to change what you're accustomed to. You need to unlearn what you've learned," Cortez declared.

"What does that mean?" Amber inquired.

"We're going to create a brand new you," Cortez replied, his tone both firm and non-negotiable.

"I have to change my name like in the witness program?" Amber asked.

"Not quite - you will keep the name Ms. Stone; your alter ego will be Agent Zero," Cortez said.

"Please call me Amber Stone - Ms. is too formal for me," Amber said.

"As you wish, we have to get you in shape, beginning with a diet. No alcohol, drugs, or cigarettes; petite sweets are allowed on rare occasions," Cortez said.

"I manage to stay thin, yet with curves, I thought I was doing all right," Amber said.

"You are not a coke addict anymore, and your appetite will increase for all the fattening foods," Cortez said.

"So you read about my vices?" Amber asked.

"Yes, soon it will all be a thing of the past - except when you see Blood. When I finish training you on willpower, you will blend in with the criminal targets and indulge, then desist immediately." Cortez paused for a second and continued.

"A spy eats, sleeps, and acts just like a criminal, but they are not. It's all about willpower and being very clear about which side of the fence you are on," Cortez said, locking eyes with her.

"I don't have a choice," Amber replied.

"Yes, you do. It's better than a life in jail," Cortez insisted.

Amber took a bite of her food and sipped her water.

"My life is ruined," she lamented.

"Look at it this way, Amber Stone: your new life is just beginning. You'll still be under the disguise of a model; only now you'll be modeling for us, and that will be your cover," Cortez explained, a cold tone in his voice.

"Do all you guys down here look like playboys?" Amber asked, arching an eyebrow.

"Don't judge a book by the cover. Your appearance can get you in and out of places. The criminals we are targeting have extravagant lives. I must make sure you blend in with the status quo to the average civilian. They are seen as wealthy, successful business bosses. The black market thrives as we speak. The only way to crack it is to go undercover as a mole," Cortez said.

"You want me to find Blood," Amber exclaimed.

"Not yet—that's part one of our plan," Cortez replied.

"You're telling me there's a part two?" Amber inquired, eyebrows raised.

"Yes, but only after you finish your training," Cortez stated firmly.

"I can't do this," Amber protested.

"You can, and you will. Enjoy your meal; we start at 5 a.m.," Cortez urged, his eyes gleaming with determination.

Amber ate her meal in silence and excused herself from the table. She could feel Cortez's eyes capturing the view of the gown clinging to her well-shaped derrière as she strutted out of the dining area and up the staircase. Blood had never looked at her in that way—only when she vied for his attention. Then again, there were no other women around, except for the maid, who was old enough to be her parent. Cortez's gaze was everywhere as she waltzed down the gallery and entered her room.

She locked the door; there was no need for him to sneak in. He had the cameras watching her, so she slipped into the bathroom.

To her amazement, it was clean, but her makeup bag, comb, and hairbrush had disappeared—along with all the personal items to which she was attached. Amber sat down on the toilet seat, contemplating how to preserve her identity.

Being sober, her once dull senses were suddenly sharp; it struck her as funny that she had taken the brush and comb she used for ten years for granted.

Now, with her personal items removed, she was astonished to feel tears running down her cheeks. Cortez acted like a mother who didn't coddle her children. He was there to toughen her up, not to offer sympathy or emotional support. Amber wiped her eyes, removed her makeup and clothes, and stepped into the shower.

Afterward, she dressed in her nightgown and climbed into her queen-sized bed. If Cortez was filming, he certainly didn't have a camera underneath the covers, and that was precisely where she buried her head and fell fast asleep.

It was 5:30 a.m., in Cortez's underground gym, which was lined with mirrors and a mat. An arsenal of weapons—spears, staffs, swords, and every kind of handgun, along with AK-47 rifles and grenades—decorated the shelves. Amber stepped in wearing a judogi. Cortez awaited her on the mat, also clad in a judogi. He glanced at his watch.

"I told you 5 a.m., sharp," Cortez said.

"Oh, I'm sorry I'm late," Amber replied.

"Don't let it happen again. Punctuality is important; a minute can save your life," Cortez warned.

"Blood always looked at his watch as if he had somewhere to be," Amber remarked.

"He was a drug addict. They glance at their watches because they lose track of time; it's a source of anxiety. I assure you that I don't do drugs. Are you ready for your lesson?" Cortez asked.

"Sure, what am I supposed to do?" Amber asked.

"Select whatever weapon you want. I suggest something unfamiliar," Cortez said.

Amber studied the weapons hanging on the wall and grabbed one staff for herself, and the other she threw at Cortez, and he caught it.

"I have never fought with a staff stick before. Shall we give it a try?" Amber asked, her eyes sparkling with excitement.

Amber charged on the mat and swung the staff at Cortez; he blocked it, hit her in the shoulder, and then knocked her off her feet.

"Amber Stone, before you attack someone, make sure you are prepared for their counterattack," Cortez said.

"I have to get used to fighting with a staff," Amber replied.

"In that case, you had no right to attack. Always defend yourself—always look into your opponent's eyes. Then you can anticipate their next move," Cortez instructed.

Amber jumped up, caught him off guard, and executed a judo throw.

"Who are you working for?" Amber demanded.

"Superior One is my supervisor; I report everything to her," Cortez answered.

Amber bolted at him; he kicked her away and sprang to his feet. He grabbed her around the neck, but she threw him over her shoulder and onto the mat.

"You are telling me you work for a she?" Amber asked.

"Who is as competent as you will be with the Cold War over and the business of terrorism. We still need spies. We can't afford to be monogenist," Cortez said.

Amber approached him, and he swept her off her feet, sending her crashing to the mat. Cortez quickly wrapped his legs around her throat, locking her in a scissor hold. Amber struggled to break free, resorting to biting his leg. Finally, she managed to escape and jumped to her feet.

"You fight dirty—old Harlem is a long way from the Middle East," Cortez said.

Amber threw punches at him, but he easily blocked her strikes. "Is that what you plan to turn me into?" she asked.

Cortez seized her in a chokehold. "Yes, and you will become whatever I make you."

Amber heaved him over her shoulder. "That doesn't say much for my own identity."

"I will teach you to live, even if you have to kill others to do it," Cortez said.

Amber extended her hand. "What about Blood?"

He grabbed her hand and got to his feet. "We're not sure—that's why we need you to get the information," he said.

"Where is Banderos located?" Amber asked.

"Blood has the information," he replied.

"How do I reach him?" Amber inquired.

"He comes into the village to have a drink at the Cantina and shop for supplies," he explained.

"Can't you follow him?" Amber questioned.

"Banderos's men have the roads blocked off," he responded.

"Capture one of his men and make him talk," Amber suggested.

Amber kicked Cortez, sending him somersaulting backward.

"Ms. Stone, you amaze me—Banderos's men would rather die than talk," Cortez said.

She smiled. "I'm full of surprises."

"Not yet. I have to get you up to speed, and then you'll encounter Blood," Cortez stated.

"What do you mean? I just beat you," Amber said.

"You need to learn how to use every weapon in this room along with gymnastics before I send you in the field," Cortez explained.

"If you say so, I am starving," Amber said.

"Shall we have breakfast?" Cortez offered.

They both faced each other, bowed, and left the gym together. Amber followed him upstairs to the dining area, where the table was spread with fruit, yogurt, oatmeal, coffee, tea, and orange juice. They sat down to eat their breakfast, and a maid approached to pour coffee into their cups.

"You've met my maid Maria," Cortez said.

"Yes, you have a brilliant setup here," Amber replied.

"I do okay. I've trained many agents; as a matter of fact, Agent Johnson is missing. Banderos has him if he's alive; we want him," Cortez said.

"If he's dead?" Amber asked.

"We need you, someone that Banderos doesn't suspect. I didn't train Johnson; my predecessor did," Cortez explained.

"That is a relief; at least I am in splendid hands. How long do you think I will be in training?" Amber inquired.

"That depends on how fast you learn," Cortez responded. They both sipped their coffee. Unbeknownst to Amber, deep in the Colombian jungle, Blood was at Banderos's mansion, practicing boxing on a punching bag in a t-shirt and sweatpants. Banderos, a handsome Latino in his thirties with slick black hair, approached him wearing a white linen suit.

"Good morning, Blood," Banderos said.

"Good morning, Banderos," Blood replied.

"I see you've quit the drugs and drinking; you're boxing and getting in shape," Banderos observed.

"Colombia is the best for me, and thank you; it's a paradise here," Blood said.

"I'm glad you're happy. When you finish, I need you to go to the warehouse and check on the shipment," Banderos instructed.

"Sure, I'll go," Blood agreed.

"Report to me in my office on how many kilos we have," Banderos said.

"All right, boss," Blood responded.

Blood removed his boxing gloves, wiped the perspiration from his face with a towel, and exited the gym. He ambled outside and waved to the armed guards in camouflaged uniforms patrolling the courtyard. They watched Blood as he entered the warehouse.

Inside, the warehouse was dimly lit, with barrels of cocaine stored along the walls. There were six females stripped down to their bras and panties at a long table, surgical masks covering their mouths and noses, goggles over their eyes, and white shower caps covering their hair. A mound of powder was in front of each of them. Particles floated up in the air, becoming visible as the beam of light from the tiny lamps shone on the narcotics. The women diligently focused on scooping the drugs into religious statues, dolls, and cans to disguise the shipment. Two armed guards stood watch, ensuring the women did not stash any product in their underwear.

The thick, humid air of the warehouse enveloped Hector as he stepped through the doorway, his eyes quickly adjusting to the dim, flickering lights. The sounds of machinery and the pungent aroma of chemicals assaulted his senses, a stark contrast to the tranquility of his cousin Banderos' hacienda.

As Hector scanned the cavernous space, his gaze landed on a familiar figure standing amidst the organized chaos. A sudden surge of relief and recognition washed over him.

"Blood!" Hector called out, his voice echoing through the warehouse.

The large man turned, a hint of a smile tugging at the corners of his mouth. "Well, well, if it isn't my old friend, Hector," he said, his excitement rumbling with a sense of familiarity.

Hector crossed the distance between them, clasping Blood's hand in a firm, heartfelt grip.

"I can't believe you're actually here," he said, his eyes shining with genuine delight. "I was hoping you'd take me up on the offer, but I almost didn't expect you to show."

Blood's expression softened, a glimmer of understanding passing between the two men. "Yeah, well, you know I couldn't pass up the chance to get out of that hellhole," he said, his voice low. "And when I heard what you were up to down here, I figured it was time for a change of scenery."

Hector's brow furrowed slightly at Blood's words.

"What do you mean, 'what I'm up to'?" he asked, a hint of caution creeping into his tone.

Blood chuckled, the sound low and gruff. "Come on, Hector, don't play dumb with me. I've heard all about how you're the 'torture man' for your cousin Banderos. Guess you've come a long way from that scared kid I met in prison, huh?"

Hector felt a pang of discomfort at Blood's words, the weight of his new role in Banderos' organization suddenly pressing down on him. "It's... complicated," he admitted, his gaze shifting. "But I'm glad you're here, Blood. I could use a familiar face in all this."

Blood nodded, his expression thoughtful. "Well, you're in luck, my friend. I was actually supposed to be here to meet you, but some business came up. Didn't want to miss the chance to see you, though."

Hector felt a surge of gratitude, his shoulders relaxing ever so slightly. "I appreciate that, Blood. It's good to have you here. I... I've changed a lot since those days in prison, but you're still the closest thing I've got to a friend in this place."

Blood reached out, giving Hector's shoulder a firm, reassuring squeeze. "Hey, whatever's going on, I got your back, Hector. We're in this together, remember?"

Hector nodded, a renewed sense of purpose and determination burning within him. With Blood by his side, he felt like he could face whatever challenges in this new chapter of his life.

"Thanks, Blood," he said, his voice steady. "I'm glad you're here."

"I have to get these keys of cocaine over to Banderos I'll see you around," Blood said, giving Hector a hug. The men break their embrace.

"If you need me I'll be in the back," Hector said.

"Sure Hector," Blood smiled and said.

Hector walked to the back of the warehouse out of sight.

Blood counted the ten already packed boxes and exited the warehouse.

He proceeded across the courtyard; the security guards watched him closely, for Banderos did not trust anyone. The drug lord was always on alert.

His previous lieutenant had told him there were eight boxes; when there were nine, he ended up being buried alive. Blood knew not to cross Banderos; money was always a means to obtain security, which he had lacked all his life. He and his mother, Irma, had lived from one day to the next, pressured by the racism of the South; as dark-skinned people, they were born in the wrong era, in an incompatible town.

Suppose they could have been born in Colombia or Africa, where color was not a problem, and the only hindrance was attaining money. It would have made things far easier. Irma would not have drowned her sorrows in a bottle, and his perspective of hate versus hate, an eye for an eye and a tooth for a tooth, could not have existed in this paradise.

How he lived was more important than cash. Banderos had offered him something no one else had: peace of mind. He no longer had to worry about being a Black man.

Blood could roam freely and spend his salary without the threat of a police officer or Ku Klux Klan member stopping him just because he drove a nice car. He could run and jog amidst the beautiful wilderness, and no one would shoot him merely because he was Black and they thought he was casing the neighborhood.

Being reborn in this existence, he felt liberated from addiction, prejudice, poverty, and the struggle for survival. He could carry large sums of money in his pocket and flash it for all to see, and no one would dare defy Banderos or take it from him.

The drug lord was the most powerful cartel leader globally, and Blood was his lieutenant, second in command. Although his duties seemed light, it was all about the title; he didn't care if he ended up shouldering the bulk of the responsibility if his boss was terminated. Until then, why not enjoy the ride and maintain harmony? Ray often spoke of himself as if Blood were an alter ego, a way to cope with the pain of his reality when it was convenient.

He could never lie to his dark lord, especially when he entered the office with that intention; Blood was protected from harm. Banderos sat at his desk when a gorgeous woman entered. She had a long cascade of lilac hair and piercing lilac eyes, with an outfit that matched her beloved color, right down to her shoes. She placed a black suitcase on the desk. Startled by her presence, Blood stood patiently, not wanting to blurt out the shipment count.

The woman opened the suitcase, revealing it to be packed with stacks of money. The drug lord checked to see if all the funds were there before closing the case.

"Blood, this is Rivera Marquee, also known as the Queen of Clubs," Banderos said.

"Pleased to meet you. What a unique name!" Blood replied.

"I run clubs all over the world," Rivera stated.

"Yes, the Queen of Clubs sells guns and launders money for me. That will be all; your plane is waiting to take you back to Morocco," Banderos responded.

"I will need more guns; the rebels and militias are also increasing in number. When they visit the club, I need drugs for my wealthy clientele—they like to indulge," Rivera said.

"My men have already loaded the guns and drugs onto the plane. I expect you to have my payment when you return," Banderos replied.

She looked at Blood adoringly. "It was nice meeting you, Blood."

"The same here, Rivera, or should I call you the Queen of Clubs?" Blood asked.

The drug lord sat at his desk, watching the sparks fly between them.

"You can call me the Queen of Clubs. I'm sorry I don't have a moment to get acquainted, but I'll be back with the money, of course," she said.

"Every penny of it," Blood replied.

Rivera sashayed out of the office.

"Are you ready to take care of business?" Banderos asked.

"You didn't tell me you had enterprises in Morocco. If they look anything like her, send me," Blood said.

"Be patient—if you don't cross me, everything will be revealed," Banderos responded.

"I wouldn't think of it. You have my devotion," Blood said.

"There is no price on loyalty. Thank you. How many boxes do we have for shipment?" Banderos inquired.

"Ten. They are ready to be shipped," Blood replied.

"Put them on the boat to Mexico tonight; then they will go to California to be distributed," Banderos instructed.

"I'll do it as soon as the sun sets," Blood said.

He exited the office and ascended the staircase leading to his kitchenette. It was well-furnished with a king-size bed set made of quality shellacked wood that shone. The spacious room contained all his amenities, including a closet full of suits and casual wear.

Colombia had spring weather, and it rained, perfect for the greenery in the winter. This was a welcome change from the oppressive heat and humidity Blood had endured in the American South. This was his space; it is not like living with the guys he misses dearly. Blood sat on the edge of his bed, carefully unfolded the letters from Jonesy, Cisco and Soupy. He read Soupy's letter first. The crisp Chicago air wafted through the open window, a welcome change from the oppressive New York summer heat.

Soupy stood before the bustling factory, sweat glistening on his brow as he rhythmically assembled the parts, his face a mask of concentration. "I've found honest work in a factory," the letter had read. "It's hard, but I'm saving up to open my own business one day. Proud to be a law-abiding citizen now."

In Las Vegas, Cisco, dressed smartly in a crisp white shirt and black vest, dealt cards at one of the lively casino tables. His hands moved with practiced precision, shuffling and distributing the cards with an effortless grace. "Vegas is treating me well," Cisco had written. "I got a job as a dealer and I'm saving up, hoping to open my own place eventually."

Jonesy was in Philadelphia and greeted an elderly woman with a warm smile, toolbox in hand, as he set to work fixing her leaky sink in a tidy apartment. "Philly ain't so bad," the letter had read. "Jonesy's found work as a handyman, doing odd jobs around the neighborhood. He said the community has been welcoming, and he's looking to put down some roots."

Blood sat on the edge of his bed and carefully folded the letters from his old friends, then placed them back into their envelopes.

A sense of pride and wonder washed over him as he traced his finger along the seals, amazed at how far Jonesy, Cisco, and Soupy had come, finding acceptance and stability within their new communities.

With the vast expanse of land and boundless freedom before him, Blood harbored no regrets. Each of his compatriots had achieved what they desired - a new life, a fresh start. Yet he alone remained entrenched in the game, having been elevated to the role of knight-protector for the kingpin. And it was on his own terms that he undertook this duty, untroubled by the constraints of Banderos's leash.

Retiring to his spacious, avocado-hued bathroom, Blood indulged in a cleansing shower. Afterward, he slipped into his sleepwear and reclined upon the bed, awaiting the arrival of nightfall to fulfill his obligations.

As the clock struck 9 p.m., Blood and six armed men, clad in navy jumpsuits, assembled at the docks. The backdrop was a moonless sky, their figures mere shadows against the inky darkness. They stood in wait for the emergence of the mini-submarine, the coke boat, to board the ten boxes of narcotics.

The hatch opened, and Blood methodically loaded the shipment as his compatriots stood vigilant. Suddenly, the stillness was shattered by the crack of gunfire - the DEA dock patrol had descended upon them. The six men returned fire with fervor, providing cover as Blood secured the final box onto the sub. In a desperate bid for concealment, one of the drug smugglers hurled a black smoke bomb, cloaking the scene in a billowing gray fog. The flicker of tactical lights was obscured, yet the relentless spray of bullets from law enforcement continued, as if an entire army had descended upon them. All was consumed by the pitch-black veil of night.

CHAPTER SEVEN

The witching hour had arrived at Banderos' palatial estate when the weathered, soaked figure of Blood returned. The crime boss approached him with a discerning gaze.

"What transpired?" Banderos inquired, his voice tinged with a hint of concern.

Blood's response was succinct. "The DEA was there - they gunned down our men. But I managed to secure the shipment in the submarine, and it's now en route."

Banderos arched his brow. "And how did you evade capture?"

"I submerged myself in the water and swam covertly beneath the dock," Blood explained, "until I had traversed a mile and could safely make my way here, unseen in the darkness."

The drug lord's lips pressed into a thin line. "I've lost six of my most trusted soldiers. We'll need to redistribute the patrols and utilize the next wave from Mexico to assist with the logistics."

"At least the product is on its way," Blood offered. "Our supply will meet the voracious demand."

Banderos nodded slowly. "Yes, you'd best discard those damp garments and refresh yourself. I'll require your presence in the warehouse at first light to oversee the packing."

"Of course," Blood replied.

"Well done, my friend," Banderos commended. "You've performed your task with distinction."

"Thank you, sir," Blood said, turning to ascend the staircase to his quarters.

The crime boss gazed after him, aware that this latest setback presented a new challenge. He knew he would need to devise an alternative method of transporting his illicit cargo or pray that the submarine could outrun any law enforcement pursuit. Banderos then made his way to the private elevator that would carry him to the sanctum of his bedroom suite.

He had alarms leading to his quarters in case an assassin tried to kill him in his sleep. Banderos looked both ways in the hallway. As he unlocked his room, he entered and locked the door.

He stepped into the lavish sanctuary of his private quarters, the ornate door sealing him away from the outside world. The expansive room was awash in a deep, regal red, the walls adorned with intricate wallpaper that seemed to shimmer in the soft light.

A massive, gilded chandelier had hung suspended from the high ceiling, its dangling crystals refracting the glow and casting a warm, ambient radiance throughout the chamber.

The centerpiece of the space was an opulent bed, its frame crafted from gleaming gold and adorned with an array of plush, jewel-toned quilts and pillows. Two matching gold-toned night-stands flanked the bed, each one topped with a delicate candelabra lamp that flickered with a gentle, dancing flame.

Underfoot, a lush, ruby-red carpet muffled Banderos' steps as he crossed the room, its soft fibers caressing his bare feet. The drug lord paused to admire the grandiose scale of his private sanc-tuary - a lavish oasis befitting his status as the uncontested ruler of his criminal empire.

Satisfied with the security of his domain, Banderos made his way to the en-suite bathroom, the walls there swathed in the same deep crimson hue. A massive, gilded tub stood as the focal point, beckoning him to indulge in a restorative soak. Banderos me-thodically bathed himself, then slipped into a pair of silk pajamas before finally sinking into the plush comfort of his regal bed, ready to surrender to the embrace of sleep.

In this ornate, palatial retreat, Banderos could momentarily shed the mantle of his ruthless criminal persona and revel in the trappings of power and luxury that his illicit enterprise had afforded him. Here, he was lord and master of his domain, immune to the constraints that bound ordinary men.

Assured that he was safe, no guards were allowed on his floor unless an alarm signaled an intruder. He would wake up im-mediately and grab his Luger gun in his bed stand drawer. Closing his eyes, the kingpin drifted off into a peaceful sleep.

It was a different story in Blood's bedroom. He tossed and turned, haunted by a vivid dream of being chased by ten Ku Klux Klansmen dressed in white hooded robes on black horses; the leader was whipping Blood as he ran through the open woods. The other Klansmen carried torches that lit up the sky and blended in with the full moon. Blood ran until he came to his house, where Irma came bursting out in a ball of fire, screaming at the top of her lungs, stopping Blood in his tracks. He couldn't turn around with the Klansmen at his back. His eyes reflected the flames as his mother burned to a crisp, along with his house. Everything he owned, loved, and knew was gone up in smoke.

Blood woke up in a cold sweat with terror in his eyes and realized no matter how far he ran or the wealth he acquired, there wasn't any protection from the memories of the past horrors that besieged him.

The following morning at 5 a.m., at Cortez's mansion underground gym, the mirrored wall slid back, revealing a gun range target practice. Amber Stone stood there with her headphones and goggles on, aiming her pistol at the revealed targets and firing away. Cortez approaches and adjusts her arm stance and grip on the trigger.

In the following weeks, Amber trained in her judogi for 160 hours, sparring with Cortez, who taught kickboxing and aikido. She and Cortez practiced in his gymnastic room, where Amber swung from bars and performed somersaults. They tossed each other all over the mat as she defended herself.

They trained in the fields surrounding the Colombian coffee farms, climbing up and down the hills to strengthen her core. For eight hours a day over seven weeks, she drilled, went to bed, got up, and trained, seeing and doing nothing other than eating a well-prepared diet provided for her. Whether she liked her meals or not, she had to eat them.

Amber had lost all control of her life; she was told what to do, when to do it, and how to do it, as if she had enlisted in the army of a communist country. With no days off and no freedom or rights of her own, Amber wondered what had happened to the girl who partied hard and lived off her father's allowance. Amber had traded one provider for another; the government had become her parent, and she remained dependent.

Far away from the Constitution and "We the People," little did she know it was changing in ways her mind could never have imagined. Amber had prepared to play a part in a world of shifting shadows. She had surmised that the New World Order was on the rise. Amber was unaware that the NWO already existed, and she had found herself ensnared in their web of manipulation and power. The question remained: how far down the rabbit hole had she gone? Would she ever be able to break free and climb out? How was it that the narcotics king, Banderos, and his accomplice, Blood, were allowed to carry on their drug business, while no one dared to immobilize them as usual?

***

Two months later, before dawn, inside Cortez's defense room, Cortez and Amber were dressed casually. He showed her some of the weapons and gadgets that she could use. He also gave her a vanity case filled with lipstick, hairspray, eye pencil, perfume, a pearl necklace, and a pair of pearl earrings.

"This is for you. Open it." Cortez said.

Amber opened the case, her eyes widening and said. "Wow, make-up wrapped in silver."

Cortez pointed to the objects and explained. "The lipstick is explosive. An eye pencil is a knockout gas. This perfume can spray acid. The can of hair spray is a blow torch."

Amber was excited and asked. "I'm going to be using all of this?"

Cortez said as his hands gently stroked the necklace, "The pearl-coated necklace covers the iron pellets. You can choke or hit a person with this. You have pearl earrings to match. Inside each earring is a tiny grenade. If they drop, they won't explode if you throw them with force - duck. A simple silver compact is a ray gun; it is also a belt buckle. A button on top - press it once, the compact opens; press it twice, a ray phasor fires. Always open it away from you if you wish to powder your nose. Remember, it is like a gun; never point it unless you are willing to fire at a target."

With eagerness in her voice, Amber said, "I'm ready to meet Banderos."

"Not yet, you have to find him, and you won't be needing your vanity case." Cortez firmly said.

"Oh, when will I need it?" Amber asked.

Cortez turned his gaze away from the objects said. "We will start with something simple." Cortez grabbed a camera off the table and hands it to Amber.

"A camera. What does it do besides take pictures?" Amber asked.

Cortez picked up the camera and said. "It's a microphone. That will record the messages into a tape recorder. It's also with a long-range magnifying lens. I can hear you. You get Blood to reveal the location. Make sure he talks into the camera. If he takes you there, even better."

Amber not surprised said. "I'm posing as a model. On vacation taking pictures."

Cortez arched his eyebrow, his face stern, hoping that she would not forget his orders. "Under any circumstances, you're not to come back here," Cortez said.

"I understand. What if I get caught by Banderos's men?" Amber asked.

"You're on your own. He's never let an agent live. If your cover is blown, you have to go through Blood," Cortez responded.

"I feel like this is a test; what will happen if I pass the exam?" Amber said.

"We will deal with it when you cross that bridge," Cortez answered.

"At least I have my name," Amber remarked.

"It belongs to the program; if you should die or we retire you, another agent will become Amber Stone," Cortez stated.

"I should hope not - at least let me keep something, and I get information only on a need-to-know basis. What about my father? Can I call him or see him?" Amber said.

"You are not allowed to discuss this case with anyone other than me," Cortez replied.

"Well, you are some piece of work. If my father discovers my drug bust, he will never forgive me. I have to prove to my father that I am not the loser in life he thinks I am," Amber said with surprising violence.

"This is strictly business," Cortez smirks.

"What I am supposed to do? I don't have back up?" Amber asked.

"Use your brain," Cortez responded.

"I have to be stern like you," she said in a sad, low tone, and hugged Cortez, desiring to be cuddled, but he remained detached and broke their embrace.

"Thank you for everything. I will keep in touch," Amber said.

Cortez said calmly and with authority. "Your objective is to stay alive. I will be waiting for your intel. Miguel will drive you to your new quarters. Take care Amber Stone."

Amber replied, her voice slightly uncertain. "Thanks."

Amber slowly put the strap around her neck, letting the camera hang from her midriff. With a bewildered expression on her face, it was clear that she was being kicked out of the nest. It was either to soar or to crash; she hadn't acquired her wings yet. Cortez gazed at her, pondering whether she would continue to survive. Lowering her head, Amber quietly exited the room.

An hour later, at the drug lord's warehouse hidden in the hills, the sun rose. In a blood-stained dirty shirt and pants, Johnson had one of the saddest faces, with bruised cheekbones and creases around his mouth as Hector drilled him.

"I am no cop?" he slowly slurred.

"Talk you, rotten Copper!" Hector griped.

Banderos waltzed in and said. "I haven't heard that expression since a Cagney gangster movie."

Hector pulled the nail from Johnson's hand, and Johnson shrieked and lost consciousness.

"Hector, you haven't had any progress getting him to talk. The DEA was waiting to block my shipment from reaching the US last night. I wonder did Johnson anticipate that was going to happen and didn't tell us?" Banderos asked.

"You want me to torture him some more?" Hector asked.

Banderos replied in a decisive tone, "Put him on ice for a while; until the next big shipment."

Hector grabbed a bucket of water and threw it on Johnson, who slowly woke up.

Banderos leaned in, calmly said. "I am going to let you live. Tell me how the DEA knew about my merchandise?"

Johnson is weak and slurred, "I swear I am not an agent."

The kingpin paced back and forth, cool as a geyser on the surface. Still, underneath, Banderos was steaming mad because Hector had tortured Johnson. He continued to say he wasn't an agent, and Banderos knew deep in his gut that the man was lying.

Johnson mumbled, "I swear I am not an agent."

The drug lord refrained from pacing, he spewed his anger, at Johnson and yelled.

"Who do you think you are talking to a fool? Are you kidding me? Your name is Johnson, and you are a DEA agent sent to destroy me. I am going to make an example of you, so they don't send another after me."

Banderos, fuming, nodded to Hector, signaling him to brutalize his victim. The drug lord lit a Tiparillo and puffed on it. Information was what he needed, yet the enjoyment of witnessing someone being beaten was satisfying. His henchman pummeled the agent relentlessly in the jaws and upper torso. Banderos watched in delight, his lips perched with a sadistic grin.

CHAPTER EIGHT

Banderos paraded back and forth across the warehouse, thinking what to do with Agent Johnson. The nagging feeling of the DEA surveilling him because he had killed policemen, politicians, soldiers, agents. This was like a hide and seek game of being sporadically attacked indirectly. However, not being busted kept him on edge about when D-day was coming.

"Lock him up eventually; he will break and tell us everything," Banderos declared.

Hector untied Johnson, yanked him up, and escorted him to the basement jail cell where the kingpin kept his enemies.

Banderos puffed on his Tiparillo cigar, baffled how law enforcement knew of his shipping schedule. Did he have a mole, or was it a coincidence he will keep Johnson hidden until the mystery unfolds?

In the town, Miguel and Amber Stone pulled up and parked in front of the old hotel; it hadn't been that glamorous, more the type of place a working model would have lived in to save money. They hopped out, and he handed her bags from the Corvette's trunk.

"Miguel, I thought you said the car was mine," Amber said.

"Yes, Amber Stone, if you complete this case, you're still a struggling model who is cabbing it around town," Miguel replied.

"Thanks for being encouraging," Amber muttered.

"Don't get an attitude; as soon as Blood sees you with a car like this, it will blow your cover, and we certainly don't want that, do we?" Miguel admonished.

"I guess not," Amber conceded.

"You have to learn to be patient and act when required - patience and action go hand in hand," Miguel advised.

"Yeah, yeah!" Amber dismissed.

Miguel urged,"Don't squawk at my advice; it will save your life. I am not just Cortez's errand boy; I am also in the field." With that, he climbed back into the car and drove off.

Amber entered the hotel, panning the empty lobby that reminded her of a haunted building. It was dingy gray with specks of white lining the borders of the walls and dusty maroon sofas. If she wanted to leave without being seen, she had to spot where the back door was; it wasn't pertinent to inquire with the desk clerk for fear of arousing suspicion.

The clerk, an older man in a shirt and pants—nothing resembling a uniform—had given her a key as if he had been expecting her. Amber had taken the elevator to room 201, located near the staircase to the second floor. How convenient! If she had to escape, it would come in handy.

She opened the door to her suite; it was spacious. There was room to dance and exercise with one queen-size bed, a dresser, a lamp stand, and a telephone. Amber inspected the lock to make sure it was strong and working. It was so old she spotted a wooden chair and placed it underneath the knob to jam or at least deter an intruder. The spy unpacked and hung her clothes in the closet, feeling secure in being undercover. However, a woman who didn't speak Spanish was a target in a foreign country, and she would be ready.

Amber searched the area for bugs and found none, relieved that no one was doing any kind of private surveillance. Outside in the streets was a different story. She didn't wish to waste energy, and being seen in public was her objective. Amber glanced at her watch, and it read 1 p.m., with her handbag, she left her quarters with the camera around her neck and went to the lobby and asked the clerk.

"Where is the Cantina?" Amber inquired.

"Señorita, it is around the corner," the clerk replied.

She put her sunglasses on and dashed out of the lobby into the bright sunlight beaming onto the narrow sidewalk. An exiguity of people walked by; some were sitting in front of buildings. There was a ghost town ambiance.

Thinking to herself, where was everybody? Banderos held such a frightening grip on the villagers that it created an annual exodus of work-seeking Colombians to America. They were instead treated like emigrants and dared not talk for fear of what would happen to the loved ones they had left behind. She had no one but her father, who opposed any unscientific civilian life she led.

Amber dreaded, at some point, having to tell him she had been an undercover DEA agent. At that moment, she had to keep her eyes on the ball and focus. Amber hoped her mission as a finder of a lost love would succeed, and that she would stay afloat as the sea of pleasure and her most painful memories flooded her heart. Most of all, she didn't want to freeze when Blood appeared. With sweaty palms and an ocean of thoughts, butterflies turned in her stomach.

She had needed a drink, but refusing to backtrack on her sobriety had been her strength in keeping herself from being transparent. Amber approached the Cantina, a purple soundproof building with a red door; the windows were blackened with steel covers.

The lack of any living soul in sight had made her leery of secluded places. She had pulled the huge handle, opened the door, and stepped into a narrow, silent black aisle. The exit had slammed shut and locked behind her. Startled by the noise, she had glanced over her shoulder. The scent of beer and liquor had seeped through the walls, tempting her to follow her nose until another red door came into view. Amber hesitated, knowing her life would never be the same once she stepped over the threshold.

The sound of her deep breathing had rumbled in her ears. It was beneficial for her to take a moment to calm herself, put her emotions on ice, and be professional. She grabbed the handle and swung the entrance open to her amazement.

She found herself in a world of older men and young women dressed as prostitutes, adorned in colorful Colombian traditional outfits splashed with vibrant reds, whites, golds, and green-blues from the past. They danced joyfully, scattered around the tables, eating and drinking. The pulsating Salsa music played by a Colombian Afro band filled the air.

The men who worked for Banderos had come from Mexico; they had to endure the differing cultures and African influence. Amber couldn't believe what she had witnessed; it had stepped into history. She glanced at the bar, and there was Blood. Looking like an irresistible dark chocolate cake, dressed in a ruby suit, he had been draped in gold jewelry, sitting on a swivel stool with his back turned, being served a drink by a distinguished middle-age male bartender. Uncannily, he had felt her stare and had swirled around, and their eyes had met. She had hoped he would have discovered her in Colombia by chance, but that hadn't been the case. Amber had been compelled to approach the counter.

"Amber Stone," he shouted.

"Blood," she surprisingly said.

"Yeah, it's me. What are you doing here?" Blood rose from the chair and hugged her.

"I decided I needed a vacation," Amber replied.

Excitedly, he said, "I'm sorry I never sent you your money, but I have it right here!"

He reached into his pocket and revealed a roll of bills, counting out fifteen hundred dollars before handing it to Amber.

"Thanks," she said, putting the money in her handbag.

"I heard you got arrested," Blood mentioned.

"Yes," Amber confirmed.

"News travels slow down here. Hey bartender, give my girl a margarita," he called out.

"I don't drink anymore; water would be fine," Amber responded.

"I neither; I have kicked all of my vices," Blood said.

"There is something different about you; there is a glow that you didn't have before," Amber observed.

"Are you saying I wasn't handsome before?" Blood asked coyly.

"Don't play coy with me," Amber chided.

"What happened with your arrest?" Blood inquired.

"Somebody told the cops that you were my boyfriend," Amber explained.

"You didn't tell them anything, did you?" Blood asked worriedly.

"No, they found the cocaine you gave me," Amber revealed.

The bartender placed the water in front of Amber, and she took a sip.

"What happened?" Blood asked.

"I beat the case; it was my only offense," Amber replied.

"Now you're here?" Blood questioned.

"It was my chance to sojourn in Colombia," Amber said.

"I can never go back. Not that I want to. I do miss the streets," Blood lamented, taking a sip of his drink.

"Ten thousand horses couldn't keep you away," Amber remarked.

"It's beautiful down here," Blood said.

"I see; what are you doing? You seem to have a lot of cash," Amber inquired.

"Believe it or not, I work. My employer is very wealthy," Blood revealed.

With a surprised expression, Amber said, "You're kidding?"

"For real," Blood affirmed.

Amber smiled and said, "I'm drug-free. Tell me you are not sniffing cocaine and gambling."

He moved charmingly close to her, and the sparks ignited between them.

"No, I quit both vices. Take my picture. I'm a star down here," Blood said, backing up from the bar and posing for Amber.

She snapped his picture. Her brows drew closer, and her face tightened. "I don't believe the Blood I knew could lie quicker than a cat can lick its behind. I want to meet your boss," Amber demanded.

"That will be difficult. He's a recluse," Blood admitted.

"Excuses, excuses," Amber said.

"Don't worry, you'll meet him," Blood assured.

"What do you mean by that?" Amber questioned.

"That depends on how long you'll stay?" Blood asked.

"I haven't decided," Amber replied.

"I'm hoping that you'll stay here," Blood said.

"Blood, I haven't been in your presence, and you are already talking about a commitment; I have a career," Amber stated.

He smiles with confidence. "Remember what I told you."

She pressed her lips together without making eye contact and said. "Refresh my memory."

"You're a part of my destiny," Blood declared.

"You really believe it, and all along, I thought you were high," Amber remarked.

"I am sober. It's a paradise down here," Blood said.

"I'm looking at the local natives, and they appear to be a blast from the past - technology has left them far behind," Amber observed.

"Don't you worry, they are fine. Every king needs a queen. I'm asking you to think about it," Blood said.

She tipped her head to one side as if she were weighing the idea and its alternatives. "Okay."

"What hotel are you staying at?" Blood asked.

"You don't beat around the bush?" Amber replied.

"Life is too long," Blood stated.

"I'm right around the corner," Amber said.

"Good," Blood responded.

"When you say that word, it's a red flag for me," Amber warned.

"I told you, baby, I have changed. I am not the man I used to be. Give me a chance," Blood pleaded.

"Prove it to me - you are going to have to earn my love," Amber insisted.

"You already love me, and I love you. Of all the joints on the planet, you waltz into mine. It's a whole new world down here, let me show you," Blood said.

Amber lowered her head. "I wasn't sure I would see you again. Word on the street was you left for Colombia. I wanted to take my vacation, and here I am."

"I believe you being that I couldn't come back to New York, I knew you would find me," Blood said.

"Still the cocky guy," Amber remarked.

"We have unfinished business. Come on, let us go and tend to it," Blood said, extending his hand.

She hesitated for a moment. Amber couldn't get over his overconfidence; he had been waiting for her arrival. If Blood had suspected her of being an agent, he could have been leading her into a trap. If she resisted, she wouldn't get the information needed to complete the case. Maybe he had changed, yet it was too late to anticipate she had to go along with his game.

Blood stared at her as if he had x-ray vision. "Well, what are you waiting for? Come on, let's go."

Amber hesitated for a moment, then grabbed his hand, and they both exited the bar.

Meanwhile, in Cortez's office, he listened intently to Blood and Amber's conversation, meticulously documenting every word. Blood burst into Amber's hotel room ten minutes later, carrying her over the threshold. She giggled and took the camera from around her neck, setting it on the dresser. Blood smiled and gently deposited her on the bed.

"Shouldn't we get acquainted with our new selves?" Amber asked coyly.

"We will," he replied, his voice tinged with anticipation.

Amber had watched, entranced, as he stripped down to nothing. She had admired his chiseled abs, taut stomach, the rippling muscles of his arms, and his perfectly formed buttocks. He had been an Adonis, and her heart had raced in eager anticipation of their intimate reunion. Amber had never been sober during their previous moments of passion, and the unfamiliarity of this sober state had caused her to momentarily freeze as he had undressed her.

His lips had tasted of sweet pineapple, and he had exuded the fragrant scent of coconut. She had run her fingers through his neatly trimmed afro, marveling at the softness, akin to spun cotton candy.

It had been an intoxicating experience as he had gently caressed her, each touch sending sensations reverberating through her being. Being alcohol and drug-free had heightened her senses, intensifying the embrace they shared. She couldn't decide if it had been right or wrong, and how she was going to resist. Amber had harbored no intentions of making love with Blood. Yet, she had resolved to compromise, to enjoy the moment and play along with his game, if only to gain the information she sought.

That afternoon, Blood had pleasured her in ways she had never experienced before. As Cortez listened intently through the hidden microphone on the camera, he documented their intimate lovemaking. The night sky still blanketed the city as the clock struck 3 a.m. Amber's eyes flitted towards the illuminated timepiece, the bright digital display cutting through the darkness of the hotel room. Beside her, Blood stirred from his slumber, rousing himself from their shared bed. Quietly, he began to dress, slipping his clothes on with practiced efficiency.

Amber had watched him through hooded eyes, the events of their intimate evening still weighing heavily upon her mind. A mix of emotions swirled within her— the lingering warmth of their passionate embrace juxtaposed with a creeping unease about the nature of their relationship. As Blood had prepared to depart, Amber could not help but wonder where he had been headed at such an ungodly hour.

"Where are you going?" Amber asked.

"I have to get to work by 6 a.m. I'll call you," Blood said.

"When?" Amber asked.

"Don't worry," Blood said.

Blood kissed her and exited the room. Amber jumped up in her purple night slip, grabbed the camera, and spoke into the mic.

"Hello, Cortez. Blood has just left the hotel. Sorry you had to hear my intimate moments. If you were asleep, you would receive this message. I had to wait to see him again - over and out."

Amber pressed a button, cut the mic off, and pushed a chair under the doorknob for her protection. She entered her bathroom and stepped into the shower.

An aura of ecstasy surrounded Amber, mixed with shame. Amber wasn't sure if she had just slept with the old Blood, who couldn't be trusted by any woman or the new man he professed to be. She had given him her all only to have gained disappointment and a ruined life.

As the warm water poured upon her, Amber had to come to terms with finally taking responsibility for her predicament. If she had never taken drugs or drank like a fish, she would have dropped Blood when he offered her narcotics. As much as Amber hated to admit Daddy was right, their affair wouldn't have started to end.

She was weak and addicted; as a result, she was trapped. Amber has to effectively solve how to attain a goal and stay alive simultaneously. Hardly a life she bargained for - the ball is rolling where it will stop is a conundrum. She exited the shower, slipped on her nightgown, and entered the boudoir; the bed was alluring. Amber slid under the covers. Blood had physically and emotionally drained her; she was tired and had no trouble falling asleep.

It was 1 p.m., when the telephone rang loudly. Amber's arm reached from under the sheets to pick up the receiver. It was Blood, inviting her for lunch and asking her to meet him at the Sabor restaurant in 20 minutes, urging her not to be late. Not being able to refuse, he hung up the phone, leaving the dial tone ringing in her ear. It felt more like an order than an invitation. She had to skip her exercise session; he wasn't going to give her space to breathe. Blood moved fast, and she had to hop, skip, and jump to keep up with him. Amber scurried to the lavatory, showered, got dressed in a sandy-brown jumpsuit, turned on her camera, slipped it around her neck, grabbed her bag, and quickly departed.

Conveniently, the diner was a few doors away from the hotel. Amber walked up to Blood; he looked sharp in an olive green suit, standing in front of a large blue entrance imprinted with yellow squares and a circle. She felt underdressed. He glanced at his watch, as he always did, except his behavior was pedantic this time.

The pair entered and sat at their table. Amber was in awe of the red, white, blue, and yellow-orange checkerboard tablecloths, along with the multicolored chairs and colorful Christmas lights hanging from the ceiling. Blood was doing his best to please her, or so she thought. The waiter approached to take their order.

"I'll have a salad," Amber said.

"No, we will have the Corvina," Blood ordered.

The waiter nodded his head and listened to Blood.

"What is a Corvina?" Amber asked.

"A type of sea bass with a Lamarinera seafood sauce," Blood explained.

"I am not in the mood for fish," Amber protested.

"Oh, you will love it," Blood insisted.

If she had refused, an argument would have ensued. The waiter wrote down their order on a pad and walked away. Blood had morphed into a control freak, or he had strongly desired to share what he loved with her. Eventually, his motives would be revealed; however, she had to get the information, the sooner the better.

"Your boss lets you take extravagant long lunches?" Amber asked.

"Yes, I finished my shift this morning. I have to go back to work tonight to complete my eight hours," Blood replied.

"What is it you do?" Amber inquired.

"I do shipment and multitask," Blood said.

"Like what?" Amber pressed.

"I am his assistant. I come into town and buy decorations for his house and whatever else he needs," Blood explained.

"In Harlem, I did all the decorating, and you and the boys helped with the painting," Amber recalled.

"What are you saying? I don't have exquisite taste?" Blood asked defensively.

"No, I am surprised to discover your hidden talents," Amber clarified.

"I am glad you brought your camera. I want you to take pictures of me. I am building a photo album of the great life I am leading," Blood said.

"To photograph the sights while I am on vacation was my intention," Amber corrected.

"The focus should be on me. Everything else is in the background. Besides, I am hoping you change your mind and stay," Blood insisted. He reached and held her hand; she gently pulled away. The server brought their food and set it on the table.

"Could you bring me a pineapple juice?" Amber requested.

"No, she will have Guarapo Costeño," Blood interjected.

"What is that?" Amber asked.

"Go ahead and bring it to her and give me one too," Blood directed the server, who nodded and hurried to fulfill the request.

"Excuse me, I never drink or eat what is foreign," Amber protested.

"It's a Colombian Sugar Cane and Lime Drink. It goes great with the fish since neither of us consumes wine," Blood explained.

Amber noticed that Blood had a recurring habit of intercepting her wishes. As if she couldn't decide what she wanted while being in a foreign country, he assumed that a gentleman would be her guardian.

Still, there was a thin line between control and protection. She received mixed signals and didn't have the luxury to decipher the situation that was Cortez's occupation; he listened to every word. Amber had to focus on the assignment.

They finished their lunch, and it had been delicious, yet she would have eaten it for dinner. Blood did everything backward and unexpectedly. That had initially kept her attracted to him, in addition to their powerful chemistry and the drugs. Blood took center stage with a group of patrons enjoying lunch, demanding that Amber take pictures of him against the artistic backdrop.

Afterward, he accompanied her back to the hotel and asked her to wait for his call. Blood got into a white Renault car and drove off. Amber entered the hotel, and the desk clerk signaled to her to approach.

"Señorita Stone, a package arrived for you," he said, handing her a manila envelope.

"Thank you," Amber replied.

Amber glanced around; her fears had been assuaged. There hadn't been anyone sitting in the dusty chairs or on the sofa tracing her conduct. As a model, she had wanted everyone to see her; as a spy she had desired incognito. With loud-mouthed Blood wishing to be the star, it would have drawn attention to her. Amber had stepped onto the elevator, clutching the package under her right arm.

She got off on her floor and entered her quarters. Looking over her shoulder, Amber placed the chair under the doorknob to prepare for any uninvited guests. She opened the package and took out a mini camera, a key to a car, and a note that said, "Be on the road to San Jeronimo at 8 p.m., change into the costume in the trunk and steal a ride onto Tito's truck at 8:15 p.m. Stay on until it stops at Tito's garage. Banderos has a shipment of narcotics - take pictures. Even if he moves the drugs around, it's imperative we have the photos. Use the key to the car we provided; the license plate is XZF603, a black Renault 1970 parked in the rear. Good luck! Miguel."

Amber folded the note and put it in her handbag along with the mini camera. She reported into the large camera.

"Cortez, you heard Blood - he'll call me. This is not going to be easy. If I push too hard to get info on Banderos, it will blow my cover. I am his woman in a box at his beck and call. Over and out."

It occurred to her that she had wandered into strange territory. Dealing with Blood was one thing—at least she was familiar with who he had been, even if she was uncertain about the positive changes he had made in his identity. She had been tired from the night before—her lover hadn't given her a chance to sleep before he had been calling again. She was thankful he never called to say hello but always demanded her presence.

That night, he was working, leaving her free to tackle the assignment. Amber lay down and took a nap to restore her energy. When she awoke, she stretched her muscles and felt confident in her martial arts skills and abilities. Yet when Blood was in her presence, she froze—he threw her off balance, and no man had ever held that kind of power over her. They had both been obsessed with each other.

However, he had the upper hand. Amber was trying to fathom the root of Blood's irresistibility: chemistry, karma, fate, or crazy love. Because she couldn't rid herself of his aura, he was connected to Amber and lording his spell over her to his advantage. She couldn't dwell on her problem; she took a shower and got dressed in a slip-on blue jumper. Amber glanced at the clock; it was 7 p.m. If her quarters were searched, the spy didn't want to lose sight of her camera, so she draped it around her neck. She grabbed her handbag and exited the room.

Taking the back stairs in the hallway leading to the yard, she found it unlit and isolated. She spotted the car, got in, drove off, and arrived in the middle of San Jeronimo Road. Amber parked the vehicle off the road, stooped low, crawled to the trunk, and slipped into a black ninja costume along with a head mask that covered her entire body, even her hands, camouflaging her sexual gender.

Slipping on the night goggles to cover her eyes, she concealed her mouth with a mask. Amber lay low, waiting in the bushes; she heard tires approaching. The truck came into view; it was driving slowly because of the steep, winding roads. As it passed, she hopped into the open back; it was covered with hay, and underneath were narcotics in boxes hidden under a blanket. The sky was starless, and no one else was on the road, not another car tailgating to protect the supply.

The truck finally pulled into the garage. The men exited and walked over to the workers, talking in Spanish; it was hard to understand what they were saying. This had been her chance to slide under the wagon. Amber crawled into position, took her mini camera, and snapped pictures of the boxes that lined the walls.

One of the men opened one and tasted the cocaine to ensure it was potent. Amber captured a photo of him. Five other men stood around the box, also tasting the product. One of the men sensed that they were being watched and drew his gun. He tiptoed over and fired his weapon under the truck. Amber emerged from behind and grabbed his gun, knocking him unconscious.

A spray of bullets aimed at her. She retaliated and shot back as she used the shipment for cover; as the bullets pierced the boxes, the cocaine sifted through the holes. The wind blew the drugs across the floor. Amber ran out of ammunition, and the men ceased shooting.

The workers feared the wrath of Banderos if his narcotics were destroyed or lost; their lives were forfeited. They knew they weren't worth a quarter to him riding or walking.

It was the cocaine, and it's always been about the abundant fast money he acquired. Amber assessed the situation and made a run for it, and the five men attacked her. One grabbed her neck, and she threw him over her head.

He flew into the boxes, hit his head, and was knocked unconscious. The other men were punching and kicking her; she blocked their blows. A man waved a knife and jabbed at her. Amber grabbed his wrist, twisted the weapon from his hand, and threw it, and it landed on the other man's forehead. She stood in the center as they surrounded her; an opponent squeezed her arms so she couldn't hit as the others made a dash for her. Amber kicked one on the side of his ear and the other up under his jawbone - hard, which caused a dizzy effect and knocked both men unconscious. It felt like she was trapped by an anaconda. Being crushed as the giant man continued to restrict her from breathing.

Death was certain if she blacked out, so she swung her head forward, then back, crashing into his nose, breaking his hold, then kicking him in his testicles. Bending him over in pain, she took her knee and jammed it under his chin; the weight of the whopping man slammed to the garage floor. Amber took her mini camera and snapped pictures of the men lying on the floor, the cocaine seeping through the packages. She spotted a door and dashed to it; a blonde woman was entering and startled by Amber, who quickly punched her right between the eyes. The woman fell to her knees, which meant other workers were on the property, and she couldn't escape through the exits on foot.

Amber jumped into the truck and sped through the garage entrance like a bat out of hell. A worker caught a glimpse of her and chased after her, throwing a monkey wrench at the front tire in an attempt to get it caught in the spokes or cause a flat. However, the wrench bounced off, and the truck sped off into the night.

Inside the truck, there had been a machete she had assumed was used to chop bushes to create off-beaten paths; no wonder Banderos couldn't have been found. There must have been millions of hidden routes. Amber drove and stayed on San Jeronimo Road until she arrived at the spot where her car had been parked in the wilderness. She went to the back with the machete, opened all six cargo packages, and dumped their contents onto the bushes. Amber quickly snapped photos and watched as the shipment was blown away by the strong wind currents. She took off her costume, slipped on her jumper, and got into her car. Amber drove away, gazing in astonishment at the silhouette of the Andes Mountains.

Gathering evidence was one thing; it was her responsibility to determine which mountain had been the drug lord's hideaway. Quitting was not an option, even though every cell in her body had told her to run off into the hills and disappear. Deep in her heart, Amber knew Blood had been the key; she had to get the information or die trying.

CHAPTER NINE

It was midnight. Amber parked the car in the hotel's yard, got out, and entered the building with her bag in her hand and camera around her neck. She sidled up the steps and entered her room and placed the chair under the doorknob, and spoke into the camera.

"Cortez, I am safe. I have the intel over and out," Amber said.

She sighed in relief, yet her body was too sore, and she didn't want to immerse herself in a blue funk. All Amber desired was to soak in a hot bath and slumber in peace, confident that if the door burst open, she would spring to her feet, ready to defend herself. After she bathed, Amber rubbed muscle ointment on her body, praying that Blood wouldn't call in the middle of the night wanting to massage her; his touch would be painful. It would certainly alert him that something was seriously wrong. Although she felt a new sense of confidence, she knew she could complete this mission by the skin of her teeth and survive intact.

The possibility of being killed loomed in her mind. There was no reason to lose sleep over the thought; she needed her rest. So, she got under the covers, and her subconscious drifted off, but her ears remained wide awake.

It was 11:30 a.m., in the living room of Banderos. Although it was spring and tranquil, the atmosphere didn't affect the drug lord, who was steaming mad. He was dressed in a white shirt and black pants. Blood, wearing a flashy, short-sleeved palm tree-printed shirt, blue slacks, and white shoes, came racing down the staircase and entered the room.

Blood approached him cautiously. "What is wrong, boss?"

Banderos paced back and forth, running a hand through his slicked-black hair. "They messed up my shipment at Tito's garage last night," he growled.

"What? Who could have done such a thing?" Blood asked, his brow furrowed in concern.

"I don't know, Blood, but I am going to skin and boil that DEA Johnson alive until he's begging to talk," Banderos threatened, his eyes glinting with rage.

"Is there anything I can do?" Blood offered.

Banderos paused his pacing and fixed Blood with a stern look. "No, take the day off; the men at Tito's will take care of everything."

"Okay, anything you say, boss," Blood replied.

With that, Blood exited the mansion and got into his 1970 Plymouth Cuda red convertible with a black top, leaving Banderos to his dark thoughts. He put on a pair of shades, made sure his gold chain hung neatly around his neck, and primped his afro in the rear mirror. Blood waved goodbye to the guards and drove off.

An hour later, there was a loud knock at the door in Amber's room.

She woke up in her bed, wearing a sheer, scanty nightgown, and asked, "Who is it?"

A woman's voice came through the door. "It's room service."

Amber paused, then got up, put on a satin robe, removed the chair from under the knob, and opened the door. She was surprised to see Maria Cortez's maid standing there in her uniform.

"Maria, come in," Amber said.

"Cortez sent me to pick up last night's photos," Maria said.

Amber went into her handbag, got the roll of film, and gave it to Maria.

"Are you going to stay and clean my room?" Amber asked.

"Sorry, I have to get the film to Cortez," Maria replied.

"Tell him I barely escaped," Amber said.

"I will tell him you take care," Maria said.

"Go in Godspeed Maria," Amber said.

Maria stuffed the film in her bosom and exited the room. When she got downstairs, she hurried to deliver the photos to Cortez. Maria collided with Blood as he entered the lobby, stepping on his white shoes. He pushed her away, and she jumped in fear.

"What the hell is wrong with you, woman?" he yelled. Looking down at his shoes and then at her only enraged him further. He screamed at the top of his lungs, alerting the maids and butler who were cleaning the lobby, along with the desk clerk, all of whom stopped what they were doing to see the commotion.

"I am so sorry, Señor pardon me," Maria said.

"Why don't you look where you are going? You destroyed my shoes, you dumb bitch," Blood shouted.

"Please forgive me. I didn't mean to. I didn't see you," Maria hysterically wept; however Blood spared her no sympathy in his fitful rage.

"Look where you are going whore. If I didn't have white shoes on, I would put my foot in your ass. Get the fuck outta my sight, idiot," Blood watched as Maria, a nervous wreck, shuffled out of the hotel.

He turned to the workers and yelled, "What in the Sam Hell are you all looking at? Get back to work!" They began to clean frantically, fearing Blood's wrath, especially since he had a gun. It was a real turn-on for him to see people squirm at the sound of his angry voice or hop, skip, and jump to fulfill his commands. He lusted for power; once the servant, now he was the master. Banderos had spoiled him and promised that he would inherit his kingdom. Blood calmly picked up the house phone and dialed Amber, growing increasingly impatient as the phone continued to ring.

While Maria stood at the curb waiting for her ride, she felt terrified that Blood would assume she was a courier for law enforcement and shoot her in the head. In an old taxi cab, Miguel pulled up to the curb. Maria got in, and they drove away.

The phone rang in Amber's room; she rushed from the bathroom in her bathrobe to answer it, and it was Blood. He wanted her to meet him in the lobby in 10 minutes and to bring her camera. Amber hung up the receiver and applied her makeup.

Blood had been capricious since he had quit taking drugs and drinking. He pranced around the lobby, tapping the sofa with his hand, sending a puff of dust dispersing into the air.

He glanced at one of the maids and calmly said, "Please come over here and dust this sofa off so I can sit down; thank you."

She finished cleaning the table, hurried over, and dusted the sofa. He sat down and waited for his lady. Amber waltzed into the lobby, her camera dangling at her midriff. She wore a floppy hat and shades, a white vintage summer dress with black and white striped pockets, and espadrille shoes.

In this part of Colombia, everyone's attire was formal or evening. A grunge dresser garnered attention, not that she wanted to be observed for being fashionable; she blended in, and so did Blood. He was desperate for the limelight. She greeted Blood, and they left the hotel, approaching his car. Like a well-mannered gentleman, he opened the passenger side door, and she slid in. He closed her door, got into the driver's seat, and drove off.

"Where are we going," she asked.

"It's a surprise you will see when we get there," he said.

Amber had thought he was finally taking her to meet his boss. It had felt like a blessing for them to be riding in a convertible with the top down. She could see the sky, smell the fresh air, and enjoy the beauty of the lush surrounding mountains and jungle. They had driven far away, and a beach had come into view.

Then she had realized that Banderos would never come to an open beach, and this was an actual intimate date between her and Blood. There hadn't been another soul walking or sitting on the sand. Amber had been poised for the unexpected, yet she couldn't panic. Cortez could hear every word. If anything had gone wrong, he wouldn't have been able to get there swiftly to save her; she had been on her own.

Blood turned and looked at her. "Are you all right?"

"Yes, If you would have said where we were going, I could have packed my bathing suit," Amber replied.

"I didn't bring you here to swim," Blood stated.

Amber's jaw had clenched; she hadn't concealed her darting eye movements. Blood had quickly hopped from the vehicle. Amber's eyes had widened as he popped the trunk, which had blocked her view of what he was grabbing. Amber had scouted for an exit in case she had to run for cover. Suddenly, he had appeared on the passenger side, holding a picnic basket in his hand.

"Surprise," he shouted.

Amber flinched. "You scared me."

"I wanted to throw you off of your routine. You are a perfectionist. You need spice in your life," Blood said.

Amber exhaled; he opened the car door and grabbed her hand, and pulled her close to him. In a low tone, he said, "I made fried chicken and potato salad with a side of greens."

"You can cook something other than spaghetti?" Amber asked.

"I've learned many things. I wanted to celebrate our memories of old Harlem," Blood replied.

"I am flattered. Do you want me to get the blanket from the trunk?" Amber inquired.

"No, you hold the basket. I'll get it," Blood responded as he handed her the basket and got the blanket.

Amber watched as Blood closed the lid with a quilt thrown over his arm. Amber was perspiring and wondered what would happen next as he approached her.

"You're sweating; the weather is nice and cool?" Blood observed.

"I am burning up," Amber said.

"When we get on the shore, there is a breeze, and I made ice lemonade," Blood informed her.

"I am thirsty," Amber replied.

She and Blood walked onto the beach and found a spot to picnic. They sprawled the cover on the sand and placed their food on top, and they sat down to eat.

"Why don't you take off your shoes?" Blood asked.

"The sand is irritating when it's in-between my toes," Amber explained.

His eyes are fixed on her. "Babe, don't be so uptight. Relax, I got you," Blood said.

"It's peaceful," Amber remarked.

"Even if you screamed, no one would hear you," Blood stated.

"Is that why you brought me here?" Amber questioned.

"What do you think?" Blood replied.

Amber gazed out at the waves that lapped against the shore, watching the seagulls soaring overhead. The endless, deserted beach stretched out before her, and a sense of tranquility blanketed the scene.

"This is what I desired to be," Amber said, turning to him.

"Alone with you on a deserted island, with no guys or women, just us."

Blood nodded. "You got what you wanted. A beach is the closest I could get - aren't you happy?"

"I didn't think it was ever going to happen," Amber admitted, a wistful note in her voice.

"Dreams do come true," Blood replied, a small smile playing on his lips.

Amber studied him, searching his face. "Blood, I can't believe you are a changed man. Our love was so unrequited."

"Satara, that witch put a curse on me, saying I would never love anyone. I was an enemy of love for so long," Blood explained.

"That is nonsense," Amber countered. "Only you can put a spell on yourself by refusing to change."

"I did transform in a lot of ways, and I have my boss to thank," Blood revealed.

Amber had hesitated, she didn't wish to seem eager to meet his boss. "Did you tell him about us?"

"Soon, you will have the honor of his acquaintance," Blood assured her.

Amber nodded slowly. "I don't wish to be pushy; we both suffered heartache, and I am still trying to find the meaning of why?"

"We expected love from the wrong people; it's all in the past; we have found each other again," Blood said, reaching out to take her hand.

Amber felt a flutter in her stomach at his touch, even as her mind raced with doubts. "I have a big appetite."

Blood chuckled. "Like me, we want too much too soon. It's a paradise here; how could we go wrong. Eat, drink lemonade and enjoy the moment."

As Amber followed his lead, she couldn't help but feel a sense of relief that Blood had revealed his intent. Yet she couldn't fully let her guard down. He seemed like a new man, but she was still trying to decipher the signals, to make a final analysis. Thanks to Cortez, who had listened to every juicy word in his office, she had grown as a woman. But the lingering heartache and disappointment—would she ever be able to leave it behind? Amber took a deep breath and decided to heed Blood's advice, living in the moment. After all, it might have been her last.

Amber and Blood enjoyed a leisurely picnic on the secluded beach after she took photos of him in different poses along the shore. The calming waves provided the perfect atmosphere. As the sun began to set, painting the sky in vibrant hues, they packed up their picnic supplies and headed back to the hotel. Blood leaned in, pressing a chaste kiss to Amber's lips before she exited the car, a flutter of anticipation stirring in her stomach. But as she watched him drive away, a twinge of the unexpected seeped in—the old Blood would have eagerly accompanied her upstairs, intent on rekindling their passionate romance.

Amber entered her quarters and ruminated over what Blood had up his sleeve. It didn't take her long to calculate his game, yet she could be wrong and didn't wish to surmise. The only way to be sure was to wait and see. The night was still young; maybe he'd double back and knock on her door, and they would make wild and passionate love. Not that she yearned for it but expected it, and with that idea, she showered and climbed into bed. Amber tossed and turned until she fell asleep.

She had awoken the following day, and there was no Blood by her side. Amber swerved to her feet and paced the floor, confused, realizing she could not predict or anticipate what he would do. For sure, he was playing a mind game, and she was the bait.

Suddenly, the phone rang, and Amber answered it. Blood was calling; he wanted to meet for breakfast at the Cantina Club in 15 minutes. At the drop of a dime, brimming with excitement, she perceived each encounter as a step toward her objective.

It was 10:30 a.m., and Blood, dressed in a navy suit and dripping with gold jewelry, was standing in front of the steel red door of the purple building that was the entrance to the Cantina.

As Amber approached, clad in a purple pantsuit with white pumps and the camera hanging on her midriff, she spotted Miguel and another male agent in a moss green car across the street surveilling the club. Blood had guided her inside; she hadn't been leery like before—the DEA agents were outside. It felt as if a boyfriend had spent the night and was taking her to breakfast.

When they entered the Cantina, soul music blasted. Men and women, young and old, danced, dressed in a vibrant array of American mod fashion—hot pants, mini skirts, newsboy caps, shiny knee-high boots, afros, and wigs. Amber felt elated at the sights and sounds, recognizing the large African and Latino influences among the clientele.

"What is going on here? It's breakfast?" Amber asked.

"It's called Soul Breakfast once a week; we do a theme on a style of music," Blood replied.

"We?" Amber questioned.

"Yes, my boss owns the club," Blood explained.

"It makes sense why you are always here," Amber observed.

"It's one of my jobs. I am hungry," Blood said.

"I am impressed," Amber remarked.

Blood had led Amber to a table, where a young waitress in a 1960s uniform on roller-skates arrived with a tray of bacon, eggs, grits, pancakes, sausages, smothered chicken livers, orange juice, coffee, and water, setting it on the table. Amber hadn't needed to order; it reminded her of Cortez taking away her choices and control. The old Amber would have loved it because she could have stayed thin with cocaine. She had to keep in shape and would have preferred yogurt and fruit.

"This is on the menu; the diners would eat it or go hungry," Blood remarked.

Amber hadn't wished to alarm Blood, so she ate what she could and left the meat, claiming her stomach had been full. Blood had devoured his portions and hers.

After they got up from the table with the camera hanging from Amber's neck, Blood had wanted the center stage, so everyone else had circled them and watched as they danced.

He had signaled to Amber to take his pictures, catching him in dance poses, and the crowd had clapped and cheered him on. When the music had stopped, Blood and Amber had been exiting the stage when an attractive Latino man with an attaché case had approached them.

"Señor Blood," the man greeted.

"Yes," Blood responded.

"I am Hugo from Miami," the man introduced himself.

Blood turned to Amber and said, "Go sit at the table and wait for me."

Amber sat down and watched as the men walked over to the bar. The bartender had handed Blood a suitcase and cracked it open slightly to give Hugo a peek at the drugs, and Hugo had done the same to provide him with a glance at the money in his attaché case.

The music played Barry White's "I Can't Get Enough of Your Love," and the patrons had been too busy dancing to notice the drug deal taking place. Amber had pretended to sing the song into the camera.

"Hugo is leaving the club, and Blood is coming this way," Amber noted as Hugo exited the club with the drugs. Amber continued rocking to the music as Blood moved toward her with the attaché case in his hand.

"I see you are enjoying yourself. We have to go soon," Blood said, joining her and starting to clap and rock to the beat. He ogled the sexy girls as they gyrated and bopped around, not noticing the bitter smile on Amber's face.

Realizing that Miguel wasn't staked out for her safety, Amber shuffled her feet, kicking at the ground under the table and hiding her disappointment behind the music.

Hugo got into a car with another smuggler outside the Cantina, and they drove off. Miguel and his partner followed them onto a deserted road where a group of DEA agents' cars had set up a barricade. Hugo's car stopped, and Miguel jumped out and made the arrest, confiscating the suitcase with drugs. Hugo had been more terrified of Banderos than the DEA. He had tried to run, but Miguel had grabbed him. They had fought furiously, with Hugo delivering an uppercut to Miguel's jaw. Determined to take Hugo into custody, Miguel had grasped his wrist and executed a judo throw, sending Hugo's body crashing onto the pavement.

Miguel then turned Hugo over, handcuffed him, and dragged him to the van, while his partner followed with the accomplice. They had pushed both men into the truck and slammed the door. Miguel had gotten into his car, and his partner had driven the criminal's car; they had all driven off, clearing the road.

Blood's car came into view, avoiding the takedown. Amber, sitting in the passenger seat, sensed that they had caught Hugo, and it would have alerted Blood. He would eventually discover the bust, but she felt relieved it would be later. He had had a suitcase full of money and wanted his picture taken in an exotic environment.

First things first, Blood had to feed his narcissism. There was no denying that there were certain aspects of his personality that Amber loved; he could be so irresistible. As for the other parts, perhaps Amber could change them, much like Cortez had changed her with a regimen. It was a trade-off of freedom of choice. Someone had to make a sacrifice; the question was, who? Blood drove onto another road, into the jungle, and pulled over.

"Where are we going?" Amber asked.

"I have a special place I want you to see," Blood replied.

He drove until they came to a waterfall with green tropical plants and trees. Amber was surrounded by nature; this was the side of Blood she admired, his eye for aesthetics.

"It's beautiful," Amber said.

"I am glad you like it; come on, take a walk with me," Blood said, getting out of the car and opening the door for Amber, helping her from the vehicle. They walked closer to the rippling water's edge.

"Take my photo; if you decide to go back to the states, you will have lots of pictures to show," Blood said, posing for Amber.

"Does that bother you?" she asked.

"I am practically in every photo, and I don't give a hoot. I am famous," Blood replied with bravado.

Amber let the camera click away as he posed.

"You always did want to be in pictures," Amber smirked.

Blood dashed to a sapling. "Take my picture next to this tree. You can show the people I'm living well."

"The same old Blood, full of bravado," Amber remarked.

"Yeah," Blood agreed.

"Guess what? I decided to stay," Amber said.

His face lit up, excited, and he swiftly reached for her, wrapping his arms around her waist.

"I knew you would like this country. Come ride with me," Blood said.

"We just got here," Amber replied.

"I have to give my boss his money," Blood explained.

"You never did tell me what kind of merchandise he sells?" Amber asked.

"Batteries for radios," Blood lied.

"Where are we going?" Amber questioned.

"It's a surprise. You're moving in with me," Blood announced, picking Amber up and spinning her around in a cloud of happiness.

"I wish this could last forever," Amber said.

"I told you dreams do come true," Blood replied, kissing her passionately. Not since their intimate encounter had he acted like a lover, and her commitment had turned him on.

He carried her to the car, and they got in; Blood drove a distance, the car's top receded. Amber stood up and leaned against the dashboard, her eyes scanning the lush, verdant landscape that whizzed by. The car sped down the winding road, cutting through the dense foliage of the jungle. Tall, swaying palm trees and tangled vines flanked the road on either side, creating a green, leafy tunnel. She raised her camera, the long lens trained out the windshield. She began snapping rapid-fire photos, capturing the blur of the jungle as they raced through it.

Sunlight filtered down through the thick canopy overhead, casting dappled patterns of light and shadow across the hood of the car. Amber's brow furrowed in concentration as she tried to frame the perfect shots, her fingers deftly manipulating the camera controls. The rumble of the engine and the whoosh of the wind filled the air, punctuated by the rhythmic clicking of the camera shutter. Every few seconds, Amber leaned back, quickly reviewing the images on the camera's display, assessing their quality. Satisfied, she turned her attention back to the lush, verdant world speeding by, ready to capture the next captivating frame.

The jungle felt alive, vibrant and teeming with unseen movement beyond the road. Amber's photographs preserved those fleeting glimpses, a visual record of their high-speed transit through that untamed, primeval landscape. Blood parked the car seven yards away from a mountain covered with leaves. "You wait here; I'll be right back," he pecked her on the lips and grabbed the attaché case before getting out and walking to the hidden gate, where a short-range security camera scanned the entrance.

He pushed the leaves aside, revealing a remote intercom, and pressed in his code.Amber aimed the long-range lens of the camera at Blood's hand, capturing the code "1446." The short-range security camera had Blood in view, standing at the jungle-covered gate as it opened, before he entered. The entrance closed behind him.The spy's camera automatically shot the photos. She sat there patiently, fumbling through her handbag and removing her compact to powder her nose. Cortez listened intently, yet she didn't dare talk for fear of someone reading her lips. Instead, she primped her hair and admired herself while waiting for Blood.

Nestled into the rugged, mountainous terrain was Banderos' palatial estate, its whitewashed stucco walls and terra-cotta tile roofs a quintessential example of classic Colombian colonial architecture. Thick, arched entryways and ornate wrought-iron accents lent an air of timeless elegance to the sprawling compound. At the heart of the estate was a grand, sun-dappled courtyard, its serene fountains and manicured gardens creating a peaceful oasis. Surrounding the central space were the multi-story wings of the mansion, their boxy, minimalist silhouettes softened by decorative plaster moldings and wrought-iron balconies.

The overall aesthetic had been one of refined sophistication, blending modern Spanish influences with traditional Colombian design elements. Towering palm trees and vibrant bougainvillea vines had climbed the whitewashed walls, adding pops of lush, tropical color to the stately compound.

Yet below the mansion's grandiose, hacienda-like veneer had lain an aura of danger and uncompromising power. Sturdy stone ramparts and armed guards patrolling the perimeter had made it clear that this was the heavily fortified domain of a ruthless criminal kingpin—a paragon of wealth and influence in 1970s Colombia.

As Blood crossed the flagstone courtyard and entered the warehouse, the imposing scale and architectural grandeur of Banderos' estate cast an undeniable, foreboding presence—a testament to the drug lord's immense resources and ambition. Bales of cocaine were scattered throughout the factory, but no half-naked girls were sitting around the cutting table.

Instead, Banderos sat calmly, sipped a cup of tea, and stared at a box of salt, while DEA Agent Johnson was chained to the wall, his back exposed.

Hector had a whip and slashed him; his flesh was sliced open. Hector stood by, waiting for his next cue from the drug lord.

"You DEA agents think you can outsmart me. Think again. What information does your government have on me?" Banderos asked.

The gangster waited for an answer, but Agent Johnson remained silent.

"Johnson, you heard the saying? Lick my wounds or pour salt in them," Banderos said, grabbing the salt and sprinkling it into Johnson's wounds. He screamed in pain and cried.

"Hector, leave him here to rot. The next time it'll be alcohol," Banderos ordered.

Blood approached. "That's going to sting," he said.

"Señor Blood. Have you ever had that done to you?" Banderos asked.

"No," Blood replied.

"Good, because if you cross me, I'll have to do the same to you," Banderos threatened.

"Don't worry, I'm never going to cross you," Blood assured him.

"Hugo nor the shipment arrived at the hangar. The pilot called me; he had to take off. Do you have any idea what happened?" Banderos asked.

"It had been an even exchange. Hugo had left. I had stayed in the club for a while before coming here with the money," Blood explained, setting the attaché case down on the table and opening it, revealing that it was packed with cash.

"It's all there, I hope?" Banderos asked.

"Yes," Blood confirmed.

"Ten percent of a million is a hundred thousand. Which is yours; thank you for your service," Banderos glanced at the cash, took his funds out, left a hundred thousand dollars in the attaché case, closed it, and gave Blood a direct order.

"Hugo has disappeared; the client is not going to wait in Miami. He's on a plane back to Australia. I want you to call him in the morning and tell him that the shipment will be on its way as we agreed," Banderos instructed.

"Sure, boss," Blood acknowledged, took the attaché case, and exited the factory.

Outside the warehouse, Blood passed the guards on his way to the gate. It opened, and he exited, climbed into the car, and slung the attaché case into the back seat.

"That was quick," Amber remarked.

"Yeah, let's go to your hotel and pack, then we'll go to the bank. I have to deposit my money," Blood said.

"You never did tell me where you lived," Amber had pointed out.

"I thought I told you I lived here," Blood replied.

"You live here with your boss," Amber stated.

"He has a big mansion. I reside upstairs, and his quarters are on the other side," Blood explained.

Amber remained silent as the sparks generated between them. She had always loved Blood despite their tempestuous relationship. Why in the hell had she been chosen to be a victim of their chemistry? His allure had been more potent than it had been when she was on drugs.

Amber had felt relieved that Cortez could hear where she was located on the camera's recorder. However, the compound had been hidden so well that she doubted he could find her. Somehow, she had had to get the photos of the kingpin's address to him.

Blood turned the key in the ignition and stepped on the gas, the car speeding off at 90 miles an hour, with no cops in sight to pull him over. He had been in a hurry to move Amber into the estate. There had been no questions asked about her apartment, father, or work. Once behind the mansion's locked gate, her lover knew that Amber Stone would disappear from the world without notice.

It was 3 p.m., when Amber and Blood finally entered the hotel room. He set his attaché case down on the floor. He grabbed Amber and gave her a passionate kiss; she broke their embrace.

"We have to get to the bank," she said.

"We don't have to hurry; it closes at 6 p.m.," he said.

"I have to pack," Amber said anxiously.

Amber placed her handbag on the chair, took her suitcase from under the bed, and put it on top.

"I'll help you," Blood insisted.

Blood opened it, removed her clothes from the drawers, and put them in the suitcase. Amber took the camera from around her neck and started to set it down on the bed table to pretend she forgot it, so Maria could find it and give it to Cortez. But he reached for it, and Amber snatched it away from his grasp.

"Let me put the camera in the suitcase. I'll go and get the film developed," Blood smiled and said.

Right then, she knew he wasn't going to give her the suitcase to unpack.

"I'll carry it. My neck was sweating," Amber insisted.

"Give it to me," Blood firmly asked.

Amber pulled the camera away from his reach.

"No, if you can take it from me, you can have it fair enough," she daringly smiled.

"Agreed," Blood said with a sly grin.

Blood moved in closer, and she put the camera behind her back and gyrated in a seductive dance, grinding her hips against his. Blood refused to be swayed; he reached for the camera. Amber quickly maneuvered as if she had a basketball and played the game. He attempted to grab the camera, but she blocked him and spun around. Amber shuffled it behind her back between both her hands. Blood laughed; he thought it was fun because he had played basketball in the ghetto and was surprised that she knew the game so well. With a grin on her face, Amber was sure he would give up and let her keep the camera.

She couldn't bounce it, yet she made every move to keep the film out of his hands. However, when she twirled around as she had done before, he hit it, and the camera crashed to the floor, breaking open and revealing the tape. Suddenly, the atmosphere grew quiet. His eyes bulged at the sight of the recording and then scrutinized Amber. Her unwavering gaze and inscrutable countenance gave nothing away. Blood stooped down and grabbed the recorder.

"You've been taping me all along," he shouted.

"Blood, please listen to me," she calmly said.

"Why?" he yelled.

"We can walk away from this in victory. Work with me?" Amber pleaded.

The anger in him began to swell, the same rage he had when he saw his Mama being torched, yet this time he could exact revenge.

"Bitch. You've been setting me up all along?" Blood shouted.

"No, they don't want you. They want Banderos," Amber pleaded.

Blood gazed at her coldly as if she was a stranger.

"Who's my boss and has given me the life of a king. Do you think I'm going to let some two-bit bitch like you blow it for me?" he firmly said.

Amber still thought she could convince him to see it her way.

"Blood, listen to me," she pleaded.

"Are you outta your fucking mind hoe? Bitch, this is my life. I am tired of you and everybody else trying to tell me how to live. All my life motherfuckers have tried to take something from me," Blood shouted.

Amber calmly said, "After we get Banderos, you can reform we have programs to help you."

Blood acted as if he was 10,000 raged caged apes who were free and now are forced to go back to the zoo - it wasn't happening.

"They took my Mama, Poppa, money, and freedom. Now you want me to believe your bullshit. Hell no! Fuck you, bitch!" Blood shouted. Then he quickly grabbed Amber and slammed her head into the wall in an angry, violent rage.

She turned and pummeled him in the jaw. He got into a boxing stance; it was his boxing versus her martial arts. She kicked and beat him, yet he could give as good as he got. He blocked every punch she swung. Blood's rage scared her and threw her off balance. He already had an instinct for anticipating her moves and seized the advantage.

"I'm tired of you trying to tell me how to run my life, bitch," Blood said.

He took his knee and delivered multiple kicks to her stomach. With his fist, he battered her face. Amber froze, and so did her brain. Blood picked her up and threw her across the room as if she were a helpless rag doll. He slammed her onto the chair; her handbag fell to the floor. Amber struggled to her feet; her face was bloody, but she had to show him she was still standing.

"I love you," she weepingly said.

"I gave you my love, and this is how you repay me?" he asked.

Blood hits her in the mouth with the palm of his hand, knocking her on the floor. Amber's tears mixed with her bleeding face blurred her vision; she wiped her eyes.

"I'm going to call Banderos and tell him you're a spy for the US government, and he'll decide what to do with your ass," Blood determinedly said.

She snapped out of her maze, realizing once Banderos captures her like all the other DEA agents, she's dead, and it's either do or die.

"Blood, one thing you are right about this is my destiny," she confidently said.

"Go to hell," he yelled.

He turned and picked up the hotel phone receiver, dialing Banderos. Still hesitating, she knew she couldn't let him make contact; it would destroy the entire operation. Amber swiftly snatched her handbag off the floor and pulled out her silencer pistol. Blood faced her, and she angrily fired a shot into his chest. He fell to the floor, dead. She crawled over to him, turning him over to confirm he was deceased. Amber was conflicted, overwhelmed with a flood of emotions as she held him in her arms and cried. She had never expected their love affair to end tragically; she had the power to influence law enforcement. Amber had hoped he was tired of looking over his shoulder and would leap at the chance to reform if given the opportunity.

Even though the signals had always been there, she had kept making excuses. Believing that he loved her and that nothing could come between them, not even Banderos, who was she kidding? Blood had been her only love, and it had been unrequited.

It had felt like he had thrust a dagger into her heart; she couldn't bear to see him turn her over to the most feared evil man in the world. Then she remembered what he had once told her - the truth hurts worse than a lie when it was said at the wrong time. It had been the answer to all her questions in the analysis of Blood. She had wiped her face and moved his dead body off her lap onto the floor. Covered in blood, she had picked up her handbag and walked into the bathroom.

Amber entered and washed her face clean. She looked at the bruises in the mirror and emptied the contents of her handbag onto the sink counter. Poorly beaten, Amber had to conceal her bruises with her foundation, under-eye cover powder, and lipstick. Painfully, she applied the makeup, and when she finished, she exited the lavatory. Stepping into her boudoir, tattered and traumatized, Amber glanced at Blood's dead body lying in the corner.

She opened her dresser drawer, grabbed the last pair of pants and a top, and changed into them. She threw her bloody clothes next to his body and closed her packed suitcase, forcing herself to pull it together so as not to appear unprofessional.

Blood's medium attaché case caught her attention. Amber opened it and glanced at the $100,000 neatly stacked inside before closing the case and setting it beside her luggage. As soon as Amber put the receiver back on the hook, the telephone rang. Amber answered the phone.

"Hello," she said.

Miguel's voice comes over the phone. "What happened? The desk clerk said he heard noises," Miguel said.

"I almost got killed by Blood. Where were you? Didn't Cortez hear the recording?" Amber asked.

"No, you had it turned off," Miguel replied.

"With all the excitement, I must have forgotten to turn it on. I am in here waiting for you guys to burst in and to save me," Amber said.

"Sorry, I wish I could have gotten there sooner. Thank God the desk clerk called me when he heard the commotion; where is Blood?" Miguel asked.

"He's here lying in the corner dead," Amber answered.

"Hold tight I'll be over with the cleanup crew," Miguel said.

Miguel hung up, and Amber placed the receiver down on the phone. She sat in the chair and gazed at her lover's corpse.

Amber surmised that Cortez had meant for her to stand alone and realized that no knight in shining armor was coming to the rescue. Remembering that Cortez was there for the cause and not for her would save her life. This brought the money issue to the forefront, and Amber definitely kept it all for herself; no questions were asked or answered. Miguel and three other male agents in black suits with a body bag entered the quarters. Amber sat patiently, still in shock.

"Amber Stone, are you all right?" Miguel asked.

"I guess so; what happens next?" Amber slowly asked.

"Does Banderos possess any information that can compromise you? Like your name what you look like?" Miguel inquired.

"No, Blood was going to tell him about me tonight, as you see; he never got the chance," Amber replied.

"Are you sure?" Miguel asked.

"Positive," Amber answered.

"I'll escort you to Cortez. He has most of the intel anything else you wish to tell him, you can add to the report," Miguel said.

"It's a lot safer in the cage than it is in the jungle," Amber said as she grabs her cases.

"Let me help you," Miguel offered.

"Thanks, I can manage," Amber said.

Amber and Miguel departed from the room with her luggage. The agents followed, carrying Blood in the body bag.

Once in the hallway, they proceeded down the hotel's back staircase into the yard. The men placed the corpse in the front passenger seat before climbing into the black car, while Miguel and Amber got into a brown vehicle and drove off in separate directions.

At 6:30 p.m., just before dusk in front of Tito's Garage, the black car sped up and came to a stop. Two agents exited the vehicle and began spraying bullets at the guards as they scrambled for cover. They jumped back into the automobile and took off while the third agent unzipped the body bag and dumped Blood's corpse onto the ground. Tito's men chased after them, firing their weapons as they zoomed away.

It was early evening when Miguel and Amber arrived at Cortez's mansion. Maria greeted them in the corridor, and Miguel left once Amber was safely inside.

"Señorita Amber Stone, welcome back," Maria said.

"Thank you, Maria," Amber replied.

"You must be exhausted. Let me show you to your room," Maria said, as she took Amber Stone's suitcase while she held onto the attaché case, following the maid. The life-sized statue's head turned as Amber Stone and Maria passed and went up the staircase to her quarters. Maria led Amber Stone to her room, and the eyes on the paintings on the walls followed them as they passed. Amber Stone couldn't see Cortez, but she felt his eyes on her as she and Maria entered her room. Maria set Amber's luggage down on the table and left.

Entering the bathroom, Amber glanced in the mirror at her bruised face. She turned on the faucet and splashed cold water on her skin. After running a warm bath, she gently touched her body, wincing at the pain. After her soothing soak, Amber returned to her bedroom in her pajamas and climbed into bed. She swallowed a few sleeping pills and downed a glass of water from the bedside table. Turning off the lamp, she snuggled under the covers and rolled over, drifting into sleep.

Amber Stone fell into a deep sleep and dreamed she was in an Underworld Cave. She glided through a misty, icy cavern, dressed in a captivating ice-blue gown. Awaiting her was Blood, elegant in a crisp white tuxedo. Candelabra were artfully arranged throughout the cave, casting a mesmerizing glow that enhanced the surreal atmosphere, as if these two souls were reconnecting from beyond. Under a spell, Amber felt an irresistible urge to walk sensually into his arms.

He embraced her tenderly, and they began to sway slowly to the haunting melody as the music swelled. Blood drew Amber closer, kissing and nibbling her neck, their connection deepening even as the music faded into silence.

"I could have loved you," Blood said, his voice heavy with longing.

"Only if I had gone your way," Amber Stone replied, her gaze steady as she held her ground.

"Why didn't you?" Blood pressed, desperation lacing his words.

"Because I am Amber Stone, and I have my own path," she stated firmly. "You were a part of it, even if I was the right one for you. Your hatred blinded you."

"Stay with me," Blood urged, his eyes pleading.

"It's too late, Blood. We don't get a second chance."

Amber's voice was a whisper, filled with finality.

Suddenly, the cave around them began to transform. The rich angelic hues shifted to crimson. Amber's gown morphed into a deep black, concealing the remnants of her once-vibrant spirit, while Blood's tuxedo blazed into a vivid red, a visual echo of his turbulent emotions. A thick mist enveloped them, swirling like memories lost to time. In an instant, Blood vanished into the fog, his figure swallowed whole, leaving Amber Stone standing alone amidst the shifting shadows, a solitary reminder of what could have been.

Amber Stone awoke from her dream, sitting up in bed, drenched in sweat and trembling with fear. She reached into the bedside drawer, rummaging through its contents until her fingers brushed against a bottle of sleeping pills. Desperate to drown out the haunting memories of past disappointments, she quickly grabbed the bottle, took out two pills, and placed them on her tongue. With a swig of water, she swallowed them down and then lay back against her pillow. As the darkness enveloped her once more, she drifted into a sleep that promised to shield her from the ghosts of her past.

Later that night at the drug lord's warehouse, Banderos received a call informing him that the DEA agents were responsible for Blood's tragic demise. Banderos yelled and screamed. Even though he had been young, he had loved Blood like a son and heir. If Blood had crossed him, he would have received the same punishment or worse.

The kingpin summoned Hector, his henchman, on the phone and demanded that he bring Agent Johnson to the warehouse immediately. Furious, he slammed the receiver down. He paced back and forth and cogitated. Who were these DEA agents who had the nerve to defy him? He would have terminated their whole families in retaliation if he could.

They were as slippery as eels and an enigma to him. His grip on the country had not been as tight as he had believed. Banderos had to send a strong message to all those who opposed him and his business. He had done this on many occasions, and he couldn't quiver or surrender in fear. Hector shoved the handcuffed and blindfolded DEA Agent Johnson into the dimly lit warehouse, making him stumble forward before roughly sitting him down on a wooden chair. Banderos stood near the barrels of cocaine, his expression grave.

"Hector, I have some terrible news. Blood is dead."

Hector's brow furrowed in confusion and concern. "What? How did this happen?" he demanded.

"We believe the DEA got to him," Banderos said, clenching his fists. "Blood's money was never found. We think they intercepted Blood and killed him."

Hector's eyes widened in shock and rage. "Those bastards! I knew we couldn't trust that pig, Johnson, over there." He gestured angrily towards the bound DEA agent.

Banderos nodded grimly. "Blood was one of our best. He was like a son I never had. We can't let his death go unanswered."

Banderos grabbed a katana sword from under his desk. Holding it in his hands, he inched over to his victim.

"This is for Blood," Banderos said as he gripped the handle tightly and swung. Johnson's head flew off his neck and rolled onto the warehouse floor, crashing into a shipment box.

The drug lord spoke in a low tone, and his anger had subsided as if extinguishing a human life had no value.

"Clean up this mess," Banderos ordered as he exited the warehouse, leaving Hector to dispose of Agent Johnson's corpse.

The rest of the night had been somber and silent, as if a light had dimmed with the death of Blood. The hotel clerk or anyone else in town hadn't dared to volunteer any information about what had led to his death or who had been responsible. Banderos had kept everyone terrified in situations like this; it had worked to the DEA's advantage.

The following morning, in the mansion's open office, Cortez had been sitting behind his desk in a charcoal gray suit and tie, with a dossier folder before him.

Amber had entered in a black pantsuit; although her face had been made up and bright with a sunny disposition, the shadows of her bruises had been visible.

"Please be seated," Cortez said.

Amber sat in front of his desk; he stared at her. Sitting straight, her shoulders back and maintaining her posture, she wished to appear professional by all means.

"Have you seen enough?" Amber asked.

"Yes, I have, and you passed the test. Do you need to grieve and mourn?" Cortez asked, his voice devoid of any empathy.

Amber took a deep breath and composed herself.

"I never wanted to see Blood again, and when I did, he was a changed man, at least I thought. A love I always wanted but couldn't attain."

Cortez leaned in, his brow furrowed with intensity. "How do you accept that rejection?" he asked, searching Amber Stone's eyes for an answer.

Amber's gaze turned distant, memories swirling within her.

"However, he refused to reform," she replied, her voice steady yet laced with sorrow. "I had a choice—I desired for him to live, yet he chose to die."

Cortez's expression didn't soften, nor did he care about the depth of her turmoil. "He was the love of your life. He had a power over you, didn't he?"

Amber took a deep breath, summoning her strength. "It's a loss," she stated firmly. "I won't be tormented, nor will I accept defeat."

Cortez's heart didn't ache for her. "That must be painful in more ways than one?"

With a determined glint in her eyes, Amber whispered, "I've decided to live with my pain."

Cortez sat back, folded his hands in his lap, arched his eyebrow, and asked, "Are you ready for your next assignment, Agent Zero?" His tone implied the gravity of the situation.

"Yes," Amber replied, her jaw set with determination.

"Excellent, let's get to work," Cortez said as the frosted glass sliding doors to his office closed shut.

ABOUT THE AUTHOR

Amina Warsuma

Amina Warsuma has been a creative writer for many years.
She started writing, interviews for Andy Warhol's Interview magazine and
The Huffington Post style blog. A former international top fashion model
for ten years, she's lived all over the world and has photographed for
Vogue, Harpers Bazaar, and many others.

Amina graduated with an Associate degree in business at Monroe College
in her hometown the Bronx, New York. She graduated at Los Angeles
City College for Cinema Production and Producing and attended UCLA
for Television pilot writing. She and her family live in Los Angeles.

Follow her on www. X.com/amina_warsuma
www.facebook.com/aminawarsuma

https://www.amazon.com/author/aminawarsuma

www.ingramcontent.com/pod-product-compliance
Lightning Source LLC
Chambersburg PA
CBHW050346030726
47503CB00008B/2636